Heart's ♥ Choice

CELESTE O. NORFLEET

Heart's Choice

ARABESQUE®

Recycling programs
for this product may
not exist in your area.

HEART'S CHOICE

ISBN-13: 978-0-373-83189-0

www.kimanipress.com

Printed in U.S.A.

Dear Reader,

We hope you enjoy *Heart's Choice,* the second book in Arabesque's MATCH MADE series. This summer, we are introducing the Platinum Society, an exclusive matchmaking service run by Melanie Harte—a third-generation matchmaker—for wealthy, high-profile clients.

In *Heart's Choice,* by Celeste O. Norfleet, the story centers around love, loss and sacrifice. Actress Jazelle Richardson, Jazz, has suffered a devastating tragedy and is finding it hard to put her life back together. Pro quarterback Devon Hayes has just signed with the Platinum Society in hopes of finding that special someone who can deal with his celebrity lifestyle. Both find it difficult to trust, but they soon learn that the heart's choice is the only one that truly matters.

Next month, look for *Heart's Reward* by Donna Hill to find out if the Platinum Society can continue to create matches made in heaven. Be sure to read the first book in the MATCH MADE series, *Heart's Secret,* by Adrianne Byrd.

Evette Porter
Editor
Arabesque

To fate and fortune

Prologue

The view of the water off Sag Harbor bay was the perfect backdrop to the Platinum Society's morning meeting. Set behind an arbor of century-old maple trees and massive azalea and hydrangea bushes, the scene created an air of peacefulness and serenity. It was the ideal setting for what was an inscrutable business—finding someone their perfect match. The Platinum staff sat in large Adirondack chairs under a veranda with a whitewashed wooden awning, facing the water as they reviewed the interview podcasts of prospective clients.

Melanie Harte, owner of the Platinum Society, watched each podcast with intense scrutiny. Every detail, every tic and nuance, helped in her matchmaking. The slightest inflection in voice or altered mannerism revealed subtle clues as to what her clients really wanted in their perfect soul mate.

Melanie believed the answer was in details and delighted in her hands-on approach. She was old school. Often she made her decision about a couple based on insight few understood. She knew most clients wanted one thing, but actually needed something else. It was her job to discern that need and satisfy it with the perfect mate. She scanned through her exclusive database, selecting promising candidates for each client.

Her two nieces, Veronica and Jessica, sat across from her. Both were extremely competent in their roles. This morning they had developed a strategy to optimize their clients' success. Veronica was the company's profiler. She had a knack when it came to matchmaking that came naturally. It was the same keen insight that her great grandmother and grandmother had. That, plus her psychology degrees, gave her an understanding few could equal. At times her matchmaking suggestions seemed unconventional, but the results were almost always right.

Jessica was the company's concierge, stylist and makeover maven. When it came to the aesthetics of romance, she was without equal. She knew fine art, food, fashion, entertainment, wines, travel and the sensory elements of romance that contributed to successful matchmaking. Her skill and connections to nearly every aspect of the art of romance were astonishing.

Vincent, Melanie's nephew, was the only male member of the staff. He was the company's business manager and financial wiz. His contacts and reputation procured many of the Platinum Society's clients.

After a brief discussion about a prospect, followed by a unanimous decision, the Platinum team moved on to their next client.

"Okay, who's next?" Melanie asked.

"Devon Hayes," Vincent said. "There's a problem. None of the dates we've sent him on have worked out."

"How did his last date go?" Veronica asked.

"He didn't feel a connection," Jessica said.

Vincent nodded.

"That's three women he chose with no success," Jessica added. "I think it's time we take the lead. He's obviously looking for someone he believes he's not seeing."

"I agree," Melanie said. "We're not a dating service. Our job is to help our clients find love in order to have a lasting, committed relationship. At this point we're obviously missing something."

"Or maybe not," Veronica said. "Look, we've had pretenders before. Exactly how serious is he about settling down?"

"Devon isn't the type of man to do anything frivolously or halfway. When he makes up his mind about something, he sticks to it. I'd say he's very serious. But the problem is he's lost perspective. His last serious relationship ended in near disaster, the one after that almost cost him his career. He doesn't trust his own instincts, and that's not good for him personally and professionally. Don't let the bravado fool you. He's really troubled by this."

"Okay. Well, then, let's see what we can do to help him. We'll start from the beginning and take another look at his profile and podcast. I want everyone's observations," Melanie said.

Veronica nodded and pulled up Devon's profile. "Okay. Devon Hayes—African-American, thirty-two years old, grew up in New York City and Sag Harbor. He's a self-made millionaire, but also comes from old money on his mother's side, new money on his father's. He's charming, intelligent, intuitive and used to getting what he wants."

Vincent continued with the profile. "He's a quarterback and designated franchise player with the Los Angeles Stallions. He doesn't follow the rules, which makes him stand out. He has an international finance background, and when it comes to making money, he's brilliant. His personal net worth is conservatively over eighty-five million."

Jessica continued as she pressed a computer key and brought up several photos to detail his physical description and personal interests. "He's six foot three inches, obviously well built, medium brown complexion, dark eyes, very handsome. He has a bad-boy reputation and his primary interests include sports, art, music and travel." She uploaded and played his podcast.

Unlike most of their other client interviews, which were usually very serious and sober, Devon's was more laid back and relaxed. His answers to the questions seemed honest and concise but lighthearted. He seemed to think he knew exactly the type of women he wanted in his life. There was nothing particularly unusual that stood out. Like most of their millionaire clients, he was a bit self-centered and conceited.

"What's his wife package sound like?" Jessica asked.

"He's looking for an intelligent, attractive woman in her mid-twenties who can easily fit into the lifestyle he's created for himself. He wants her to be demure, quiet and completely devoted to him and his career. He also wants her to stay as far out of the spotlight as possible. With that in mind, we've sent him out on dates with two prominent businesswomen and an end-of-career supermodel. None of them worked for him, although it seems that all three women instantly fell in love."

"Let's see the podcast again," Melanie said.

Veronica pressed the laptop keystroke and played the podcast again. One thing in particular immediately stood out to her. "Anybody know anything about his parents?" Veronica asked.

"They're divorced. There was no pre-nup, and it got very, very nasty. There were charges of infidelity and abuse countered by theft and emotional cruelty and abandonment. He and his sister were front and center for most of it," Vincent said. "His father is an ex-football player, and his mother is in real estate now. Both are remarried. He lives in Dallas. She's here in Sag Harbor."

"So not exactly happily ever after," Jessica chimed in.

Melanie nodded. "Apparently Devon learned some pretty difficult lessons about love and commitment in all that drama. That's why he's only interested in women who are totally wrong for him. With them he never has to worry about falling in love and repeating his family's history."

"That would explain his previous dating pattern— starry-eyed groupies who are totally into him. There's never a chance of him getting emotionally involved," Veronica added.

"He's never going to have a lasting relationship like that," Jessica said.

"And we're feeding his fears by giving him exactly what he wants—more of the same," Vincent said.

"I say it's time for him to break the cycle," Jessica replied. Melanie nodded in agreement.

"Exactly," Veronica said. "What he needs is a woman

who is just as much a celebrity as he is. She also needs to match him dollar for dollar or be well-off enough to hold her own."

"Think bigger. He needs more than that. He needs someone totally different, someone who doesn't care about his celebrity, someone who has her own life," Melanie said. She stood and walked over to the far rail. The view was breathtaking, but she had little time to contemplate it. Her line of vision did connect with something, or rather someone. "He needs someone who's not caught up in the trappings of fame and thus doesn't necessarily need him to define herself. He needs a woman who's self-sufficient and couldn't care less about his money or his career." Melanie turned and smiled. "Can it really be that simple?" Vincent, Veronica and Jessica looked at each other, confused. "I believe our answer has been right here all along."

"What do you mean?" Vincent asked.

"She means Jazelle Richardson," Veronica said, smiling.

"She's perfect," Jessica added. "Not to mention they'd make a great couple."

"What's our strategy?" Vincent asked.

"Good question. It's been almost three weeks, and Jazz has yet to leave the house. How do we introduce them?" Jessica asked.

Melanie thought a moment then smiled. "Is Devon coming to the party this weekend?"

"Yes," Jessica said, quickly checking her list.

"Good. We'll introduce them at the party. If there's chemistry, and I'm certain there will be, then we'll proceed from there. Jessica and Vincent, I want you to take the lead on this one." Melanie looked at them with a knowing smile. They were all on the same page.

"Okay, we gave him what he asked for and what he said he wanted. Now I think it's time that we give him what he needs. We'll match Devon Hayes with Jazelle Richardson. Are we all agreed?" Everyone nodded. "Okay, we're decided. Let's do it."

Chapter 1

FADE IN:
INTERIOR PARTY—NIGHT
Camera.
Roll sound.
Scene one. Take one.
Cue background.
Action.

She was alone. Jazelle Richardson stopped at the foyer mirror and spared one last glance at her reflection before going downstairs to the party. She had to admit, she looked like her old self again, almost. With her signature diamond-stud earring in the shape of a star, she sparkled like the precious gem she was. She turned to the side, examining the black cocktail dress she'd finally decided to wear. It was perfect, not too bold, not too daring. It made a statement: she was back.

Six months of reclusiveness had been enough. In those months she'd traveled and spent a lot of time thinking about her life, something she seldom had time to do before. As a successful actress and entertainer, she'd moved from character to character without much time to be herself. Her brother's death forced her to do just that. After he died, she walked away from her charmed life with a definite purpose in mind: to find herself again. Somewhere along the way she had become a parody of herself, playing a role, being someone she no longer recognized.

Turning her body, she took a deep breath then tilted her head from side to side, examining her face closely. She looked completely different now. Few people would even recognize her. She'd trimmed her long honey-blond hair and dyed it back to her natural color, her face was thinner and her eyes were far less brilliant. But she still had the deep rosy blush that seemed to always tint her cinnamon-toned complexion. The glint in her eye never reached her heart. But always the consummate actress, she knew she could pull it off for one evening. After all, they were all waiting to see her. And who could blame them.

She knew rumors had been flying about her for months. The tabloids loved her because the tragedy that was her life sold papers. Every time she stepped out of the front door another story had been concocted in the media. One had her in a suicide pact with her brother. Another had her locked away in a psychiatric hospital and yet another had her moving to Tibet and joining a monastic sect.

The absurdity of the reports made her chuckle as it always had. Her brother, Brian, taught her that. They always made fun of the tabloid stories. It was their private joke on the rest of the world. Brian… The thought of him brought it all back like a movie trailer caught in an endless loop. She chuckled again, remembering Brian mimicking a booming baritone voice-over detailing her life.

> VO: The melodrama that is Jazelle Richardson's life is scripted daily. The star of this tortured existence lives a never-ending drama, performing for the entertainment and amusement of the media and anyone else who feels the need to partake of her tragedy. Tonight we find our heroine attending a lavish soirée, the first in years. Will she succeed in rejoining society or turn and run away again?

Her life, she mused, was the perfect juggling act of melodrama, comedy and tragedy. The precarious balance, she sometimes found, was now a little wobbly. It had been that way since birth. Dialogue, locations, cast, crew and extras changed all the time. But she remained the tragic heroine; that part never changed.

Jazz turned, hearing the sound of laughter coming from the party downstairs. She sighed, thinking that she was not looking forward to the next few hours. But a promise, was a promise especially to Melanie Harte. She owed her. Not just for herself, but for her mother. Melanie had come to the rescue when she needed her. She was also a godsend in helping her mother, and if going to her party would even begin to repay that debt, it was the least she could do.

Everyone knew that when Melanie Harte threw a cocktail party, you best believe it was going to be the talk of Sag Harbor for the next week. Mel's lavish party tonight marked the opening of the Hampton's summer season. Soon the small resort town would be inundated with celebrities from New York, Boston and as far away as L.A. and London.

Despite its size, the party was strictly for friends, a few locals and, of course, a nice smattering of her most successful clients. After all, what would a Melanie Harte Platinum Society cocktail party be without a little matchmaking? But matchmaking and the thought of falling in love was the last thing Jazz needed or wanted.

Love was not in the cards for her. In her twenty-nine years, she'd climbed higher than she ever imagined. She pushed herself constantly to be the best, knowing that it was more to prove to the naysayers and critics she could do it than for the money and celebrity. Now she had proved she could make it. She expected to be happy, but she wasn't. She was lonely, and now, with Brian gone, the realization was even more obvious.

She sighed, refocused on the image in the mirror and stiffened her chin. The sadness in her heart echoed the sadness she felt earlier that day, but she refused to give in to it. "I can do this," she assured herself, forcing a smile to her lips. She wore very little makeup, with her hair styled flat-iron straight with subtle highlights that gave her hair a sun-kissed look. Hers was the face of numerous cosmetic ads that touted radiant beauty, lustrous skin and flawless makeup. Funny, she didn't feel particularly radiant or lustrous right now. She didn't particularly feel much of anything.

She'd long since relinquished all hope of being happy. The best she hoped for was pleasingly attractive. After all, it was appearances that mattered in her world. Her mother's words suddenly came to mind. *"If you look the part, then you are the part. Always appear above it all, so even if your heart is breaking, they should never know."* But they did know, and now the words that had always shadowed her had suddenly become meaningless. The media saw her heartbreak and used it against her.

Hiding out was the only thing left to do, so she traveled. Fiji, Tahiti, Madagascar, anywhere they'd never heard of her, but she knew she couldn't hide forever. So for the last three weeks she'd kept a low profile at her friend's in Sag Harbor.

Tonight would be her first public appearance in months. "I can do this," she repeated, puckering her gloss-covered lips. "Okay, Jazelle, you're on." Then childishly she stuck her tongue out at her reflection. Hearing laughter, she looked quickly.

Jessica Harte stood smiling. "Now that's the Jazz we all know, love and adore."

"Hi, Jess," Jazz said, seeing her friend's reflection behind her in the mirror. "I'm glad that was you and not someone less understanding."

"Why, everybody knows you have a wry sense of humor."

"Not everybody," she said, finally turning around and nervously smoothing the perfectly fitted evening dress.

"Girl, check you out, you look fantastic," Jessica said, walking up behind her. Jazz smiled then touched her hair, which was already perfectly in place. "See, I knew there was some spark of the old Jazelle Richardson in there somewhere."

"Thanks, but I don't feel particularly sparky."

"Are you okay?" Jessica asked.

"Yeah, I guess. I'm just not up for one of these mega parties."

"Don't worry. You'll have a fantastic time, trust me."

"Are Ronnie and Vincent here yet?"

"They're already downstairs. Now come on—most of Mel's guests are already here. You're late. And I'm your designated handler, so let's go."

"You think I'm gonna need one?"

"No, but just in case, I'm here," Jessica said as she linked her arm with Jazz's and proceeded down the hall to the staircase.

Jazz nodded, grateful for Jessica's presence. The two got to the top of the stairs and stopped. "You ready for this?" Jessica asked. Jazz nodded, then shook her head no, then nodded and shrugged. "You can do this." They started down the steps. Then, midway down, the lilt of laughter and sound of music hit her. Jazz stopped. Jessica stopped.

"I'm suddenly not so sure I'm up for all this."

"Yes, you are," Jessica said, continuing down the steps with her arm still linked with Jazz. "You're a Tony-nominated, Emmy and Golden Globe Award-winning actress. You've been in front of the cameras and audiences since the day you were born. You had your own TV show at eight years old, and you starred in movies at twelve. You practically grew up with a camera in front your face. I bet you even had a sound crew, a few grips and full makeup trailer on standby when you were in diapers. So don't tell me you're not up for this. I know better."

Jazz laughed. That was her entrance, and as soon as they walked into the room, heads turned. Her joyous laughter radiated, and those in the immediate vicinity smiled with delight. It looked as if Jazelle Richardson, movie star and entertainer, was back. "Thanks, Jess," Jazz whispered.

"For what?" she asked.

"Only you could make me laugh just as I walk into the lion's den."

"Don't mention it. Now relax and have some fun—the food is delicious, and the guests are interesting and entertaining. Remember it's just friends, locals and clients here tonight. I'll get you something to drink."

"Wait, which ones are the clients?" Jazz asked quickly.

"They don't have a special nametag on—they're mingling around. Most of them are businessmen, entrepreneurs and athletes. Why?"

"Athletes, millionaire athletes," Jazz said woefully as she looked around intently. "Crap, that's all I need."

Jessica knew exactly what Jazz meant. It had been widely publicized that Jazz had a huge public breakup with both of her last two boyfriends, both of whom were professional athletes. "Don't worry. There are no professional soccer players or tennis players here tonight. Just enjoy yourself and have fun."

"Easy for you to say. I don't want to be mistaken for one of Melanie's clients. The last thing I need is to be matched up with a millionaire looking for love."

"You say that like it's a bad thing."

"Not at all. For most people, finding love is the greatest thing in the world. It's just not for me."

"Sure it is. Do you know how many women would love to be standing in a room surrounded by handsome millionaires looking for love? You just have to have a little trust," Jessica said.

"I trust that as soon as I get my heart broken it will be splashed across the tabloids and on the Internet for the next few weeks. No, thanks. I've been there and done that. Believe me, I have no intention of falling in love ever again."

"Jazz, love can come at any time and in the most unexpected places. And yes, it could even come packaged in the body of a handsome millionaire athlete. Don't let a couple of bad experiences wound your heart and spirit. Just be open to it—the rest is our job. Now, we're going to have company in a few seconds so turn around and smile. Action."

Jazz turned. She instantly smiled as several guests walked over to her. She greeted them warmly as Jessica introduced them. A few more joined them. Some she knew, others she didn't. Pretty soon she was surrounded by an adoring crowd, fans and well-wishers. Jessica eased away, smiling. She'd planted the seed, so her work was done for now.

Although everyone seemed genuinely concerned about Jazz the next few minutes were a high-wire act of nerves and determination. It was taking every bit of acting ability she had. She smiled and greeted people all the while wishing she hadn't let Melanie talk her into coming.

Of course Jazz's instinct was to turn around, run back upstairs, wash her face and crawl back in bed. But she promised she'd attend, so she couldn't back out now. Still, the last thing she wanted was to be at a matchmaker-organized cocktail party. But being the houseguest of a prominent yearlong Sag Harbor resident, she didn't have much choice. Besides, saying no to Melanie Harte was clearly not an option.

So she smiled and laughed, and smiled some more and did all the things a good house guest was supposed to do. She listened to lame jokes and did her best to be as pleasant as possible. After a particularly awkward conversation with an L.A. plastic surgeon who suggested she have several very elaborate facial procedures, she excused herself and headed toward the buffet table. Midway, she was stopped by her hostess.

"See, I told you you'd enjoy yourself once you joined the party," Melanie said, smiling happily as she walked over to stand beside Jazz. "And FYI, I have three clients here tonight who would love to meet you."

"Meet me, fine. Anything more, no thanks. You know I'm not exactly in the 'looking for love' mood."

"Not a problem, just thought I'd mention it," Melanie said, glancing across the room nonchalantly toward the man who'd just walked in to the party.

Jazz followed her line of sight. He, whoever he was, was impossible to miss, and not just to her. A crowd of women immediately gathered around him. Heads turned and guests stared, smiling. Who could blame them? He was incredibly handsome. He was tall, amazingly built and dressed stylishly in a dark blue suit with matching shirt and tie. He had a casual ease that was both relaxed and sexy. Melanie smiled and waved. He waved and nodded just as Jessica walked over to welcome him. He instantly turned his attention to Jessica, while still glancing across the room.

"Who is he?" Jazz asked of the man staring across the room at them. "He looks familiar," she added.

"I'm sure he does. That's Devon Hayes, or 'Bolt' to most of his fans. He's the star quarterback for the Los Angeles Stallions football team. His face is on just about every sports-related merchandise there is. He's single, thirty-two years old, rich, handsome and currently negotiating to sign another multi-million dollar NFL contract." Melanie watched Jazz's expression closely. It **didn't change, but Melanie nodded happily, seeing that** neither Jazz nor Devon took their eyes off each other. "He is magnificent, isn't he?" Melanie whispered.

Jazz didn't realize she'd been holding her breath since she first saw him. She didn't know about the rest of Melanie's description, but when it came to the handsome and magnificent parts, she was right on the money. He was definitely magnificent. Jazz nodded without responding.

"He's also one of my newer clients, but I don't know for how long," Melanie said, then added, "I've been having a difficult time finding his match. I'm headed to the city tomorrow to do a more intense search."

"A client, really?" Jazz said with interest, seeing Jessica walk away from Devon as a very young woman in a red micro-mini dress immediately move in to take her place beside him. "So, why would a professional football player who looks like that need your services?"

"He wants to find love and companionship, same as all my other clients."

"Actually, Mel, it doesn't look like he's having any trouble finding female companionship, unless of course those three women connected to his arm are the ones you'll be hooking him up with."

"You know there are dozens of reasons why wealthy clients come to me for assistance. You, for instance— you've never had a problem attracting men. Still, you were once a client."

"But that was something different. My mother initiated it, and I had my reasons for staying."

"Exactly," Melanie said as another two women walked over to Devon's side. "Devon's reasons are just as valid and just as compelling, so I agreed to work **with him.**"

"Hmm," Jazz said. "Looks like he already has quite a harem."

"Looks are deceiving. You of all people should know that. Did I mention that he lives just a few doors down the beach?"

Jazz noted the intense way he still looked at her. He'd smile and talk with a guest, then glance across the room at her. Melanie caught the frequent exchanges between the two as well. She smiled and nodded then leaned in to whisper into Jazz's ear. "Would you like to meet him?"

"No, that's okay. I was just curious because he looked familiar. Athletes, all athletes, are definitely off my list."

Melanie nodded. "Try to enjoy yourself, sweetie."

"I will," Jazz said. "I promise."

"I'm going to hold you to that promise."

Jazz watched as Melanie walked across the room. Gliding through the throngs of guests with ease, a wave here, and kiss-kiss there, she seemed to be in her element. When she got to Devon, he turned his attention to her as he opened his arms.

Their interaction was instant. Melanie kissed his cheek and laughed, apparently at something he'd said. They talked a while, and then Melanie greeted and introduced Devon to another guest, an older gentleman accompanied by two young girls dressed in next-to nothing with six-inch stilettos that threatened to topple them at any moment. They immediately gave Devon the universal "I'm feelin you" signal. One touched his arm playfully, getting his attention. The other pouted, then nearly broke her neck flipping her long straight hair back over her shoulder. It was obvious they were literally throwing themselves at him. It was a pathetic attempt at getting attention, and it was obviously working. He couldn't keep his eyes off them.

Jazz shook her head as she watched the brazen seduction. Witnessing the typical male ego always amazed her. She wasn't sure why, but it did. Maybe it was because she'd seen it all her life. Her brother, her friends, her co-workers, but her father was the worst. Fluttering eyelashes and pouty lips did it every time. Unconsciously she continued to stare until she noticed that Devon had turned his attention to her again. As soon as she realized it, her breath caught and she immediately turned away.

Unfortunately, she turned as the plastic surgeon approached her again. He seemed thrilled she had turned to him. He talked for the next fifteen minutes. His conversation was mostly about her. He seemed to know everything—her career, her movies, her mother, her father, her brother. It was like taking a long, torturous trek down memory lane. It was a journey that she'd had enough of. Seeing the patio doors and her exit so close, she politely excused herself. She'd had enough. It was time to leave.

When Devon Hayes decided it was time to marry, it seemed to be an easy enough decision. He considered it, analyzed it and then came to the conclusion that it was time. He needed stability and the assurance that his personal life was just as successful as his professional life. But at this point it wasn't. His life was out of balance.

Being on injured reserve last season and standing on the sidelines while his team lost game after game brought him clarity. He was the team's franchise player. Because of the drama in his personal life, he'd lost focus on the field and gotten hurt. After that like dominos, things around him began to tumble and fall apart. He needed balance again. He needed to get married.

Always analytical, he did what seemed like the logical thing to do to get what he wanted. He'd signed with the Platinum Society four weeks earlier, hoping to make his search easier and more effective. But he was wrong. If anything, it had gotten even more complicated.

Word had gotten out that he signed with Melanie, and every single woman from L.A. to New York's five boroughs knew what that meant—he was looking for a wife. Suddenly he became the winning lottery ticket, and women came knocking on his door, ready to cash in. So far he hadn't met anyone even remotely compatible. They all seemed to be looking for a diamond ring and an easy life. He'd had it with all that. He came home to Sag Harbor just to get a break from it all.

Melanie was the best at what she did, but even she was having a hard time finding the woman he wanted in his life. He wanted someone real, who loved him because of who he was and not what he did for a living. Of course, there had been many women in the past. He never considered himself a choirboy—far from it. He had sowed his wild oats. Being who he was, and in the position he was in, made it easy. It was the media hype that was making it more difficult. He knew he had to limit all the publicity. But could he help it if the papers loved to write about his relationships with various women?

Since his freshman year in college he'd been a front-page headline, so it wasn't like he purposefully went after the attention. It just came to him, mainly because his exploits on the field were legendary. He was known for breaking records as well as hearts. When he got to the pros, everything hyped up a notch, including his popularity. Unfortunately, they didn't print a lot about his foundation and the scholarships he'd given to deserving students. They only printed the scandalous reports, whether they were true or not.

But now that his career was coming to an end, he knew he needed to settle down. His publicist, agent and manager all recommended it. Correction—they insisted on it. *Minimize distractions. Change the focus to on-field ability and stay out of the tabloids. No negative publicity, only positive.* So he left L.A. and New York and came home to keep a low profile. And tonight he came looking for his future.

"Hey, you made it, finally," Vincent said.

"Barely," Devon said and smiled as the two shook hands. "Nice party."

"Yeah, well, when my aunt throws a party, she goes all out. You need to mingle. There are a lot of women here anxious to meet you."

"I've noticed," Devon said, seeing a woman in red standing close by as he and Vincent talked.

"So, what do you mean *barely*? What happened?"

"I opened my front door to come here this evening and there was a woman standing there. She wouldn't leave. She clamped on to my car and refused to move until I took down her phone number. Thankfully security was driving by and saw the whole thing. They sent her on her way. Man, I'm almost afraid to go home tonight."

"Ah yes, the hazards of fame," Vincent joked.

"Don't start," Devon warned as the two chuckled. Then slowly Devon's expression changed. He was focused and worried. "You know, I didn't think it would be this difficult to find a woman. Hell, I've been dating since middle school. There are always women around me. But as soon as I decided to settle down, I started seeing women differently. None of them were who I wanted in my life permanently," Devon said as he looked around the room, scanning more slowly. Melanie told him she had invited several prospects. He didn't have a lot of faith, since the last three women she sent him hadn't worked out. But he knew it wasn't them. It was him. He was looking for someone he probably would never find. "I guess the bad boy in me has finally grown up."

"Dating is one thing, finding love is another. It's not always quick and easy. But when you see that one woman, you'll know instantly she's the one for you. Be patient. She might just be here tonight looking for you, too."

Devon nodded. Still, no one had stood out as far as he was concerned, except for that one woman. As soon as he walked into the party he spotted her. She was impossible to miss. She was stunning in the sexy black cocktail dress. It hugged her slender body to perfection. But it was when she turned around that his breath caught in his chest. Her back was completely exposed and the subtle sexiness of the halter front quickly turned to a teasing seduction in the back.

He recognized her. Except for her hair, she looked exactly like she did on television, on stage and in the movies. She had delicate features, full, sexy lips and soft mocha-caramel skin that he wouldn't mind licking for the next few years. He smiled as his imagination hung on that stray thought. It was unlike him to fantasize, but when it came to Jazelle Richardson, it was all good.

She stood out like a dazzling diamond. The brilliant luster that surrounded her came so naturally that it outshined everyone in the room. He couldn't help wanting to wrap his eyes around her luscious body for the rest of the evening. She seemed distant, yet still approachable. She smiled and even laughed at times, but he could see that the joy never reached her eyes. They shined, but never sparkled. He wondered what it would take to see the real woman behind the cleverly constructed façade.

Vincent noticed Devon staring. He turned casually to his line of vision. "That's Jazelle Richardson," he said quietly.

"Yes, I know. She's stunning."

"Yes, she is. She's Melanie's houseguest. Would you like me to introduce you to her?" Vincent asked.

Just then Devon saw a man walk up and start talking to her. She smiled warmly. It was obvious they knew each other. The man touched her bare back. She inched away. It wasn't exactly obvious, but he noticed. Devon's eyes narrowed and his jaw muscle tightened. "No, that's okay."

"Okay, if you change your mind, let me know. Enjoy the party." Vincent walked off, and the woman in red immediately took his place, standing possessively beside him. She began talking. Devon didn't pay much attention. He acknowledged her presence, but he still glanced across the room. His thoughts still wandered to Jazz and the man standing too close.

Jazelle Richardson had been his first love years ago. He remembered watching her television show. He was enamored of her. Posters and photos of her adorned his walls through most of his teens. As a kid and teenager she was cute and funny in sitcoms. As she matured she starred in movies and performed on stage. As a dancer and singer, she was unequaled, and her fans loved to watch her. He loved to watch her.

He looked away momentarily as the young woman beside him called his name and started talking again. She grabbed his arms and smiled brightly as if it were the most natural thing in the world. Her juicy red lips, which matched her vibrant red dress, puckered then pouted. She said something that didn't matter much, so he spared another glance across the room. Jazz was looking at him now. He smiled and half nodded. She looked away casually, as if she'd been looking at someone beside him. But he knew better. She was staring at him just as he was staring at her.

Women drifted in and out of his life constantly. They appeared out of nowhere and made their intentions abundantly clear. It was a fact of nature in his profession. There was a blur of pretty faces and lovely bodies, but after a while even the most attractive women faded. They were interested in his fame and celebrity, and then they were gone. Few had ever kept his attention longer than a month or two, and none had gotten his complete attention until now.

He glanced across the room again. The same man was still with her, and another had joined them. It was obvious they flocked to her like hounds to a bone. He decided to take a different approach. He did what he got paid to do on the football field. Timing was everything, so he waited.

Melanie brought a woman over to meet him. They talked a few minutes, but he felt absolutely no chemistry. Jessica introduced him to two other women. The result was the same. There was still no chemistry, and they seemed too young and oblivious to anything other than money and status. Later he mingled, greeting a few friends, and walked around meeting other guests. He glanced over each time a man came up to her. His gut tightened until he witnessed them walking away. He smiled. They didn't have a chance. The time was right. He walked over.

Chapter 2

EXTERIOR PARTY—NIGHT

The party continued, and Jazz did her best to remain cheery and cordial. Surrounded constantly she talked easily with guests, with the grace and charm of the seasoned actress she was. She shared funny backstage stories and amusing anecdotes and those around her loved it. But she'd never stay too long with any one group. She kept moving, sometimes meeting men who wanted more than friendly conversation.

One after another they tried their best to impress her. They failed. Businessmen, professionals, millionaires, they all gave her their best pickup lines. She shot them all down. She wasn't interested. Deciding that she needed a break, she headed for the patio. As she turned to head outside, her path was obstructed. Jazz looked up right into the face of Devon Hayes. He stood just inches away. His smile was mesmerizing, like he knew something everyone else didn't. Her senses escaped her for a brief moment. "Excuse me," Jazz said, angling to get around him.

"You're not leaving, are you?" Devon asked.

"Yes, I am."

"Do we know each other?" he asked.

"No, we don't. Excuse me," she repeated, then took a step back to walk around him.

"Are you sure?" Devon asked, stepping directly into her path again.

She looked up at him and smiled, knowing a pickup line when she heard one. "Positive," she said, then stepped around him.

"Because," he said, turning to face her. Jazz stopped and turned back to him. He leaned close and spoke softly, in nearly a whisper. "From the way you were staring at me all evening, I assumed we knew each other."

She chuckled. "Don't flatter yourself," she said quietly.

"So you're saying that you weren't staring at me all evening?"

"On the contrary, it's the other way round. You were staring at me. But then, you already knew that." She glanced momentarily behind him, seeing a woman standing, obviously waiting for his attention. Devon didn't have to turn around. He knew there was someone—there was always someone. Jazz smiled knowingly. "I believe your fan club is waiting for you. Excuse me." She began to walk away again.

"Oh, okay. I get it, typical diva," he said softly, knowing she'd hear him.

She did. She turned again and moved closer. "I beg

your pardon," Jazz said stiffly. Being called a diva was something that always annoyed her. She was anything but a diva, but somehow the word always circled around.

"I know you heard me, sweetheart," Devon said. He stepped closer and lowered his mouth to her ear. His voice trembled low and deep. "You stare at me all evening and then when I come over to talk, you blow me off. Yeah, that's typical diva behavior."

Jazz shuddered. His hot breath near her ear and neck sent a quiver through her body. She steadied herself quickly. "First of all, there's nothing typical about me, and secondly, I am certainly not a diva. If by chance I was looking in your direction earlier, put on your big-boy pants and chalk it up to coincidence." She stepped back and glanced behind him again. The young woman waiting seemed impatient. "But I guess with the groupie-fest going on, I can certainly see how you got confused."

"My apologies. I assumed you wanted me—" he paused purposefully "—to come over."

"You know, given your bad-boy status, I expected your pickup line would be a bit more toe-curling. 'Do we know each other' is pretty pathetic."

Devon laughed heartily, drawing polite smiles from guests standing nearby. "Sorry to disappoint, but it wasn't a pickup line. I was curious. You were staring at me, so I naturally assumed that perhaps we'd met before and I should know you."

"No, trust me, you shouldn't know me," she said.

"Why is that?" he asked.

"Because the only reason you want to get to know me is so that you can get into my pretty black-lace panties, and, of course, add another notch to your belt."

He chuckled. "That's a wildly outrageous assumption and also the sexiest invitation I've gotten in a long time."

"It wasn't an invitation," she assured him.

"Are you sure?" he asked.

"Positive."

"That's a shame," he said, then smiled that smile she knew made women buckle at the knees, "because I really like pretty black lace. And for the record I don't do notches."

"Yeah, right, all athletes do notches."

"I'm not that guy," he said very seriously.

The stern seriousness in his voice gave her pause. "Okay, if you're not that guy, then you need to let me pass." He immediately stepped aside, allowing her to pass. "Thank you." He didn't reply, and she didn't wait around to hear one. Just twenty more feet away and she'd be outside. Suddenly the guy from earlier was back.

Smooth as crinkled sandpaper, Larry continued their previous conversation. He prattled on about his business, his money and himself, none of which seemed of particular interest to anyone except him. He laughed at his jokes and answered his own questions. Still Jazz smiled at all the right times and faked vague interest out of politeness. She knew Devon was still watching, so she kept up the pretense. Thankfully, Vincent walked over.

"Hey, there you are. You look stunning," Vincent said.

Her once-plastered smile turned genuine instantly as she greeted Vincent with a kiss on the cheek. "Thank you. You look handsome yourself. I assume you know Larry."

"Of course, Larry's a good friend. Jazz, if you'll

excuse Larry, Jessica has someone she'd like him to meet. Larry, Jessica's waiting for you in the library." Larry nodded grudgingly and left. Vincent turned his attention back to Jazz. "So, having a good time?" he asked.

Jazz nodded. "Yes. That's two I owe your sister," Jazz said.

"Two. What's the first one?"

"Never mind. I think I need to step outside and get some air. It's getting a little too stuffy in here. I've been hit on by practically every man in the room."

"You're a hot commodity."

"Oh, that makes me feel much better," she quipped.

Vincent chuckled. "A'ight, I get it. Come on," he said as he guided her toward the open patio doors. "Do you want some company?"

"No, I'll be fine. I just need to get out of here for a few minutes."

He nodded. "Here, take this—you'll look less conspicuous," Vincent said, offering her a glass of champagne.

She accepted it with a broad smile. "Thanks."

They stopped at the open doors and talked a few more minutes. Then, after one last glance across the room, Jazz casually continued outside as Vincent turned to rejoin the party. She only stopped once more, quickly dismissed the extralarge man who approached, and then passed nearly unnoticed through the French doors and onto the patio.

A sense of freedom washed over her instantly. Looking around, she noticed there were several other guests already outside. She breezed past them, smiling pleasantly, and continued toward the secluded gazebo near the far end of the property. Laughter rang out. She turned, glancing back at the party going on inside. The place was packed, but she would have expected nothing less. Few parties in Sag Harbor could rival those given by famed matchmaker Melanie Harte.

She continued walking down the path, admiring the veranda aglow with tiny white lights as she went. Candles floated in the pool, and the garden path was brilliantly illuminated. It was dazzling. *When Melanie throws a party, you can best believe it's going to be fabulous.* She stood at the entrance to the gazebo.

Fortunately she was alone. The air stilled around her. She took a deep breath, then exhaled slowly. Alone wasn't so bad.

She stepped up onto the platform and leaned back against the far post, then took another deep breath. The sweet, salt-air filled her lungs. She closed her eyes and tried to remember the last time she felt peaceful and contented. It was too long ago to even remember. All she could think about was her loss. It didn't help that today was her mother's birthday. Tears threatened. Thankfully no one noticed she'd left.

Devon walked over to the bar as he watched Jazz head toward the patio doors. Midway there she was stopped by the same man she'd been talking to all evening. Devon was tempted to go over again, but he stopped himself as he heard a familiar voice. "Yo, man, what up?" He turned to see his friends Scott Rembrandt and Armand Fuller walk up. Two women followed closely, but stopped just short of approaching them. The three men pounded fists and bumped shoulders in greeting. "So, how you doing, man? Ready to get back on the field?" Armand asked as he finished his drink and ordered another.

"Definitely," Devon said.

"I know you are. Last season was ugly, man, ugly. What was the ending, nine, ten losses, something like that," Scott said. Both Devon and Armand looked at him sternly. The rule was never look back at a losing season; he knew that. "Hey, I'm just saying," Scott added defensively.

Scott was part Irish, Italian, French Creole and German. He was hard and fierce. Meeting him across the line scared most men to death. He grew up in Compton with an attitude to match his massive size. Few knew and even fewer saw his friendlier side.

"Yo, so what are you doing here, man? I thought you'd be back in L.A. selling your soul for that fat contract they're offering you," Armand said.

"Offering?" Scott quipped jokingly. "I hear they're pinning you to the wall with some bogus threats. Rumor has it they're holding up your contract in negotiations until you get your act together."

"What's up with that?" Armand asked, looking at Devon.

Scott answered quickly. "It's the same thing they tried to do to me, man. They dumped some morals clause in my last contract. Fools wanted me married and out of trouble. They said I was in the papers too much. Stay out of the spotlight, get married, settle down." He laughed loudly. Several guests nearby turned and smiled. "Like that's gonna stop me from being me. I hear they're doing the same thing to you. So, is that why you signed up? Looking for a wife, right?"

Devon scoffed. Scott was loud and obnoxious, but as a defensive lineman there was no one scarier. His personal life was a mess, and he loved living in the spotlight. "Don't believe everything you hear," Devon said dismissively, neither confirming nor denying the rumors. But most people knew his contract was in trouble and his personal life was an issue. The team owners felt he'd lost focus. It was his job now to prove them wrong.

Armand chuckled. "Yeah, that's right. Everybody knows Devon's got it like that. So his personal life took a couple of hits last year. He'll recover."

Devon nodded. Armand had been his mentor when he first entered the NFL. He and his wife, Shelia, were the best. Unfortunately, they were no longer together. Armand was an old-school player. He was the personification of charming. Women fell at his feet constantly, and he loved it. He had girlfriends in nearly every city he played. His wife finally divorced him.

"So, for real, why are you not in L.A. takin' care of your business?" Scott asked.

"That's why I hire agents, lawyers and managers, so I don't have to stress the small stuff," Devon said cockily.

"I heard that," Armand said, pounding Devon's fist again as he scanned the room for anyone interesting.

"Still, man," Scott said, "they've come down hard on players lately. That morals clause is some bull. I lose five thousand dollars for every negative article, fifty thousand if it's a major scandal. That's some bull. They had me walking down the aisle for a contract. Like that's supposed to stop me from doing my thing."

"Scott, just stay out of the tabloids," Devon said simply.

"They hound me, man. They're always on my case looking for dirt. Nah, they thought I was gonna be stepping to their tune." He chuckled then laughed again. "Listen here, as soon as that signature ink on the contract dried, all bets were off. All that dictating my life off the field is a bunch of bull," he stressed.

"Well, at least y'all two got a contract," Armand said dryly. "Yo, retirement is a joke, for real. I'm ready to grab my helmet again."

"You must be joking," Devon said.

"I'm serious," Armand assured him.

"I don't know about ya'll two, but I'm serious about needing me some food. I gotta find me something to eat. A brother be starving up in here," Scott said then immediately headed to the buffet table across the room.

"So, what are you doing here? Three years retired and you're getting bored already? I thought you were headed to Hawaii to lie out on the beach for the next forty years," Devon said.

Armand shrugged. "I changed my mind. I figure that I have a few more years in me, so why not. I talked to some people, got myself a trainer to get me back in shape, I got the knees feeling good and I'm about to be stepping up in training camp next month. Can't have you keep getting all the glory."

"Training camp, whoa, man you've been in the league for almost fifteen years then out for three. Why are you talking about trying out at training camp?"

"A brotha's got to do what a brotha's gotta do. Besides, I've seen some of these wet-neck rookies coming into the league. They look all pumped up on roids. Trust, they'll deflate during camp, I'll make sure of that. It'll be all over for them."

"Yeah, I know the steroids and all, but some of these rookies look like they've been pumping iron since birth."

"A'int nothing to them, trust me," Armand said

confidently shrugging it off. "Don't worry, Bolt, I'll be taking the ball from your tired butt as soon as the season starts."

"Man, it's a different game out there," Devon warned.

"Yo, I got that. I'm about to hit it large. Get me some bank and be right back up there. This time I'ma do it right. No more skanks to turn my head. I'ma get my lady back same as how I got her before. She's gonna see me on the gridiron, and bam, we'll hook up all over again."

"Yeah, I heard about Shelia walking out. I'm sorry, man."

"Ain't nothing I can't fix. Ya see, I wasn't focused on what was important. I know now." He downed his drink and ordered another from the bartender. He took a deep gulp and continued. "Look here, take a tip from somebody who's been around the block. You find that one lady, keep her, no matter what. Don't let all that other stuff turn you around. There's nothing more important than finding love and keeping it."

Devon nodded and glanced across the room. "Yeah, love, important, got it. Just watch your back and your knees."

"Oh, you know that. Here's to having it all, and then getting some more," Armand said, raising his half-empty glass to toast. Devon nodded, clinking his glass. Armand finished his drink and got another.

"You're hitting that pretty hard. Did you drive tonight?"

"Me? Nah, man, I'm fine," Armand said, smiling.

Devon frowned, and then nodded skeptically, not quite sure he believed his friend. He knew that since his wife left him he'd been having problems. He'd even gotten stopped on a DUI a month ago, but an ex-teammate covered it up and made it go away.

Devon hated seeing his friend like this. Armand was devastated when his marriage ended, and it seemed that he was still hurting. But now he thought he had a second chance. Devon hated to burst his bubble. Still, he knew that he needed to say something. "Armand, drinking isn't helping this. If you're in condition and training, you shouldn't be drinking. You know that."

"Come on, Devon, back off. I know what I'm doing, man."

"Armand..."

"Shelia will come back to me, and everything will be like it was before."

"I hope so. But do me a favor and chill with the drinking, okay?"

"Cool." He downed the last of his drink and then ordered a diet soda. "Is that better?" he asked.

Devon nodded and smiled. Armand was much different than the man he met years ago. Living alone had changed him. Moments later, Scott walked back over with three plates filled high. "Whoa, man, you got enough on those plates," Armand said, knowing that Scott, at nearly three hundred and fifty pounds of solid muscle, ate like a vacuum. He knew he didn't bring the three plates back for them.

"You bring those for us?" Devon joked.

Scott didn't bother to answer. Within the next ten minutes all three plates were completely empty. He nodded to a passing server, piled the three plates on his tray and dismissed him. "Hey, Devon, I heard your girl Trina just signed her divorce papers," Scott said, wiping his mouth with a cocktail napkin.

"Divorced?" Devon said, surprised to hear the news.

"Parker in Houston told me about it. You know Trina was good friends with his ex-wife. Apparently her ex wasn't the billionaire he told her he was. She started going through the cash, and he put the brakes on. I'd say she went with the wrong meal ticket." Scott laughed heartily. "Yep, she's single again. So watch your back, bro. A'ight now, so what we got up in here, any lovelies of interest?" Scott asked, rubbing his fat hands together greedily.

"Just the young and dangerous kind," Armand warned.

"A'ight, now that's what I'm talking about."

Devon and Armand looked at each other and shook their heads. Everyone knew Scott was the biggest hound in the league. He lived in family-court. He had three children by three different women and another one on the way. He often joked that he intended to start his own team.

"You live too dangerously for me, man," Devon said, then pounded fists with Armand, who obviously agreed with him.

Scott continued laughing. "Nothing wrong with that."

"I pass," Armand said.

"I've got two on my tail already," Devon said. He turned to see the two girls in micro mini dresses and stiletto heels. They smiled, giggled and waved as soon as he glanced at them.

Scott turned around, too. "You need to work that, man. Ain't nothing wrong with getting a piece of the action."

"Nah, you know I don't play that. They may be young, but they know exactly what they're doing. They specialize in playing innocent when they need to. I'm not about to be chased down by some girl and her lawyer talking about baby daddy and child support."

"Two words," Scott said. "Paternity test."

"These girls be sweating a player doing hard time. I'd rather go up against a three-hundred-and-fifty pound lineman than to be up on all that drama," Armand added.

"See, that's why I'm about to get myself hooked," Scott said as he glanced around the room again. "Yo, yo, is that who I think it is? I heard she was here. Damn, it is her. She's lookin' good." Armand turned to see who Scott was talking about.

Devon didn't have to look. He knew exactly who Scott had asked about. He was talking about Jazelle. Suddenly he felt an instant sense of possessiveness, but said nothing. He didn't really blame them. Jazz was every man's fantasy.

"That's Jazelle Richardson. Damn, but she's still hot. I never saw her in person before. Damn," Armand reiterated, "she is sweet."

"Yo, when did she come back out to play?" Scott asked.

"What do you mean?" Devon asked.

"Check the tabloids sometimes, man. One of my girls was cracking on that for months. So, like her mom dies, then her brother and then some D-list actress started crying that Jazz stole her man out from under her."

"Did she?" Devon asked curiously.

"Who knows? The actress got her fifteen minutes of fame. That's all I remember," Armand said.

"Yo, didn't she check into some rehab center in Arizona or New Mexico or someplace like that?" Scott asked.

"After all that drama, she probably needed to get her head together," Armand said.

"Yo, check it out, she's looking over here. She's checking me out. I'ma see if I can break off a piece of that."

"Don't bother," Devon said.

Both Scott and Armand turned to him. Then they looked at each other and laughed. "Yo, man, Devon, she shot you down, didn't she?" Scott said. Devon nodded. Scott and Armand laughed riotously.

"This has got to be a first," Armand said. "Devon Hayes shot down by a woman. I never thought I'd see the day that happened." They laughed again.

Devon smirked. "It was only the first down. You know that I don't give up the game that easily," he vowed.

"Step aside, young blood. Let a man show you how it's done."

"Oh, please, fool, like you got game," Armand said.

"Let it go, Scott," Devon said possessively.

"Yo, man, you snooze, you lose. You had your shot. For real," Scott said, "I got this."

"Let him go," Armand said. "I'm sure she's been shooting them down all night."

"With the scrubs working this room, I don't blame her," Scott said confidently. "But check it out. I'm the real deal."

"Hold up. I thought you were about to be hooked up. Aren't you supposed to get married in a few weeks?" Devon asked.

"Yeah, man, but I ain't dead yet. Check it out. She's looking over here again. Yo, I'll talk to you later." He held his fist out to pound. "I'm gonna hit this."

"Good luck," Armand said, shaking his head and laughing as Scott strolled over. "Poor fool doesn't have a snowball's chance in hell."

They watched as Scott stepped up to Jazz just before she left the room. He said something. She nodded and smiled, and then they shook hands. He held her hand then leaned in too close, dipping his head to her neck each time he spoke. Devon took a step forward, then stopped himself. Scott raised her hand to his lips and kissed it. A second later, Jazz nodded then walked away. Scott was instantly besieged by the two young girls that had been behind him earlier. He beamed happily, obviously not at all fazed by Jazz's rejection. "Like I said, not a snowball's chance," Armand said, chuckling knowingly.

Devon smirked and shook his head as he continued to watch Jazz. She was definitely intriguing. Just then she turned and glanced back at the party. Their eyes locked. His narrowed as his smile crept ever so close to a grin. Seconds later, she slipped outside. Armand noticed the interaction. "It seems Scott was right about one thing. She was staring over here. But not at him—at you. Looks like the game's back on."

"I'll see you later," Devon said.

Devon looked around for Melanie. She had informed him earlier that she'd invited several possible matches for him to the party. She had introduced him to several women, but none of them impressed him like Jazz. She was who he wanted. He made his decision. He wanted Jazelle Richardson.

He scanned the first floor for Melanie and found her across the room. He headed over. Midway there he was intercepted by a young woman who'd hovered around him all evening. Overly confident, she'd been aggressively pursuing him since he walked in the door. He had discouraged her several times, but it appeared she just wasn't going to take the hint, so this time he blatantly told her that he wasn't interested, hoping that would put her off. It didn't.

When he got to Melanie, she introduced him to her other guests in the small group, then excused them for a private word. "So, Devon, have you decided which lady you'd like to spend some time with?" Melanie asked quietly. She looked around the room, seeing the three women she and Jessica had introduced to him earlier. The women were all the type of woman he'd initially asked to meet, but she secretly hoped her alternate plan had worked instead. "Which one of them would you like me to bring over?"

"Actually, none of them," he said. "I'm sorry, Melanie. I didn't expect this. I'm just not seeing the woman for me."

"Are you sure no one here caught your eye?" she queried.

Devon considered her question. He couldn't actually say that no one had caught his eye. Someone very definitely had gotten his attention. "Actually, there was someone. But I'm not sure if it's possible."

"In love, all things are possible. Who was she?"

"Jazelle Richardson."

"Interesting. You want to be matched with Jazelle?" she asked, inwardly pleased by his decision.

"Yes, is that a problem?" he asked.

Melanie looked at him, gauging his sincerity. The firm, narrowing glint in his eye told her exactly what she needed to know. He was very sincere. But she knew that when it came to Jazelle, he was going to have his work cut out for him. She was perfect for him, that much was true, but she was also vulnerable and wary. "Tell me what you know about her."

"She's an actress. She has blockbuster movies. She had her own TV show when she was a kid, then again in her teens. Her mother was entertainer Yelena Brooks and her father is actor-director and movie mogul Frank Richardson. Her brother died last year. She's in the tabloids off and on."

"Is that why you want to be matched with her?"

"No. There's something about her—she's intriguing. She's got a lot of spirit. I like that. She's quick and smart, and, as my grandfather would say, she's got moxie."

"Exactly. And, if you noticed, she isn't the type of woman you wanted to meet according to your profile. As a matter of fact, she's the exact opposite. She has her own very successful career. She's famous and constantly in the public spotlight. And as for demure and quiet—" Melanie shook her head "—well, let's just say Jazelle has a good head on her shoulders and uses it."

Devon smiled, remembering their brief conversation. "I realize that, but seeing her tonight sparked something inside of me I hadn't expected. I'm attracted to her. Not just physically, but something else, something more."

"Have you spoken to her?"

"Yes, briefly." He smiled, then chuckled. "She's got spirit."

"Yes, she does."

"The thing is, I remember her so well from when I was a kid. Like every other teenage guy, I had her posters and photos taped to my bedroom wall. I saw every show she ever did."

"Devon, I'm not running a childhood wish-fulfillment-dating service. She's not the girl next door anymore. So don't let the fact that you watched her grow up influence you."

"I know that. I also know that, so far, none of the women you introduced me to even came close to what I felt when I first saw Jazelle across the room."

"Jazz is my houseguest. She's not here as my client."

"Is she married or engaged?"

"No."

"Is she seeing someone?"

"No, but she isn't looking for a relationship at this time."

"At this time," he repeated, picking up on her phrasing. "So at one time she was a client?"

"Yes."

Devon nodded and looked to the patio doors. "What is she looking for?"

Melanie smiled. "Truthfully, she's looking for serenity."

"Serenity," he repeated. Melanie nodded. "Okay, I get it."

"But first and foremost, she needs a friend. Her heart is damaged from loss and betrayal. She's in pain, Devon, more than either you or I can even realize. She hides behind a façade. You've obviously heard about her brother last year and her mother the year before." He nodded silently. "She was extremely close to both of them. She's afraid of getting close to anyone else right now. Bombarding her with what you want will not endear you."

"I understand."

"I hope so, because if you truly want her in your life, going full speed ahead isn't going to do it. She's struggling to hide her grief, pain and sadness from the rest of the world. She's vulnerable. Don't believe everything you think you know about her."

"So, do I have your blessing?" he asked.

Melanie nodded and smiled. "She's probably at the old gazebo at the far end of the property."

"Thank you," he said quickly.

"Devon, there's one more thing you should know. Jazz despises athletes." Devon's jaw dropped. Melanie nodded.

Devon nodded and headed straight across the room and out the patio doors. He didn't stop until he reached the path leading to the gazebo entrance. Ever mindful of Melanie's words, he decided to be even more cautious. He spotted Jazz instantly. Her back was to him as she stared out at the bay. Seeing her sexy silhouette made his body immediately react. He took a deep, calming breath to relax, then noticed that someone else was with her. It was the man who'd been with her earlier. Devon overheard the tail end of their conversation. She was callous and shot him down cold. A few seconds later, the man turned, called her a few choice names under his breath and stomped away.

Devon stepped up onto the gazebo platform. "That was pretty brutal," he admonished. "He probably practiced talking to you all evening. It takes a lot of courage for a man to walk up to a woman like you and introduce himself."

Jazz rolled her eyes in the quiet darkness as she shook her head. Another intrusion. She didn't look up or even turn around this time. She'd been getting clichéd lines all her adult life. Tonight's party was no exception. For some reason, some men seemed to think that attempting to seduce her was a national pastime. Sometimes she was nice about shooting them down, sometimes not so nice. Right now she didn't particularly feel like being nice, but she knew she had to curb her tongue. "Not exactly my problem, and for the record, I was being very nice, considering his proposal."

"That bad, huh?" he said.

"Yeah, you could say that," she said.

"I'm sorry to hear that," he said.

"Why are you sorry?"

"I could say I'm sorry because men are insensitive jerks or that we're cocky, self-absorbed idiots, but you'd only think I was still trying to get into your black-lace panties."

The phrase was familiar. She turned, seeing Devon leaning against the far post across from her. "You," she said.

He nodded once. "Me. Or I could say I was sorry that you had to deal with all this drama when all you want to do is just be left alone. But I have a feeling you still wouldn't really believe me."

"Probably not," she said.

"Probably." He repeated her word, encouraged. "So I guess that means there's a chance you might just believe me."

Jazz grimaced and shook her head. "Why don't you tell me what you want from me?"

"Do I have to want something?"

"Most people do."

"You're right, I do want something. I just want to talk."

"There are about a hundred people in there to talk to. Half are women, and I'm sure they'd be delighted to chat."

"But they're not you."

"You don't know me."

"True, but I'd like to."

"You're an athlete, right?"

"Yes."

"I don't date athletes anymore."

"Do you talk to them?"

She smiled. "Yes, I guess I do."

"Good, 'cause that's all I want—to talk. That's all."

Okay, he was certainly different. She'd grant him that. His response definitely wasn't what she expected. They usually turned and left after she'd coolly dismissed them. He didn't. "You're tenacious, aren't you?"

"Actually, I prefer the term 'persistent.'" He smiled that smile she knew curled women's toes. He lowered his head shyly then looked back up at her. "You left the party and I was getting a little lonely inside without you," he said in quiet sincerity.

"Somehow I doubt that."

"No, don't doubt it. It's the truth."

The fact that he knew she had been staring at him didn't bother her anymore. "There are plenty of women in there to stare at."

"True, there are, but then there'd be no point, would there? Devon Hayes," he said, stepping closer holding his hand out.

"Jazelle Richardson," she said as they shook.

"It's a pleasure meeting you."

"So, Devon Hayes, you're one of Melanie's clients, right?"

"Sometimes," he said cryptically. "Right now it depends."

"It depends on what?" she asked.

"On whether or not you are," he said, flirting shamelessly. She opened her mouth to speak, but instead said nothing. She smiled and looked away. "Was that too honest?"

"Not at all. It was direct," Jazz said, then stared at him, wondering what he'd say next. This man, this modern gladiator, was nothing like she expected.

"We got off on the wrong foot earlier. I'd like to make it up to you."

"That's not necessary."

"Yes, it is."

Jazz had to admit his smooth talking, self-assurance and bravado came from a quieter place than she was used to or expected. There was something about him she felt connected to. She glanced behind him, seeing a young woman dressed in red standing on the lit path with her lips pursed and her eyes zeroed in on him. She'd obviously followed him. "Your fan club has arrived."

Devon turned briefly, seeing the same young woman in red who had plastered herself to his side all evening. Earlier he'd tried to make it clear that he wasn't interested, but she obviously hadn't gotten the message. "I assure you, she's not with me," he said. "I think one of Melanie's guests brought his daughter along."

"And let me guess, you're babysitting?"

"Not exactly. She wants me. Her words, not mine," he clarified quickly. "Discouraging her has proved to be difficult at best. I told her I wasn't interested."

"I don't think she got that message." Jazz leaned back to perch against the gazebo's rail. She tilted her head, seeing the young woman take a few steps closer, obviously to try and hear what they were saying.

"No, I guess not," Devon said, walking over to lean back against the post beside her.

"Maybe you should go back inside and talk to her," Jazz suggested, still hoping to be left alone.

"I'd rather not. It's obvious that talking isn't going to work. Some people believe only what they see."

"I know a few people like that," she said.

"It's difficult sometimes," he confessed truthfully, "not being cruel when you just want to be left alone."

"Yeah, I kinda get that a lot," she commiserated.

"I'm sure you do," he said looking admiringly at her profile.

"Devon, let's cut to the chase, shall we? I know who you are and you know who I am. I'm here to get away from the drama. I don't need more."

"How do you equate me with drama?" he asked.

She tilted her head and purposefully looked at the woman waiting for him. "Oh, I don't know, perhaps it's the enamored teenager standing there, panting breathlessly and waiting for you."

"You seem to be an expert at getting rid of unwanted attention, so any suggestions would be greatly appreciated," he said. She stared into his eyes, seeing his sincerity. "Look, you don't know me, and it's not your problem. I get that, but…" Jazz looked away quickly. Devon stopped speaking. He leaned away from the post and moved toward the gazebo entrance to leave. He stepped down the one step.

Jazz knew a solution, but that would mean putting herself out there, and she wasn't sure she wanted to do that until she saw the young girl's face. She was smiling victoriously, like she'd just won a prize at the county fair. She seemed too young to look as cocky as she did. Jazz knew girls like her. They got whatever they wanted, by looks, by plastic, by connections.

Suddenly striking a victory for the rest of the population who didn't trade in on their father's wealth and advantages prompted her to call out. "Devon," Jazz said before she could stop herself. He turned. She got up and walked over to him. They stood nearly eye to eye. She reached out slowly and stroked the side of his face tenderly. Then, without a word, she leaned in, drew his face closer and kissed him. Their lips met, once, twice, three and four times, each touching and tasting just enough to make a point. Jazz leaned back, more surprised by his nonaction than her impulsiveness. He hadn't touched her. He'd barely even returned her kiss. "I think you're gonna have to do better than that if you want to make your point."

Before she could continue, his arm instantly encircled her waist, pulling her body flush against his. She gasped, surprised by his strength and feeling the solid hardness of his body. She looked up into his dark eyes. He smiled, seeing his own wanton thoughts reflected in her eyes. He stepped forward and pressed her body against the nearest gazebo post. He cupped the back of her head as his mouth descended. He paused a brief instant and then kissed her as if their lives depended on it. Deep and sensual, his kiss instantly set her on fire, searing her body from the inside out.

She opened her mouth to him, and he entered. The sensuous feel of his tongue dipping into her mouth was intoxicating. Her body shuddered as the kiss intensified. She met the pressure of his kiss with equal fervor. Her insides tingled and her pulse accelerated as every nerve in her body sizzled. She felt a rush of excitement that slashed through her body. It had been a long time since a man kissed her like this.

She felt her body mold to his as her senses floated far beyond. Passion began to swell. Her heart pounded, her stomach fluttered and her body ached for him. She was losing control, and she realized that right now she just didn't care.

A soft moan of utter satisfaction hummed deep in her throat as she wrapped her arms around him, holding on tight. It felt as if every part of her body was on fire. The kiss was so much more than she had expected. It was mind-blowing, and he was insatiable. It staggered her, and in their passion they'd long since forgotten the woman in red. Then, suddenly mindful of what she was doing, Jazz leaned back and away. "Devon," she said breathlessly. "Devon, wait—we need to stop."

He stopped, but still held her close. Then, seeing her face, he grew concerned. "Are you okay?" he asked. She nodded then took a deep breath. "Are you sure?"

She nodded again. "Yeah, just a little breathless," she said, smiling.

"So I took your breath away. I like the sound of that."

She looked at him, not at all surprised by his bravado. "Calm down. I was only acting," she said.

He smiled and shook his head. "That kiss was not acting."

"You are so…" She paused. "So…," she said, easing back.

"Charming?" he suggested. She laughed, shaking her head. "Dashing?" She laughed again. "Charismatic?"

"How about conceited?" she said.

"Is it conceited to know the difference between a real kiss and acting?"

"I'm a very good actor."

He nodded, conceding the fact. "That'll work for now," Devon said easily as he wrapped his arms around her waist and held tight. The conversation had somehow turned to slow dancing. They swayed, languishing as the scant breeze swirled around them.

Jazz peered down the path toward the patio. The young girl in red was gone. "I do believe your friend got the message."

He glanced back. "You did it. Thank you," he whispered.

"You're welcome."

"Now, how do I repay you?"

"You don't."

"I have to. I always pay my debts. My grandfather used to say that a man in debt is a man in trouble. You don't want me in trouble, do you?" he asked, swaying their bodies effortlessly.

She could feel her body yielding to him again, but she didn't want to lose control. "I don't usually dance," she said, stepping back.

"That's not exactly true," he said with a smile knowing that she was well known for her moves.

She smiled. He was right. She danced all the time in her videos and onstage. "You're right, but I don't usually slow dance, particularly when there's no music," she said.

"Ahh, but there is music," he whispered quietly. "Listen."

Jazz listened. "All I hear are crickets and maybe a frog or two."

"No, close your eyes and listen closer. What do you hear?" She closed her eyes. He began detailing the sounds around them. "A gentle breeze, crickets, a woman's laughter from the party and…"

Jazz opened her eyes, smiling. "My mother's voice."

He nodded. "Exactly."

She smiled and stepped back again. He opened his arms to free her this time. Putting distance between them, she purposely went to the far end of the gazebo. "I take it back," she said, feeling emotion beginning to sweep over her. "You're not conceited. You're…"

"I'm what?" he asked after she went silent.

She moved to the gazebo's entrance then turned and looked back at him. Standing there she could see how he was every woman's fantasy. But he was also too "…complicated."

His eyes narrowed with focused intensity. "Not at all. We both know how this goes. I want you," he whispered, barely audible.

"But you can't have me," she said.

"Not even as a friend?" he asked. She didn't respond. He nodded. "Okay, Then stay—we can talk some more." She smiled and shook her head slowly. "Please, stay with me."

"Tempting, very tempting, but as much as I've enjoyed the evening's entertainment, I think I need to go now. Good night, Devon. Thank you for the dance."

"Jazz," he called out softly. She stopped but didn't turn around. "I still owe you, and I always pay my debts." She didn't reply. Moments later she was gone. Devon didn't move or try to stop her. He sat back on the rail in the darkness and smiled.

Chapter 3

INTERIOR—DEVON'S HOME—EARLY MORNING

Hours later Devon woke up on fire, his arms and legs tangled in the silk sheets, his pillows tossed to the floor. He sat up and looked around the room. The quiet darkness assured him that he was in his bed alone. He lay back and closed his eyes again. Kissing Jazz earlier that night had set his body ablaze and he'd been laying awake most of the night thinking about her. She had burned into his blood, and each time he closed his eyes to sleep she came to him in his dreams.

In this last dream she was the essence of a warm, gentle mist. The scent of her sweet perfumed body surrounded him. She was everywhere, touching every inch of his body. He reached out to hold her. She vanished. Then the mist slowly cleared, and she appeared again. She was a shadow at first; then her smooth brown skin formed her slender body. He reached out and touched her, feeling the smooth curve of her back. His body hardened with need as he drew her close. Soon her seductive body pressed against his and they were lying down on a white sand beach. She kissed him, and her full soft lips released his passion. They made love shrouded in the mist. It was surreal and erotic.

He smiled as he lay in the darkness. The memory was perfect, them together making love on the beach. Slowly he drifted back to sleep with that thought. The constant buzzing sound made him look to the side table. His cell phone was vibrating. He grabbed it and quickly answered. "Yeah."

"Hey, am I interrupting something?"

"No, I was asleep, dreaming," Devon said, sitting up quickly. Hearing his sister Terri's voice immediately concerned him. Although she called to stay in touch, she wasn't the type to call this late unless something was wrong. "Are you okay? Is Debbie okay?" he asked.

"Yeah, I'm fine. Deb's fine, nicely tucked in at college. I just needed a break. You sound stressed—that must have been some dream."

"It was. So, what's going on?" he asked.

She sighed heavily. "Just a crazy day, that's all."

"Is the exciting world of advertising getting too stressful for you all of a sudden?" he asked, already knowing better.

"Today it was. I had a shoot, and two models didn't show up. I was stuck on the San Francisco wharf waiting for the fog to lift. I finally talked the client into making it a night scene."

"How'd it come out?" he asked.

"Even better than I originally planned," she said

proudly. "My client is thrilled. He already agreed to do more work with us."

"Congratulations. That's why you get the big bucks."

"Yeah, right," she joked. "Hey, I've got some really good news. I found out today that I'm up for a creative advertising award. It's not as big a deal as the Addy Awards or the Clios, but it's still a nice accomplishment."

"Hey, that's great, fantastic news. Congratulations again. When do you get the award?"

"I'm nominated. I still have to win."

"You'll win. Just make sure to mention me in the speech."

"There's an awards dinner, but I'm not going," she said.

"You should go."

"I don't know, maybe."

"No maybes. Go, I'll escort you. It'll be fun."

"All right, we'll go together. It's quiet there—where are you, exactly?"

"I'm home."

"Home where?"

"I'm at the beach."

"Which beach?"

"Sag Harbor."

"Hmm, Sag Harbor—that sounds like a good idea. I could use a few days of R & R, and I haven't seen Grandmom and Granddad in months. Why don't you send a jet to come get me?"

"Like you'd actually come."

"I might," Terri said, but they both knew better. She'd just started her own advertising firm and even though she had her brother, the number one face in America, on speed dial, she wanted to make it on her own. "So, what are you doing home already? It's what—three-thirty a.m. on the East Coast?"

He glanced over at the clock. "Yeah, about that. I went to a party then came home early."

"That doesn't sound like you."

"It was at Melanie Harte's house. I left early."

"Really? So you're really going through with it?"

"If you're referring to Melanie's matchmaking services, yes, I am," he said. "Melanie's track record and reputation is the best."

"But a professional matchmaker, Devon, it's so old school. Why not use a healer or a witch doctor the next time you need knee surgery while you're at it? You don't find lasting love like that. It's a crapshoot at best. Besides, I still don't get why you need to get married all of a sudden. Is it because the contract negotiations are stalled?"

"Where'd you hear that?"

"Internet, radio, newspapers," she said.

"Yeah, they're stalled. And it's not all of a sudden and I don't *need* to get married. I *want* to get married. It's time. It's what's missing in my life."

"Fine, whatever, it's your life. You know what all this is really about, don't you?"

"This has nothing to do with what happened."

"Of course it does. You don't trust yourself anymore. It's understandable. Trina, your ex-fiancée, dumped you, and you got hurt. You thought she was the one, and then she goes and does that. It's only natural to feel mistrustful. You were together for a long time, and then to have her turn on you like that."

"I realize not all women are like Trina. And my

wanting to get married has nothing to do with what happened."

"Yes, it does. You jumped out of the frying pan into the fire. After Trina, there was Tasha. Heaven knows what you were thinking when you hooked up with her. Talk about fatal attraction. She was nuts and fixated on you. She lied to you constantly and then attacked you publicly. I still don't see why you didn't press charges."

Devon closed his eyes, fighting the memory of the hell Tasha put him through and how she almost cost him everything. Terri was right—her attraction was definitely fatal. But three o'clock in the morning wasn't the time to rehash his mistakes. He'd gotten over it and was trying to move on with his life. He just wished the rest of the world would, too. "Are you done strolling down memory lane?" he asked.

"Devon…"

"Terri, let it go," he said in that tone he always used to end the conversation. Devon had had this same discussion with his sister several times before. They went around in circles. She didn't understand how important this was to him. He knew in his heart that what he was doing was necessary. This was his future.

"Okay, fine." Terri yielded, knowing she'd never be able to convince her brother what he was doing was another impulsive act. "I'm sorry, Devon. It's just that you're my big brother and I hate seeing you like this. You don't need a matchmaker to find love. You just need time to trust yourself again." He didn't respond. "So, how was Melanie's party?" she asked, knowing it was best to change the subject.

"Interesting. There were a few familiar faces. Armand and Scott showed up. Also, I met Jazelle Richardson."

"Jazz Richardson? Get out, really? How'd she look?"

"She looked beautiful," he said, smiling.

"I can definitely believe that. She's got that reserved style and class that few people have, especially in her line of business. Most entertainers are crass and tacky. She's not. You know, she'd be great for this new cosmetic client I'm trying to land. I wonder if she'd be interested?" she thought out loud.

"You'd have to ask her."

"Is she one of Melanie's clients, too?"

"No, she was just at the party," he said.

"She'd be perfect for the perfume campaign. She's an independent woman, strong, focused. She's got her own career, she's talented and she's famous, and did I mention that she'd be perfect for this new ad campaign?"

"Yes, I believe you mentioned that," he said.

"So?" Terri asked.

"So what?" Devon questioned.

"So, what happened at the party?"

"The party was nice. There were a lot of people and—"

"No, I mean with Jazz. The tabloids say that she went to rehab for drugs and pills. Did she?"

"I don't know. She seemed fine when I talked to her. You know how the tabloids love to sell papers. They'll print anything about anybody. It doesn't necessarily have to be the truth. You've read the things they write about me," he said.

Terri laughed. "Yeah, but the stuff they write about you is usually true."

"Not funny," he said, "and not all of it."

Terri paused a moment. She didn't mean to remind him again of the scandal that had led him to his current predicament. "I didn't mean to…Tasha was a clear case of a crazed, obsessed fan, everybody knows that."

"Now, yes, after the fact. But not then," he said.

"That's not true, Devon. You got a lot of support. It was just her father that kept pushing it. He wanted his fifteen minutes of fame, and now he has it. Extortion, blackmail, perjury—he has all the fame he can handle for the next several years, and so does she."

"Yeah," he said, fighting the bitterness of the memory.

"So tell me, Jazz looked well?"

Devon locked his thoughts on her smiling face and nodded. "She looked," he said, then paused, thinking about her in that dress and their kiss, "stunning."

"Beautiful, stunning—sounds like the two of you hit it off. Actually, she'd be an interesting match for you."

"You think so?" he said coolly.

"You're attracted to her, aren't you?"

"I can't believe you just asked me that question. Since when do we discuss my personal life in detail?"

"Since now. Answer the question. You're attracted to her."

He sighed loudly. "Yes, I am. So what? Half the men in the country are attracted to her," he added.

"You can both be in the ad campaign. It'll be romantic."

"Whoa, slow down. We just talked and then…" He paused before saying too much. "Besides, I thought you said that matchmaking was old school."

"I stand corrected. What else happened? You were going to say something. What was it? Something happened between you, didn't it? Come on, you can tell me," she prompted.

"I don't know what you're talking about. She and I

only talked a few minutes. I don't know much about her other than what I've heard," he said.

Terri yawned. "I don't buy it."

"I don't care. It's late, go to bed. You sound delirious. Get some rest and I'll catch up with you later."

"I know there's more to your story than you're telling me, but since it's late and I am tired, I'm gonna let it slide for now."

"Good idea. Get some rest. I'll call you in a few days."

"Okay, take care. Good night."

Devon closed the cell phone and looked at the time. In a few hours it would be dawn. He lay back down then looked up at the high ceiling, thinking about the dream. It had been a long time since he'd had a dream that vivid and that sensual. Making love to Jazz was all he could think about now. He had tasted her, and he knew that nothing and no one else would satisfy his need except her.

He sat up, knowing a peaceful sleep was out of the question. He got up and walked out onto his balcony. The cool night air was exactly what he needed. He sat on the wooden rail, thinking about the recent changes in his life. Thoughts of Jazz quickly returned. He thought about his sister's concerns. After witnessing their parent's disastrous divorce firsthand, neither one of them ever intended to marry. They even vowed to each other that they wouldn't. But he was tired of being alone. Fame and fortune were wonderful, but having no one to share them with was an empty feeling.

He went back into his bedroom, changed into his sweats and went downstairs to his gym. This was his sanctuary, the one room in the house where he could fully concentrate. His work ethic was simple: the harder he worked out, the more focused he became. Nothing ever distracted him when he was in here. A rigorous workout was exactly what he needed to get his mind off Jazz and his desire for her.

He flipped the light switch, and the room was immediately bathed in bright light. Just as he dropped a CD into the player, the phone rang. He answered. "Devon, it's Vincent. You need to get over to the police station."

"What's going on?" Devon asked.

"A friend of mine at the hospital told me Armand Fuller crashed his car."

"Is he okay?"

"Yeah. He refused medical attention, but the police took him in just in case. He's fine. He's got a few cuts and bruises. They already discharged him. The police took him to the station a few minutes ago to give a statement on the accident. I don't think they're gonna book him, but they might need someone to vouch for him."

"I'm on my way."

"All right, I'll meet you there."

Fifteen minutes later, Devon and Vincent arrived at the police station at the same time. They walked into the building and saw Scott talking to a few uniformed officers. "Hey, what's going on?" Devon said as he approached. They shook hands, and Scott introduced Devon and Vincent to the officers.

"Mr. Fuller is fine. He's in the office giving a statement. He didn't appear to be intoxicated, so there shouldn't be a problem," one of the officers said.

"So, he's free to leave after that?" Devon asked.

"Yes, there should be no problem."

Scott and Devon looked at each other and then to

Vincent. They all knew that Armand was upset and had been drinking heavily at the party. "We'll make sure he gets home safely," Vincent said.

Armand was released soon after. He had bruising around his eye and a small bandage on his forehead, but other than that he looked fine. Scott volunteered to drive him home. Vincent and Devon stayed behind in the police station parking lot talking. "He's really messed up," Vincent said as Scott waved and drove away.

"Shelia leaving him hit harder than I thought. It's amazing what they do to us."

"Nah, man, we do this to ourselves."

"See, you have a much different perspective. You work with Melanie. Your business is love."

"It's not a different perspective—it's a clearer perspective. Women are just as confused about men as men are about women. We don't know how to communicate with each other. We never learned that in school. We talk at, not to, each other."

"So you're saying that all Armand and Shelia had to do was talk and their marriage would have been fine?"

"No, I don't know their issues, but what I am saying is that we all want the same thing—to be loved. We each go about it differently. The Platinum Society doesn't just match couples. We teach clients how to stay together and build strong bonds."

"I remember all the conversations with Jessica and Veronica when I first signed on. But does any of that really work?"

"What do you think?" Vincent said proudly.

"Since I know the company's impressive success rate, I'd say it speaks for itself."

"I agree. Did you enjoy yourself last night?"

"Yeah, it was nice. It was lot more crowded than I expected."

"It's the first party of the season. It's always larger, and also most of our clients prefer a more social atmosphere. They usually feel more comfortable."

"I spoke with Melanie last night."

"Did you meet anyone interesting?"

"Yes."

"Good."

"Don't you want to know who it was?"

"It's your selection. They were all three chosen with your profile in mind. Any one of them would very easily make you a very happy man."

"But would I fall in love with them?"

"You were very specific about your ideal woman. Presumably you would fall in love, since she's exactly what you wanted. The question you should ask yourself is, is she what you need?"

"Opposites attract," Devon said.

Vincent nodded. "Sometimes, but not always. But I'd ask myself why these specific qualities were important. Look, I know you've had issues with women in the past. Some saw you and immediately saw a dollar sign. Finding someone to love is hard."

Devon considered Vincent's comments. "Women were never a problem, you know that. They'd come and go in and out of my life constantly, most thinking of being my wife. But I'd never promised them anything, ever. Then two years ago I met Trina. I thought we were perfect together. She was beautiful, poised, demure and intelligent. She was a wealthy socialite who spent her time doing charity work and shopping sunup to sundown. She loved partying and spending money. She was selfish and vain and lived to bask in the spotlight. She was seriously high maintenance. I knew it and accepted it.

"We got engaged, and I thought everything was fine. The breakup took me completely off guard. I found out she was getting married on my way down the tunnel to play my last game. It was exactly what you read in the papers. She dumped me for someone with more money.

"I met Tasha a month after the breakup. She was the exact opposite. She grew up poor and did everything imaginable to claw her way to the top. I thought that was admirable at the time. I didn't know that meant lying, stealing and cheating to get what she wanted. I don't have to tell you how badly that ended. Now lately, women come and go like the weather, hence the bad-boy rep. So as you can see, my track record isn't exactly top notch when it comes to the women I choose. What does that say about me?"

"That you're human. That you've been protecting yourself. They were beautiful, intelligent women. How could you possibly know they had ulterior motives? Melanie's instincts are sharp, and her approach works. Attraction is the key. When you see a woman, and you can't take your eyes off of her, then there's something there. You can't fake feelings, and you can't fool the heart, not for long."

Devon shook his head. "I want to marry, but I don't trust my instincts when it comes to women anymore."

"That's why you have us. We've got your back. So, with all that said, I have to go. Some of us actually have to work for a living. I have three appointments in Boston today," he joked.

Devon chuckled as they shook hands then walked to

their cars. "Hey, thanks again for the phone call. Good looking out."

"Anytime." Vincent waved as he drove off. Devon pulled out of the parking lot, thinking about what Vincent said. He'd made some valid points. He'd met the women he had asked for and turned each one down. Then Jazz showed up and instantly captured his attention. She was nothing like what he thought he wanted. But his attraction was undeniable. He drove home thinking about Jazz. She was far different from any woman he'd gone out with.

It was still dark when Devon got back home. He headed to his gym and started his workout. Heart-thumping music blasted through the speakers. He warmed up then walked over to the wall of mirrors and looked at his reflection. He looked the same, perhaps a bit more tired than usual. He picked up some weights and, holding one in each hand, began his workout routine.

Already in peak athletic condition, he did not need to exercise much, but he did it anyway. Not because he had to, but because he needed the release and the physical exhaustion. Exercise had always been his mental distraction, and right now he needed all the distractions he could get.

The grueling regimen he set up for himself was intense. Free weights, push-ups, pull-ups, dips—he did them all, back to back. He hit the treadmill, the elliptical bike and the lat dorsi station. His angry muscles pulled tight then released in agony. Gluteus maximus, quadriceps, biceps, triceps, abs, they all burned with the added demands.

With training camp coming up, he knew he needed to be in better shape than ever. This was a contract year, and after last season and knee surgery he had something to prove both to himself and to his team. Right or wrong, he felt responsible for last season's losses. Had he not been distracted, none of that would have happened.

He lay back on the bench and grabbed the long bar. The large black weights had already been set. He held the bar securely above his head then took a deep breath. In one smooth motion he heaved the weights upward, releasing them from the bar stand. He straightened his arms. Flexor and extensor muscles tensed as biceps and triceps pulled through. He pumped the weights slowly, took a break then repeated the action several more times. Finally he let them rest back on the bar stand. He lay back down and, taking a deep breath, looked up at the ceiling. His body ached, his muscles throbbed and his pulse rate soared…and still Jazz was on his mind. He sat up, grabbed his towel around his neck and gulped from his water bottle.

After a quick shower, he wrapped a towel sarong style around his waist and walked out onto the deck and stood staring at the approaching dawn. The deck was perched high, with a breathtaking view. He stood looking around. The cool morning air was refreshing after the grueling two-hour workout and shower. Dawn had barely touched the sky in the distance. He sipped his energy drink and perched on the wooden rail, looking out at the picture-postcard moment. The beach was empty except for a lone figure strolling by with her dog. She reminded him of Jazz.

He touched his finger to his lips and smiled. The taste of her had long since gone, but he still sensed the intense pressure of their kiss. It had sparked and then ignited a flame inside of him. His body was still on fire. She thought she was helping him, but in actuality she had started a blazing inferno. He tipped the bottled water to his lips and swallowed hard.

Assessing his life was something he seldom did, but lately he found himself doing it more and more. His life was envied by many. He watched the silhouette of the woman and her dog at the water's edge. He thought about the dream that woke him up. Jazelle was in his blood the same way she was when he was fifteen years old. An adolescent crush on a television star was one thing, but he was a grown man now. Still, the deep well of feelings he'd tapped into earlier had begun a raging flood of desire. How to quench a need so strong?

He picked up his cell phone, then paused. It was early, but he needed to be proactive. He decided to leave a message, but to his surprise she answered instantly.

"Good morning," Melanie said brightly.

"Good morning," Devon answered. "I didn't expect you to pick up. After the party last night, I thought you'd sleep in."

Melanie laughed. "Hardly. There's a ton of work to do. You left early. Did you enjoy yourself last night?"

"Yes, I did. I had a great time," he said.

"Good, I'm glad to hear it."

"I spoke with Jazelle briefly."

"Have you changed your mind?"

"No, not at all," he assured her. "She's a lot different than I expected—she's quiet and more introspective. I'd like to get to know her."

"Surprised?" Melanie asked.

"Yes. She was kind enough to help me out of a jam last night. I'd hoped I could invite the two of you over this evening as a thank-you."

"I have to be in New York this afternoon, but I should

be back barring any unforeseen circumstances. And I'll make sure to relay your invitation."

"Thanks, I'd appreciate that. I'll see you this evening around six."

"Sounds good," she said.

Devon smiled and hung up.

Chapter 4

EXTERIOR BEACH—EARLY MORNING

Jazz stood in darkness and waited until she saw the dawning of the new day. She took a deep breath then held the phone to her ear and listened. The sound of her brother's voice penetrated deep into her heart. She closed her eyes and listened closer. His voice was slow and methodical. He enunciated each word with clarity and purpose. There was no denying he knew exactly what he was doing. He wasn't drunk or stoned or high as he was so often when he called her that early in the morning. On the contrary, he was calm, rational and resolved, and that scared her even more.

She listened to his words, but also to the sounds in the background. She heard people yelling and shouting, the early morning seagulls screeching, the hum of highway traffic in the distance, the car horns blasting and the emergency sirens blaring. It was the sirens that always gave her a chill. Their loud and incessant wailing screamed continuously like earsplitting whines from grief-stricken mourners. Then, when they stopped, there was the explosive sound of a car engine and the screech of tires peeling on asphalt. After that, there was nothing. Silence hung in the air.

The time between that instant and the next seemed immeasurable. Minutes, hours, perhaps days passed, but she knew it was only a few seconds. Then suddenly there was a loud, piercing scream. High and shrill, it released before she even knew it was her own voice. The terrifying sound stabbed into her heart. And even now, months later, her heart still pounded in her chest and her hands still shook with rage and helplessness.

She looked out at the rising sun in the distance. The skyline was scattered with a few yachts and sailboats. It was another day and another time. She took a deep breath then closed her cell phone and stood silently. It was over. Waves lapped onto the sand and birds called from above. It was over. It was an ordinary day much like all the days since. But still each morning she awoke to the last moments of his life. It was over.

Another day had dawned, and she wondered how she was going to get through it. She looked down at her bare feet pressed into the wet sand. It wasn't the Pacific, but it would have to do. Jazz quietly watched the slight slit of sunrise widen across the bay's horizon. It was the stillness of the moment she anticipated each morning. She took a deep breath and released it slowly. She knew she was lost and empty inside. But this was what she hid from the rest of the world: her pain. She had to be strong. The façade was important. She could never let them see her cry again.

After a few moments, she walked down the beach eventually joined by her usual morning companion, a scruffy-looking mongrel that had appeared by her side a week ago. There was never a formal greeting or salutation. He appeared, stayed at her side, and then moved on. For some reason they each seemed to find solace in walking together. She had no idea where he came from or where he went when he left her. He had no tags, and it looked as if life had knocked him down, too. They were the perfect pair, two lost souls in search of solitude.

About a mile and a half down the beach the two waywards climbed up onto the rocks and sat in the smooth cradle she'd found a few weeks ago. She braced herself securely against the ill-fitting chair then relaxed. The mutt, finding his place, cuddled protectively at her feet. It wasn't particularly comfortable, but it wasn't uncomfortable, either. It was, however, the perfect perch from which to watch the world go by while still isolated. She saw everything and everyone, but no one saw her. And just as morning light brightened the sky, the usuals came out.

From her lofty perch she watched an old man with his earphones and metal detector search the beach for lost trinkets and treasures. He stopped occasionally to sift through the sand for nothing much, then continued on. There were a few nondescript joggers, with and without dogs. A runner ran by at top speed, and two women in designer sweats power-walked and power-talked, loud and nonstop. Farther down the beach she watched the morning gathering. At first there was one, then two, then a few more; after a while it was a small group. On the same spot each morning they did their tai-chi exercises.

Jazz watched the graceful movements. It was these peaceful moments that refueled her. She felt her body completely relax. Her thoughts drifted, then centered on the party the night before. Since the summer season hadn't officially started, most of the guests were residents. Still, the guest list had been a virtual who's who of Sag Harbor society. Some were direct descendants of the original settlers, while others were Sag Harbor's nouveau riche.

After a while she started thinking about Devon. She smiled for no particular reason. When she first saw him across the room, she expected him to be a typical egomaniac jock. She'd often found that athletes were like that and assumed that he'd be the same. Instead she found him charming, funny and unpredictable. He made her laugh.

She'd seen him before. It was impossible not to. His charismatic smile was everywhere, and he sold everything. He endorsed cars, power bars, clothing, shoes, even his own gym equipment. He was handsome, and women flocked to him as soon as he walked in.

A seagull swooped down, landing on a rock near them. The dog's head bopped up, and he growled. The bird flew off instantly. "You're a great bodyguard. I should have had you with me last night. Dr. Larry was driving me nuts." The dog sat up and looked around for more intruders. "And you missed a great party," she said. The mutt looked up at her lazily, his floppy, wayward ears only half-perked. "Maybe next time I'll invite you as my date. What do you think about that?" The dog yawned wide then turned and lay back down. "Yeah, great idea, I totally agree."

Just then her cell phone rang. She looked at the time stamp before answering. It was just after six o'clock.

Few people had her personal cell number and even fewer would call her at this time in the morning. She answered.

"Please, please tell me I woke you up and you're lying next to a hunk of man and the two of you just had hot 'n' sweaty butt-naked scream-his-name-over-and-over-again sex."

Jazz laughed. It was her best friend, Savannah. "Does a dog at my feet count?"

"A dog as in a man, or a real barking mutt?" she said.

"A real barking mutt, actually a mongrel, I'd say," Jazz clarified, humored by her friend's constant hopefulness of getting her in bed with someone, anyone. Just then the dog's head bopped up and he looked at her. Jazz smiled haplessly and shrugged as if apologizing for hurting his feelings by calling him a mongrel. "Sorry to disappoint you."

"Yeah, yeah, but you always do. Honey, when are you gonna throw caution to the wind and enjoy your life a little?" Savannah asked with mock disappointment. "You need to get out of the lovelorn slump and find yourself some new blood, preferably coursing through the veins of a six-foot-five inch hunk of a man."

Savannah always thought a man was the answer to all her problems. In actuality, men were the main thing contributing to the problem. She'd been married three times already, and she and Jazz were the same age. She was wild and uncontrollable and had been that way ever since they'd met in boarding school. Jazz had attended for only a few years, whereas Savannah had grown-up there.

She was part Cherokee Indian and part African-American. Her father, unlike most Native Americans, sat on a ton of money. Her mother was a model who owned an international modeling agency and lived in London. Looking at Savannah was like looking at perfection. She had the beauty of both parents, and she used it to her full advantage.

"Please tell me that I, at least, woke you up and you're still in bed."

"I'm up sitting on some rocks in Sag Harbor."

"Good Lord, woman, what the blazes are you doing in Sag Harbor already? The season hasn't even officially started yet."

"I know, and it's the perfect time to be here."

"So, what do you do there?"

"Read scripts mostly, walk along the beach, relax."

"I bet you haven't even been out of the house, except at dawn, have you? Speaking of which, where are you renting?"

"I'm not. I'm staying with a friend, Melanie Harte. You've heard me talk about her."

"Sure. She's a matchmaker, right?"

"Right," Jazz said.

"Well, that at least sounds promising."

"I'm not here to see her professionally. I'm just visiting."

"Have I taught you nothing? Find thee a man, get thee sexed up then get thy butt back to L.A." Jazz laughed at Savannah's creed. "You think I'm kidding. I'm not."

Jazz laughed again. Talking to Savannah was exactly what she needed. They had always been there for each other. After her mother died, they went to New Jersey and stayed with her grandparents for a month. Afterward they went to Santa Fe and stayed with Savannah's grandmother for another month. When Savannah's mother got sick, they stayed in London for months.

Whenever she married or divorced, they celebrated. Then, when Brian died, they traveled together for three months. She was always a lifesaver. "Where were you last night when I really needed you?"

"Why, what happened last night?" Savannah asked.

"Mel threw a preseason party."

"Sounds intriguing. Anybody interesting show up?"

"Have you ever heard of Devon Hayes?"

"L.A. football player, gorgeous, rich, body of an African warrior?" she said, describing him perfectly.

"Savannah, do you know every eligible man on the planet?"

"You have your hobbies, and I have mine," she said by way of explaining her extensive knowledge of just about anything concerning men. "What about him? Was he there?"

"Yes."

"Did you do him?"

"You are absolutely obsessed," Jazz declared.

"Thanks," Savannah said, laughing. "Now answer the question. Did you?"

"No, I didn't do him. He's not exactly my type."

"Honey child," Savannah said in her most Southern accent, "if my memory serves correctly, that man is everybody's type. My advice to you is to find him, do him and then do him again."

"I don't have to find him. He lives close by."

"Ohh, how convenient. Nothing like ordering some takeout."

"I swear, you have a one-track mind. It's way too early for this conversation. Half the states aren't even up yet. As a matter of fact, where are you now, still on location in Brazil?"

"No, London."

"You're visiting your mom?"

"Yeah, she had a crash and burn. I'm helping her out."

"Okay, I'll catch the next flight out," Jazz said, sitting straight up.

"No, don't, she's fine. I just popped over to confirm."

"Are you sure you don't need me?"

"Positive."

Jazz nodded, knowing there was never false pride between them. If Savannah really needed her, she'd have no qualms in saying so. Their friendship was based on honesty. If there was a problem and she needed her, she'd ask Jazz to come, knowing she would without question. "What happened?" Jazz asked.

"The usual—overworked, near exhaustion. She collapsed. I'll tell you about it later. I'm headed back to the States, hopefully, in a few weeks."

"New York or L.A.?" Jazz asked, referring to where they would meet up.

"Let's do New York," Savannah said. "I need to shop American."

"Sounds good. Call me when you get in."

"I will. I gotta get ready to go."

"All right, take care. Tell your mom I asked about her."

"Will do, and take care of you. Remember, baby steps."

Jazz closed her cell and sat back thinking about Savannah's mother. In a lot of ways she was like her own mother. They had both fallen in love with impossible men, and they both had been devastated when they turned away.

Her mother, Yelena Brooks, had everything: beauty, brains and talent. Her one and only movie had been her downfall. Meeting and falling in love with Frank Richardson had ruined her career and, in the end, her life. She loved him to the end. He came to her when she was dying and professed his love. He asked for forgiveness for choosing his career over her. She died in peace knowing that.

Unlike her mother, Jazz still hadn't forgiven her father and she saw no reason to ever forgive him in the future. She closed her eyes and lay back, letting the early morning light bathe her in warmth as a gentle breeze rustled around. She hummed the song she'd heard last night. It had been on her mind ever since. It was her mother's song. It wasn't the most popular, and it hadn't won any awards, but it was special because it had been written for her by her mother. Her mind drifted back to happy memories with her mother. A few minutes later she heard playful screams. She opened her eyes and saw a couple frolicking on the beach.

The man chased the woman, and she squealed each time he caught her. He grabbed her waist, and she held tight when he picked her up and spun her around. He slowly stopped and sat her back down on the sand, but not before kissing her. Jazz watched as the kiss intensified then stopped when a jogger ran by.

Being outside, yet still away from the prying eyes of the public, was a pleasure. That's why she loved walking on the beach at dawn and dusk or sitting out on the patio. Going beyond those boundaries meant the possibility of being recognized. She had changed her hair, highlighted it and wore large hats and dark sunglasses. Few people bothered when she looked so closed off. And if they stared, it was on her terms, because of her outrageous hat and glasses, and not because she was who she was.

Months ago, when Melanie had suggested she come and spend a few weeks at her Sag Harbor residence, Jazz turned her down. Being alone was more to her liking. Then some tabloid concocted an elaborate tale about her suicide watch and subsequent mental breakdown, and she knew she needed to do something different. The scary thing was the story had an inkling of truth.

Staying with a family friend had seemed to be a good idea at the time. Now she wasn't so sure. Melanie was a matchmaker. No, correction, she was "the" foremost matchmaker to the wealthy. Not just wealthy: millionaire, billionaire wealthy. Her clientele ranged from sports figures to movie stars to CEO's. Anyone with at least a seven-digit bank account could request her services. Thankfully, she was no longer on Melanie's hit list.

"Jazz, is that you?"

Jazz leaned up, seeing Jessica in jogging shorts and ear buds. She was running in place beside the rocks. She waved good morning.

Jessica climbed up and collapsed down beside her. "Now I remember why I hate jogging. I was going to call you later. I looked for you last night. I guess you left early. Was everything okay?" she said breathlessly.

"Yeah, fine. I had a nice time. I'm glad I went. But I didn't leave that early. You probably missed seeing me because I was outside in the gazebo toward the end of the evening."

"You, too. Wow. Apparently that gazebo was pretty popular last night. A woman at the party told Veronica she saw a couple kissing passionately in the gazebo.

Then afterward they danced slow and seductively. She said it was like a scene from a movie. She had to pull her husband away, 'cause he wanted to stand in line to use the gazebo next."

Jazz groaned inwardly. "Actually, that was probably me."

"That was you?" Jessica repeated, obviously surprised.

"It's not what you think. I was helping Devon out."

"Devon, as in Devon Hayes? Nice, very nice," she said.

"Some pint-sized Lolita was on him all night, and we kissed to cool her jets. It worked. She left him alone."

"I like my version better."

"I didn't realize there were other people that close."

"No one recognized you. But they did see Devon coming back to the party alone. He left shortly thereafter. His bad-boy image is still intact. Everyone assumed he was meeting his kissing partner somewhere more discreet."

"It's amazing how these things start."

"This is Sag Harbor. It's a small town, and everybody knows everybody's business. Devon is a hot ticket."

"So I've been hearing."

"There are few men to equal his intensity and abilities on the field. His football stats and his career records are incredible. They're already talking about him being inducted into the Hall of Fame when he retires."

"Is he really that good?" Jazz asked curiously.

"Better. He's probably got a dozen-plus endorsements. And they say that he makes more money off the field than on it. He was injured four games into last season. The Stallions crashed and burned after that. Everybody thinks he blames himself."

"Was it his fault?"

"No. It's football. It happens. A key player goes out for the season, morale drops and it's like treading the Atlantic trying to get back again. The harder they tried, the more they failed."

"So he chilled out all season, huh?"

"I doubt that. It was a bad hit right to the knee. It was what they call a career ender. He had surgery, worked hard to recover and now he looks as good as new. I know he's been working with his youth foundation and scholarship programs in his downtime. He's a good guy, not the average athlete."

"Maybe, maybe not," Jazz said, still skeptical.

"Okay," Jessica said, standing and looking down the beach, "I gotta get back to running. I'll catch you later." She jumped down onto the sand, jogged in place, checked her neck pulse and started jogging again.

Jazz watched her a moment then lay back and closed her eyes. This time she thought about the kiss last night with Devon. She'd only kissed him to help him out. She knew any woman, no matter what age, couldn't just stand and watch the object of her infatuation being kissed. So she did it for him. At least that was the story she insisted on telling herself. But she knew better. She kissed him because she was curious and because she wanted to feel his arms wrapped around her. Last night the kiss had swept her up. What was meant as a taste had devoured them. When their lips parted and she looked into his eyes, she saw what she knew was reflected in her own eyes: passion and desire.

Every part of her wanted him. It had been a long time since a man had touched her, and having Devon's solid body and strong arms holding her had made her feel protected and secure. She liked the feeling. For so long she had felt helpless, but all of a sudden with him she was strong and in charge again.

She smiled as her thoughts wandered to daydreams and then to fantasies. The kiss from last night became more than a kiss as his mouth traveled down her body, setting her skin on fire. She drifted away with that thought.

She awoke alone. It was twenty minutes later. She looked around. Her amiable canine companion had long since disappeared.

She got up and walked back to the house. Beachfront, the sprawling mega-mansion, sat on a bluff surrounded by nature's perfection. It was beyond exquisite. As she approached the large structure, she admired its beauty and aesthetics. Melanie had told her the huge three-story mansion had been built in the mid-twentieth century. It was first owned by her great grandmother, then her mother and now her. It was her home and her workplace. She spotted Melanie sitting out on the patio with her laptop. "Good morning," she said.

Melanie looked up from her laptop and smiled happily, bracing her oversized straw hat against the warm breeze. "Good morning. How are you feeling?"

Jazz took a deep breath and nodded. "Great. You?"

"Wonderful. There's coffee in the pot. Help yourself."

"Thanks," Jazz said as she walked to the marble-topped buffet and poured herself a cup. She carried the china cup to the seat across from Melanie and sat down. "You're working already?"

Melanie smiled. "I'm always working. My grandmother once told me that matchmaking is a calling, not a nine-to-five job. She was right. I didn't quite understand what she was talking about until I took over the business from my mother. And our Platinum Society's morning meetings are the best part of my day." She smiled contentedly.

"I still don't see how you do it."

"It's a joy, and I really love what I do."

"Are you setting up a match now?" Jazz asked, seeing Melanie focused on the laptop's screen again.

"No, actually this is something neither my mother nor my grandmother had to contend with. I'm blogging."

"You blog?"

"Of course. This is the twenty-first century, and there's a whole new world to communicate with. That means keeping up with technology. I use MySpace and Facebook. I blog and I Twitter."

"What are you blogging about this morning?"

"Last night's party, of course. It was a huge success. I arranged two very promising in-person meetings and got several potential clients."

"In-person meetings?" Jazz asked, instantly thinking of Devon. "You mean where the two people actually meet for the first time?"

Melanie nodded. "You know that my clients are very wealthy and very busy people. Some of them prefer to meet their matches in less formal ways. For them I throw small parties. I also invite friends and associates to make the evening less obvious and more enjoyable."

"So, a few of your clients met their matches last night?" Jazz asked. Melanie nodded as she checked her cell phone for text messages. Knowing that Devon was one of Melanie's clients, Jazz wondered if he'd met his match and, if so, who she was. "Devon is one of your clients. Did he meet his match?"

"He met several," Melanie said.

Jazz wasn't sure what that meant or how she felt about

it. She just knew that it made her uncomfortable. Of course, it wasn't that she liked him or anything like that. She didn't know him. It was just that he was the first man to make her feel anything in a long time.

"Did you enjoy yourself last night?" Melanie asked as she finished texting and looked across the table.

"Yes, I had a nice time. Thank you for insisting that I attend."

"Is that what I did, insist?" Melanie asked innocently.

"Yes, you did, adamantly," Jazz said, smiling.

"I'm a smart lady," Melanie said, congratulating herself shamelessly. Jazz smiled and nodded in agreement. "It was good to see you out and with people last night. Now, what are your plans today?"

Jazz had secluded herself in Melanie's house for weeks. The farthest she'd gone was down the beach a bit then back to the house. The whole idea of seeing her face on the cover of another tabloid sickened her. "Nothing major, why?"

"We have a dinner engagement this evening."

"We?"

"Yes, Devon Hayes asked you and me to dinner this evening. I already accepted."

"Melanie…"

"Ahh," Melanie said, holding her hand up to halt her next comment. "You said you were ready to get back out into the world. A nice quiet dinner with friends is the perfect setting. Besides, I couldn't turn him down. He wants to thank you for last night. Apparently you rescued him from a tricky predicament." Jazz half smiled. "Do you know what he's talking about?"

"Yes, I helped him with a pest problem."

"I see."

"But inviting me to dinner isn't necessary. He's your client, and I'm sure you two have things to discuss."

"Not really. This is purely social. That's why it's the perfect outing for you."

"I don't do sports."

"I doubt we'll be playing sports this evening."

"You know what I mean."

"Jazz, two athletes broke your heart. It doesn't mean every man will, does it? Nor does it mean every man who plays a sport will. Trust me on this."

"Fine, I'll go with you."

"Excellent. I should be back in time, but if not, I'll meet you there."

"What do you mean, meet me there? Where are you going?"

"Into the city. Veronica and I have a few clients to see, and I'm holding a look-see for potential clients. Dinner's at six." She gathered her laptop and cell phone from the table. "Don't worry. I've known the Hayes family for years. Devon's one of the good guys. He may come off a bit macho at times, but he's definitely a nice guy. Here's the address in case I'm running late." She handed Jazz a piece of paper then looked at her watch. "It's getting late. I had better get started. I'll see you this evening."

Jazz took a sip of her coffee. She let the hot liquid slip down her throat, warming her insides as it went. She'd told Melanie that she was ready to get back out into the world, but all of a sudden she wasn't so sure anymore. Melanie was a matchmaker, and it was obvious what she was doing.

Last night's party was a rude awakening. It didn't bother her that she was at times stared at and even ogled; she was used to that. What bothered her was Devon. Her impulsiveness was so unlike her. She had never just walked up and kissed a man she didn't know. Why she did it last night she had no idea. No, she did know. It wasn't necessarily to help Devon, although she used that as an excuse. It was because she wanted to know what it felt like to kiss him. And then it wasn't just a kiss. Now she'd be spending the evening with him. But thankfully Melanie would be there with her.

By the time afternoon came, the weather had turned dismal, overcast and drizzly. Jazz's mood, not surprisingly, had turned with it. She spent most of the day in quiet meditation. That morning she sat out on the covered patio with a stack of scripts in front of her. Her agent, Simon Wells, had assured her she'd love them all. She read the first few. She didn't.

Simon called with his usual end-of-the-world-as-we-know-it speech. "I'm headed to L.A. and meeting with the studio. Is there anything you want me to tell them?"

"Not particularly," Jazz said nonchalantly.

He went on to extol the virtues of getting back to work and the fact that there were hundreds of young starlets clamoring for a chance to take her place on the set. Her response was simple. "Fine, let them."

"I know you don't mean that, so I'm gonna let it slide."

Jazz smiled. Simon was so predictable. He used the same scare tactics every time. He would tell her about projects that had been put on hold and the studio could no longer afford to wait for her return. She had already lost a role she'd been interested in doing and was on the verge of losing another one. She told him to pass on both of them, much to his chagrin.

"Are you sure?" Simon asked in earnest.

"I'm sure, I'll pass," she said.

"Jazz, listen to me, this is possibly the role of a lifetime. It could do for you what *Carmen Jones* did for Dorothy Dandridge. You can't keep turning these roles down. I spoke to Barbara, and she agrees."

"You talked to Barbara?"

"Yesterday. We met for lunch. She's concerned about you. We both are."

"Wow, I must be in really bad shape," she joked. Jazz shook her head at the reality of that comment. Barbara and Simon didn't get along at all. They were like fire and water. As ex-husband and ex-wife they were civil, but as manager and agent they fought and constantly disagreed. So for them to meet and discuss her was monumental. They had to really be concerned.

Simon was a phenomenal agent. To those who didn't know him, he was calculating, vicious, and ruthless. But to his clients, he was practically a saint. His stable was small, but most assuredly they were some of the best and most promising talents in the business. He was more or less bequeathed to her when her mother left the business years ago. Although at the time Simon didn't represent child actors, he made an exception and they'd been together ever since. To say he had his finger on the pulse of Hollywood was putting it mildly—his fist wrapped around its throat was more accurate.

Barbara, on the other hand, was the exact opposite. She was kind and nurturing and an excellent manager. Her job was to anticipate drama before it happened. In that capacity she was brilliant. Her instincts kept her clients ahead of the typical business as usual Hollywood hurdles. Thanks to her insider knowledge and connections, she had managed some of the most successful clients in the business.

"Jazz, I just hate to see you pass on another one,"

Simon said. "I read the script. It's perfect for you. The thing is, it's got a small window of opportunity. But if you want it, I can still get it for you. The studio really wants you for the lead."

"No. There will be others, I'll pass."

Simon took a deep, exasperated breath. "What do I have to do to get you back here?"

"I'm coming back, Simon. I just need a little more time."

"You said that three months ago and then again six months before that. Look, I don't mean to sound thoughtless or insensitive, but I'm worried about you. We're all worried about you."

"Simon, I'm fine. Trust me. I'm coming back. I just need a little more time and the right project."

"Okay, but are you absolutely positive you want to pass on this role?" he asked again.

"Yes."

"Okay, I'll tell the studio."

"Thanks. Is that it?"

"Actually, I was told about another script. It's very special. Barbara told me about it yesterday. It sounds wonderful. It's yours, but there's one small catch."

"What's the catch?" Jazz asked.

"Your father's producing and directing it. That part's set in stone."

"Then I pass," she said, barely letting him get the words out.

"Jazz, believe me, you're not going to want to pass on this after reading the script. It's not just good—it's brilliant."

"I pass," she insisted.

"Jazz, just do me a favor and keep an open mind about this one. I'm going to try and get my hands on a copy and send it to you. You should really consider this one."

"Fine, I'll consider it." She relented, knowing of course that anything her father was attached to, she wouldn't be. Their relationship wasn't toxic or volatile like the one he had with her brother, but that was only because she made a point of avoiding him completely. "Is that it?"

"Yes. I'm headed back to the Coast, so call me there. And please think about what I said. You need to come back."

"Have a good flight. I'll talk to you soon," she said then closed her cell. She took a deep breath and held the phone to her chest. Agents and managers talking about her father were unavoidable. He was *the* Frank Richardson, movie mogul. He had three Oscars. He started out as an actor then went behind the camera to direct and produce. His production company was responsible for some of the most profound films in the past ten years. Still, the mention of his name infuriated her.

They hadn't seen each other in over ten months, and they hadn't spoken in nearly two years. The last time she spoke to him was at her mother's funeral. The fact that he showed up caused the same madness each time their paths crossed. Newspapers, bloggers and tabloids never forgot the past. Each time they were in the same space, the past was dregged up in the tabloids.

As expected, the day after her mother's funeral the media ran every story imaginable about them. If it wasn't for her brother, Brian, she didn't know what she'd have done.

Jazz spent the rest of the afternoon reading scripts. Every so often she'd look up at the clock, anxious about the evening. She considered cancelling, but she didn't. When the time came she dressed in comfortable pants and a sweater and her usual dark sunglasses and large floppy hat. She waited until exactly six o'clock before going to his house. She still had no idea why she had agreed to go.

Chapter 5

INTERIOR—DEVON'S HOME

Curiosity made her go.

"Baby steps," Jazz reminded herself as she walked up the path to the front door. It had been a long time since she'd gone to a man's house. She took a deep breath, rang the bell and waited. "Okay, Jazelle, you're on." She straightened her back and smiled.

A few seconds later, a smiling Devon opened the front door. "Hey, hi, come on in," he said, obviously happy to see her. At least his friendly demeanor put her at ease.

"Hi, thanks," she said and walked in, hoping to see that Melanie had already arrived. She hadn't. Jazz glanced at her watch. It was a little after six o'clock. Melanie was never, ever late for anything.

Jazz paused in the open airy foyer while Devon closed

the door. One quick look around gave her a sense that nothing about Devon Hayes was what she expected. She looked up. Blue sky showed through skylights. The white marble floor sparkled and led to immaculately polished hardwood floors.

She looked up at the grand stairway leading to the second floor. It was stunning. Stately columns flanked the entrance along with lush green ficus and palm trees.

"I'm in the kitchen. Come, join me," he said.

Jazz nodded and followed. Devon didn't stomp or stroll, but he did walk with a definite swagger that looked as if it were rooted in extreme confidence. He was barefoot and wore a white button-down shirt and blue jeans. It was classic beach style yet still casual. She passed a mirror as they proceeded. She instantly regretted the outfit she'd chosen. But the extralarge knit sweater and wide-legged tan pants weren't intended to be appealing. Neither were the dark sunglasses and wide-brimmed hat, both of which she hurriedly removed.

She smoothed her hair and changed focus. She watched, admiring the broadness of Devon's shoulders as he walked. His waist was narrow, and the almost-tight jeans accented the firmness of his butt. She smiled. Seldom did she have the covert pleasure to so freely admire a man's body. Instantly the thought of seeing him naked occurred to her. Her smile broadened. Kissing him the night before had planted a wayward seed of sexual interest she hadn't realized was even there. She wondered what it would be like to feel him inside of her.

She knew he was interested in her. At least he was last night. She was right. The looks they gave each other across the room were pure heat. But seduction was never her forte. The assumption that she was her mother's daughter couldn't be further from the truth. Her mother was the seductress men couldn't resist. She had her mother's talent for singing and dancing and acting, but that was all. Anytime she tried to pull off sexy, she came off embarrassingly bad. There was no way she was going to hear another man ask her why she wasn't more like her mother.

She pushed aside the sexual fantasy of being with Devon out of her mind. What could she possibly offer a man like him? "Melanie's not here yet?" she asked as they continued down the wide-open hallway past what looked like the dining room and library.

"No, not yet. She called a while ago. She was running late. We're on our own for a while. Is that okay?" He turned briefly and smiled as they entered the brightly lit kitchen.

That wayward fantasy she'd just tried to push aside came bursting back again. Her throat went dry. She needed a drink. "Sure, great," she said, sounding more like a frog croaking than her real voice.

Brilliant sunshine streamed from the large picture windows and open sliding glass door in the kitchen. Jazz looked around slowly. Everything seemed pristine and new. The pale marble countertops glistened atop the solid white wood cabinetry. The brushed chrome appliances shone perfectly. She assumed he was like her and never cooked.

"Have a seat," Devon instructed before he circled behind the center island counter and headed toward the glass door refrigerator. Jazz paused at the counter and placed her sunglasses and hat on one of the stools lined up. "I'll get us a glass of wine."

"Actually, something nonalcoholic would be preferable."

"Sweetened iced tea okay?" he suggested.

"Yes, that sounds good, thank you."

He opened the refrigerator and pulled out a large glass pitcher. Ice cubes and lemon slices jingled around as he brought it back to the counter. He grabbed two glasses from a cabinet and poured their tea. After giving her a glass, he held his up to toast. "To my hero," he said.

"Your hero?" she asked before sipping the tea.

"You saved me last night."

"I wouldn't say all that."

"I would, you did and I thank you." He nodded nobly.

She nodded as well. "In that case, you're welcome."

They each sipped the sweetened tea. "I'm glad you came, even if it wasn't of your own volition," Devon added as he set his glass down and turned back to the refrigerator. He began pulling items out and putting them in a large colander on the counter.

"Did you think I wouldn't?" she asked curiously.

He turned to her and smiled. "Yes, the thought had occurred to me. I'm sure it was a very real possibility, wasn't it?" He glanced at her briefly then went back to what he was doing.

Jazz smiled and looked away. The fact that Devon knew she'd had second thoughts about coming tonight didn't really surprise her. She assumed he knew she was a private person. "I'm more of an introvert. I don't go out much."

"Seriously, I would have never guessed that about you."

"Why not?" she asked.

"Because you're an actress and in show business. I would assume it would take an extrovert to accomplish everything you've done."

"Performing is different. When I'm onstage or on set, I'm a different person. On set I'm the character I'm playing, and onstage I have an alter ego that takes over. I just do my job."

"Really?" he asked. She nodded. "That's interesting. So, is this the real you here tonight?" he asked, looking at her intently.

She had no reason to lie, so she told the truth. "No."

"I didn't think so."

"Disappointed?" she asked.

"No, but someday I'd like to meet the real Jazelle." They looked at each other as his words filled the room. He knew her letting go and just being herself was asking a lot. He was sure few people knew the real Jazz. But he hoped to be one of those people one day soon. "So, that pretty much means that the real you isn't a performer. Who is she?"

Jazz considered his question. No one had ever asked her that before. Her family knew her, and Savannah knew her. Others just assumed they knew, but really didn't. "A lot of things, but I guess I'm more like a bookworm."

He laughed. "No way. I don't believe that."

"It's true," she said. "I read and write, and I..." She quickly stopped herself.

He turned. "And you what?" he asked. She went silent. "Come on, tell me."

"It's nothing." He waited patiently. "I can't believe I'm actually telling you this. Origami," she finally confessed.

"Origami? You fold paper?" he asked.

She nodded. "Strange, right? I create my own pieces. I've done it for years. It's very cathartic. I started with horrible scripts that I hated reading. It felt good to make them into something better."

"Actually, that's very interesting. I would imagine that it would take a lot of imagination and engineering skills to create origami."

She looked at him, surprised. "Few people actually understand that part. Most think it's just folding paper and that's it."

"No, I would imagine that it's a lot like sculpting in a way, but with only two-dimensional materials."

"Yeah, it is," she said.

"So, how do you go about it? Do you choose the paper then see what you're going to make, or the other way around?"

"I choose the paper and work with it until something comes to me."

"That sounds really interesting. I'd love to see some of your work."

"We'll see." She stood and moved to the kitchen's sliding glass doors and looked out at the view. The house was higher up on a bluff, so the view was far more extensive than Melanie's. "Is Sag Harbor home for you all the time?" she asked.

"No, not all the time," he said. "I have a place in L.A. I'm there most of the time. Speaking of which, how long have you been here?"

"In Sag Harbor?" she asked. He nodded. "About three weeks."

"What do you think of it so far?"

"I haven't really seen much of it. I've been kind of

hiding out at Mel's. I guess one of these days I'll stop in town and have a look around."

"So you haven't seen any of the sights?" he asked. She shook her head. "You're missing a unique experience. Sag Harbor isn't just a playground for the wealthy and famous. It's a cultural haven. Long Wharf Harbor, the place where celebrities dock their yachts, was once a major seaport in early America's whaling business? As a matter of fact, Sag Harbor was actually the first Ellis Island."

"Really," she said, surprised by his knowledge.

"Eastville is considered the first purely African-American community. That's where you'll find several historical sites like the AME Zion Cemetery and St. David Church, which was actually a stop on the Underground Railroad before and during the Civil War."

"Impressive," she said.

"Yes, it is. You should check it out while you're here."

"I was talking about your knowledge of the area."

"Was that a compliment?" he asked slyly.

"Just don't let it go to your head," she warned.

"I'll try not to." Devon took the glass pitcher, walked over and topped off her glass with iced tea. "I gather you don't drink alcohol," he said.

"I hold glasses at parties very well. I seldom drink."

"Is that by choice or by design?" he asked.

"If you're talking about AA, then it's definitely by choice," Jazz said, moving away from the outside door and going back to sit at the counter. Devon followed. "When I was fifteen I went out partying and drinking with my brother. He was celebrating a movie wrap, and

I was celebrating my third season wrap. I begged him to take me with him. He finally said yes. I was thrilled. He let me have whatever I wanted. So I drank tequila shots. It was big mistake. After the third one I got really sick. I think he expected that."

Devon smiled and nodded. "You're probably right."

"Now I can't even look at a bottle of tequila without nightmares."

Devon chuckled. "Your brother was teaching you a lesson."

"It was well learned, I assure you."

"That's what big brothers do. They impart wisdom."

"It sounds like you're a big brother, too. Are you?"

He nodded. "I have two younger sisters. I'm pretty hard on them, too, particularly when it comes to the men in their lives. One of my sisters actually stopped bringing them around me."

"Why did she do that?" she asked.

"I have no idea," he said innocently.

"What did you do?"

"Well, it might be because I asked my defensive line to introduce themselves to her last boyfriend."

"So you got five or so burly football players to introduce themselves to a prospective suitor. I don't suppose that went over well."

"Go figure, right?" he joked.

She chuckled. "Yeah, go figure. So, why did you do it?"

"Seemed like a good idea at the time," he said.

"No, why did you really do it," she asked.

He looked at her and nodded. "I needed to send a message."

"To the boyfriend? Why?" she asked.

"I'd heard things about this particular guy, and I wasn't impressed. He was a player. I needed him to understand my position."

"Did he understand?"

"Yes, very well. He never called her again."

"Imagine that," she said sarcastically.

He moved to the refrigerator and pulled out a large platter. "Is seafood okay for dinner? Any allergies?" he asked.

"No allergies, and seafood sounds great," she said. "Do you know what you're doing, 'cause I'm not about to be rushed to the E.R. with ptomaine poisoning."

He laughed. "You'll be fine, trust me."

"Famous last words," she muttered, loud enough for him to hear.

He laughed again. "So, do you cook at all?" he asked.

"Me? No, not very often. I eat out, mostly."

"What about when you're in the mood for home cooking?"

"Then I just go home," she said. He looked at her, surprised by the statement. He knew of course that her mother had died years earlier. "I visit my grandmother and grandfather. They moved to my mom's old house in Alpine, New Jersey. It's a small community about twenty miles from Manhattan. They're incredible cooks. They're always in the kitchen cooking together. My grandfather says that it keeps the spice in their marriage."

Devon laughed. "Yeah, I can see that."

"My grandmother's always after me to get in the kitchen and cook. She says that you learn a lot about a person when you're cooking together."

"She's right. I think I'm gonna I like your grandparents."

"Don't say that. They're huge sports fanatics. I'm sure they already adore you."

"Okay, now I know I like them. I guess then I just have to convince their granddaughter to adore me, too."

She tried to ignore his last statement, but she couldn't. "They're old-fashioned in a 'the way to a man's heart is through his stomach' kind of way."

"How long have they been married?"

"To quote them accurately, 'Since the dawn of time.'"

"Well, in honor of your grandparents, you're going to be my sous chef tonight."

"You're kidding, right?" she said.

"No. Seriously, you can do it. Don't worry, I'll walk you through each step. You're going to be in charge of stirring and tasting. Think you can handle that?" he said patiently as if talking to a novice.

She looked at him and laughed. "You asked me if I cooked," she explained with precise terminology. He nodded his agreement. "I answered that I didn't cook, not that I couldn't cook."

"Oh, so you think you got skills?" he said, chuckling.

"About as much as you, probably," she boasted proudly.

He nodded. "Okay, let's do this, then," he challenged.

She walked over to the sink and began washing her hands. While she was sudsy, he came up behind her with an apron. "May I?" he whispered too near her ear. She nodded and took a step back. He was too close. Their bodies bumped intimately. "Was that good for you, too?" he joked. She didn't respond and tried not to smile. He reached around slowly, exaggerating every move, and wrapped an apron around her waist. His large hands lingered at her sides and back just seconds longer than necessary. "A little protection is always a good idea, don't you think?" he whispered while reaching around to hand her a towel.

His innuendos were clear. She turned while drying her hands. He was still too close. "Thanks. So, where do you want me first?" she asked simply, but then realized that the innocent question could be taken very differently than she intended.

He smiled rakishly. "Now, that sounds promising. What options do I have?" he asked, giving her the sexy look that had nearly taken her breath away the night before.

"Are you finished?" she asked.

"Actually, I'm just getting started," he said even closer.

"Okay, enough," she said, smirking, then pushed him back and tossed the towel at him. He anticipated and caught it effortlessly while they both laughed easily. When the laughter died down, they stared into each other's eyes, much like they'd done from across the room the night before. But now they were close, too close, and their bodies were too tempted. Heat permeated the room.

All she had to do was reach for him and she knew they'd be making love right there. Her heart pounded thunderously, and every nerve ending in her body seemed to quiver. His eyes never faltered or wavered. He looked straight at her as if searing her to his body. She knew exactly what was going through his mind. It was the same thing she was thinking. They wanted each other, but being with him would only complicate her life more than it already was. There was no question but to—

He leaned in and kissed her quickly. Then he leaned back and smiled. The slight, unexpected peck was innocently playful, but seemed to profess everything they were feeling. It was the certainty of their passion and the uncertainty of going further. She smiled, too, and then something in his eyes told her that he was waiting for her to make the next move. She did. She walked away. He took her hand and held tight. She turned and looked into his eyes. "Are you sure?" he asked.

Those simple words were more than a question. They were a plea, a promise of something that could be. Jazz took a deep breath and then looked at her watch. "Okay, I don't know what's keeping Melanie. Did she say how late she'd be?" Jazz asked, hoping that a change in conversation would cool their heated bodies.

Devon was just about to remark on what was happening between them when his cell phone rang. Impatiently, he picked it up from the counter and looked at the caller ID. "I need to take this. Why don't you walk around, have a look at the rest of the house? I won't be long."

"Sure," Jazz said, and then quickly left the kitchen.

Chapter 6

INTERIOR—DEVON'S HOME

She'd never been so thankful to hear a cell phone ring in her life. Her body was on fire and her head was spinning in every direction. She wanted him, and the only thing stopping her was the knowledge that this would be a disaster just like every other relationship in her life. But there was no denying the heat between them. One glance across the room had started it; now she was nearly out of control with desire.

She headed back down the open hallway toward the foyer. Her heart was still pounding. She stopped, closed her eyes and walked to the hallway's marble-topped table. She placed her hands on the cool, hard surface and looked up at her reflection in the bevel-trimmed mirror. She looked exactly the same except for the slight added blush in her cheeks.

Leaving right now was the perfect solution. She was a runner and proud of it. Conflict, stress, anxiety, drama—she ran from them all. Why should now be any different? Then just as quickly the answer came: because it is.

"Baby steps," she repeated. "You can't keep running all your life," she chided her reflection. "Chill." Moments later she reached up and adjusted her hair, her earring and necklace. Then, just as she was about to walk back into the kitchen and excuse herself from the evening, she saw the reflection of a painting. She turned.

Curiously she walked into the living room and looked around. The room was long and stately, much more stylish than she'd imagined it to be when she first breezed by. For some reason she expected chrome, glass and black lacquer, a typical bachelor pad. What she saw was far from it. The furnishings were exquisite, and the priceless antiques scattered about would make any dealer green with envy. It was an eclectic mix of traditional, modern, antiques and beach-house comfort.

Seeing the painting that first got her attention, she walked over and stared up at it. It was secured to the wall above the fireplace. It wasn't exactly a painting, but instead a photograph on canvas with multimedia effects. It was beautiful and truly remarkable. Its brilliant colors were breathtakingly fluid and rich and seemed to melt onto the canvas.

Done more in a modern style, the seascape was vivid and dramatic. The brushstrokes against the photo were lavishly, freely flamboyant. They intensified the high, foam-laced waves that crested and exploded against the rocks in a crescendo of vibrant colors. She looked at the signature, but couldn't make it out.

Now curious, she continued her tour. She looked

around, poking her head into any open door she found but staying on the first level. She saw the game room, dining room, library and gym. The last room with the door open was obviously the office. She walked in and looked around. It was definitely a man's office, with large leather chairs and dark rich mahogany furniture.

There was a desk and credenza, bookcases and curios with dozens of trophies. Sunlight streamed in from the skylights above and massive palm trees with wide-fingered leaves arched high toward the ceiling. Dark wooden beams divided the ceiling, matching the floors, large coffee table and desk.

She walked over to the large curio to see the trophies and then to the fireplace mantle to check out the framed photos. She picked one up and looked closer. Devon smiled happily, with two women on either side of him. She presumed they were his sisters. She replaced the photos then turned to leave. That's when she saw the massive fish tank on the opposite side taking up nearly half the wall. How had she missed that?

She walked over to examine it more closely. The blue water was crystal clear. Miniature coral reefs seemed to grow along the sides with cascading hues ranging from dark purple to vibrant yellow. The gravel at the bottom seemed to almost shimmer, reflecting the tiny jewellike stones freely tossed across the watery terrain. Everything in the tank seemed perfect, except there were no fish.

Devon took a moment to regroup before he picked up the cell to answer. It had stopped ringing, but he knew his agent would call back almost immediately. In the meantime he took a deep breath and released it slowly. Jazz had rattled him again. Resisting the need to touch was more difficult than he imagined. He had kissed her, but he wanted so much more. It wasn't all about sex right now. Yes, he wanted that, too, but being with her, talking to her, had surprised and delighted him.

The instant he saw her that need started all over again. He needed her. He wanted her. Maybe if they just had sex, he could get her out of his blood. The thought instantly brought the dream back to mind. His cell rang again. This time he grabbed it up quickly, knowing who it was. "Yeah, what do you have for me, Reed?"

"Devon, it's Melanie," she said through the chopped static connection.

"Melanie, we have a bad connection. I can barely hear you."

"I know. My phone keeps going out. Listen, I'm stuck here in the city tonight. There's a bad storm, and the roads and highways are insane. I heard there's major flooding on twenty-seven just outside of Queens. Did Jazz get there?"

"Yes, she's here."

"Good. Give her my apologies."

"Sure, no problem, be safe. See you later," he said, but the signal had already been lost. He put the cell down and walked toward the hallway to Jazz. The phone rang again. He backtracked and picked it up. "Reed?"

"Devon, I've got good news, and I've got great news. First of all, the Stallions front office recognizes your caliber of talent and your commitment to the team. That said, I've got several options, including a big fat contract," he said.

"Yes," Devon exclaimed as he smiled and laughed. "Excellent. So they went with everything we wanted?"

"No, not quite. The Stallions front office wants

to extend your current contract and give you twenty million dollars this year and twenty-five million dollars next year. They're also putting five million dollars in incentives on the table."

"Is that it?"

"No, there's more. They definitely want you here when you decide to end your career. They're willing to cut you a deal right now, putting you in the front-office after two years. So that's fifty million, plus a guaranteed front-office job. The position is substantial, all inclusive even up to retirement options down the road."

"What's the other news?" Devon asked.

"New York wants you now, and they're willing to match your numbers one hundred percent. That's a brand-new contract just like you wanted. We're talking sixty million with incentive options, signing bonus, the whole package."

"New York," he whispered. "New York. I can't play for New York. There's no way they want me for first-string quarterback. I'm not backing up some newbie, not with my career numbers."

"Devon, they recognize your talent. So what if you cruise or sit out a few games? You've earned this time to take it easy."

"Reed, you're kidding me, right?"

"Look, Devon, cards on the table. They've seen you take the hits. The concussion two years ago, followed by the broken wrist and your knee surgery. They're looking at everything. It's a good offer."

"You're saying that they've lost faith."

"I'm saying that you need to look at this like the business it is. Truthfully, word is they're looking around. Penn State, USC and Alabama, they've got some incredible QBs on the roster this season. I'm not going to sugarcoat this, and I don't know any other way to say it. You know this is a business. My opinion, New York is a good deal. They're willing and ready to take care of you and give you exactly what you want. They also want to lock this up right now."

"Reed, I'm a six-time Pro Bowler with ten years in. I've spent all that time in a Los Angeles Stallions jersey. I've taken them to the playoffs the last seven years in a row. I'm an all-time leader in passing yards. I'm a franchise player. I want to end my career in L.A. I'm not leaving."

"I got your back," Reed said. "Let me figure a few things out. I'll call you in a few days. But listen, the papers, the media are gonna do their thing. Nothing's final until you sign your name."

"Yeah, I got that. Thanks." Devon hung up and placed his cell on the counter. The idea that his abilities were in question was a serious blow. He'd been with the team for over ten years, and there was no way he intended to leave now.

He looked around the kitchen, seeing Jazz's hat and sunglasses on the chair. He took a deep breath, grateful for Reed's interruption. Not that he particularly wanted to talk to his agent at that moment, but he needed some time to regroup. And their conversation had gotten Jazz off his mind, at least for a few minutes. He left the kitchen looking for her.

It took him a few minutes to find her. She was in his office, standing in front of the fish tank. He spared a few seconds just to observe her. It was obvious she had purposely dressed down tonight. She wore a loose-fitting sweater that was at least two sizes too big and unflattering pants. And if she thought that would quell his excitement, she was very wrong. He knew she was beautiful no matter what she wore, or didn't.

He saw the desire in her eyes. She wanted him as much as he wanted her. But something held her back. She needed time. He decided to take a step back and allow her to lead. She was obviously skittish, but the knowledge that their time would come was a certainty. "There you are," he finally said. "I thought you ran off and left me."

"No, I'm still here."

"Melanie called. There's a storm. She's stuck in the city until morning. She sends her apologies." Jazz nodded. "So, you got a chance to look around. What do you think of the place?"

"It's beautiful, very cozy and comfortable. It's big."

"Unofficially it's about eight thousand square feet or so. It has five bedrooms, seven fireplaces, a three-car garage, gourmet kitchen, salon, greenhouse, and…"

"…a really big gym," she added.

"Yeah, it's my sanctuary."

"And this room is wonderful. But what does a professional football player need with a home office this elaborate? You have everything a work office needs."

"Football isn't my only career."

"The endorsements, right?"

"I have a number of foundations, both sports related and not. I run year-round sports programs and camps for kids and I sponsor several major scholarship programs. I also invest."

"When do you have time to actually play football?"

"You find time for what you love and for what's important. Remember, I'm only one lucky sack away from ending my career."

"No, you'll be fine," she said, touching his arm for added assurance. He looked down at her hand on his arm. She dropped her hand and stepped away. "And what happens when you decide to retire? You can't play football forever, right?"

He nodded. "I hope the transition will be as smooth and painless as possible."

She took another step back, then turned and walked around the room again. The dark rich furniture mixed with the lush vivid trees, and the aquarium was surprising. She stopped at the plush damask sofa. The light satiny fabric was sophisticated and exuded glamour and chic styling. She didn't expect something so beautiful in an office. But everything about Devon and his house was unexpected.

He walked over and stood beside her. "I bought this painting years ago. It's called *Sag Harbor* and reminds me of something my grandfather once told me about finding home."

"What's that?" she asked.

"If you keep home in your heart, you're always there."

"He's right," she said, turning to meet his eyes only to see that he'd been looking at her instead of the painting.

Devon smiled. "The artist was unknown at the time, but his work fascinated me. It's actually a multimedia photograph."

Jazz recognized its similarity to the painting she saw in the living room. "It's stunning. Is this by the same artist as the painting above the mantel in the living room?"

"Yes, I have about seven of his pieces. He's an amazing talent. His works are worth a fortune now."

"It's beautiful, different. It's real and comfortable. Your home is like that, too. It's not at all what I expected. Neither are you. You surprise me, Devon. That's a pretty rare thing."

"Really?" he asked.

She nodded. "Not many people surprise me. You do."

"I like that idea, surprising you. But I can't take all the credit. I actually live in L.A. I come here when the season's over. It's like a retreat. My great-grandparents originally owned the land and the structure. They lost it years ago. I was able to buy it back. My grandfather was thrilled. He gave me two garages full of furniture and possessions from his mother and grandmother. So I guess a major part of my ancestors are still connected to this house."

"That's so cool. I like that idea, a true family home. I guess that's why you have so many antiques around."

Devon laughed. "Antiques? Oh, no, my grandfather would have a fit if he heard you talking like that. To him they're still brand-new."

Jazz smiled. "I'll make sure not to mention it if ever I run into him. So, you said that Sag Harbor is your home. Do you mean you actually grew up here?"

"Yes, mostly. My father's family has been coming to this area for decades. I'm talking the mid-1930s. My mother's family goes back even further."

"Really? They had amazing foresight."

"I don't think it was necessarily foresight. When I used to come up here to visit my grandfather years ago, he talked about how much his father loved this place. It was a melting pot long before there was a name for it."

"It's so surprising to me that African-Americans were here so long ago."

"Don't let the nouveau riche fool you. African-Americans, Native Americans, European settlers, they all lived and died here together for centuries. I'm not saying that everybody lived in harmony all the time, but back then it was about survival, not race. This was considered the first Ellis Island. It's the recent arrivals that want to claim that it was always a playground for the rich. It wasn't. It was and is still just a small town."

"Wow, your family has been here a long time."

"My grandfather was an engineer. Now he's an historian. He once traced our ancestors back to the original whalers."

"They never moved away?"

"Some did at one point, when the town had begun to die. But they always stayed connected. Years later, in 1946, just after the war ended, they returned and bought land on the beach. Things in the country were getting ugly, and that was the only place African-Americans could live in this area—the beachfront. Ironic, isn't it? The real estate here now is considered prime. My great-grandfather built a home on the beach. My grandfather was actually born in that house."

"What did your great-grandfather do for a living?"

"He was a doctor, and my great-grandmother was a teacher."

"So, your family was moving on up way before Weezie and George Jefferson."

He chuckled. "Exactly. My grandfather used to tell us stories of how our ancestors were whalers. As a matter of fact, our family actually helped build the First Presbyterian Church in the early 1800s. It was referred to then as the Whalers Church. Later they helped build St. David AME Zion Church."

"You know a lot about the history here."

"Only what my grandfather would tell us. He's an amazing man. He's over eighty years old now, and he's still active."

"He sounds like a wonderful man."

"He is. He enjoys your music."

She laughed. "Somehow I doubt that your grandfather even knows who I am."

"You'd be very wrong. He's a pretty cool old guy."

"He sounds like it. So, I guess this is where your mother and father met and fell in love. He sees her from across a crowded room and they know instantly that they are destined to be together forever, the perfect happily ever after."

He laughed. "Not quite. I forgot that the other part of your life is movies and make-believe. No, they definitely didn't have a happily ever after. My mom got pregnant with me, and my grandparents forced them to marry. They divorced a few years later. They seldom speak and are never in the same room."

"So much for a nice Sag Harbor romance," she said.

"Is that why you came here, looking for a Sag Harbor romance?"

"No, not at all," Jazz said. She smiled tightly. The conversation had turned to a topic she didn't want to pursue.

Devon got the message. "So, are you ready to get back to work?" He stepped aside to allow her to lead the way back to the kitchen. When they got there they split the jobs up. They'd decided to grill everything, so when all the preparations were complete, they went outside on the deck.

"Wow, that's massive—it's like mission control at NASA. Are you sure you know how to work this thing?"

she asked, seeing the dozen or so knobs and levers on the grill.

"Of course. It's mine."

"Yeah, I get that it's yours, but that doesn't necessarily mean you know what you're doing."

"Do you doubt my grilling skills?" he asked, appalled.

She smiled amused by his mock offence. "No. Of course not, I'm sure you're brilliant."

"That didn't sound very convincing."

"It's the best I could muster."

Devon adjusted the heat and placed the seafood on the grill. The instant sizzle added to his confidence. The next few minutes were magical. He was indeed brilliant. He seasoned and cooked on the side burners, then basted and grilled like a true master on the main burners. Jazz was indeed impressed.

The meal was delicious. "I have to admit, everything is wonderful. You're not too bad in the kitchen." She helped him take the dishes back into the kitchen.

"Thank you. Neither are you," he complimented. They put the food away, and he loaded the dishwasher while she sat at the counter and watched. "You're pretty good at that, too. You'd make an excellent househusband."

He turned and glared at her. She laughed. "Come on," he said, taking her hand and escorting her back out onto the deck. They stood at the rail and looked into the darkness. The sun had long ago set, and heavy storm clouds were moving in as the wind picked up.

"I had a good time tonight. This was really fun," she said.

"I'm glad. I guess your grandmother and grandfather were right about cooking together."

"Yeah, I guess they were. Umm, smell that," she said.

"What?" he asked.

"It's going to storm. I love the smell of a coming storm."

He looked at her, knowing that the something about her that he'd always found attractive had nothing to do with her face or her body. She wasn't Jazelle Richardson, actress and entertainer, tonight. Tonight she was an irresistible woman.

She turned to him, sensing his silence. "What?"

"I'm just admiring you," he said. She turned away and shook her head. "No," he added, placing his hand on top of hers as she held the rail, "not the entertainer or the sexy woman, but you, the person, origami queen. I really like you, Jazelle Richardson."

"You sound surprised," she said. He didn't respond. She turned back to him, smiling. "I really like you, too, Devon Hayes, regular guy with no fish in his tank."

"What?" he asked.

"What's with the no fish in the fish tank?"

"You mean in the office?" he asked. She nodded. "I'm taking it down. It's being donated."

"It's a beautiful tank. I'm surprised you're getting rid of it. I've never seen anything so grand."

He reached his hand out to her. "Come, I want to show you something."

"What?" she asked.

"You'll see. Come on."

Chapter 7

INTERIOR—DEVON'S HOME

Jazz took Devon's hand and followed as he led through the kitchen, down the hallway then up the stairs. They walked down the hall to the end. He opened the double doors and stepped aside. She looked at him, assuming it was his bedroom. She went inside. She was right. His bed was stunning. But that wasn't the astounding part. There was a nearly wall-size aquarium above the bed. The tank downstairs in the office was beautiful, but this one was astonishing. The colors were even more vibrant, if that were even possible. "Wow, this is insane. It's incredible."

She walked toward the bed. The dimmed lights throughout the room accented it beautifully. Small iridescent fish swam carefree and luxuriously as if still miles beneath the sea. She turned. Surprising, he was still standing in the doorway. "How do you sleep with the tank's lighting?"

"Lie down on the bed," he instructed.

She sat then lay back. The room was completely cloaked in darkness. She sat back up and looked around. "How is this possible?"

"I have a friend who's a lighting engineer. He contracts out to movie studios, dance clubs and even NASA. He designed and patented this new system."

She lay back down. The sensation was remarkable. It was as if the room was completely dark, but she knew it wasn't. She sat up and looked back at the fish tank close up. There were more and different varieties of fish than she'd first thought. Some she recognized, some she didn't. She stood and walked back to the door. Devon smiled as she approached. She touched his hand. "Thank you for tonight. I'm really glad I came."

"I'm glad you came, too," he said in an almost whisper. He opened his mouth to speak again then clamped it shut. She noticed instantly.

"What?" she asked curiously.

He shook his head. "Nothing."

"No, tell me. You were going to say something. What is it?"

"Actually, I was going to ask you a question."

"Sure, as long as I don't necessarily have to answer."

"Fair enough," he agreed. "Why are you alone?" he asked.

She considered exercising her option to not answer, but spoke too quickly. "Because alone is safe."

"Safe how?"

"I grew up busy. There were always people around me telling me what to do, what to say, how to think.

Somewhere in all that, the I, or I guess more like the me inside, got lost. I learned that I needed to be alone to find myself again. After every movie or every tour I go away to be alone, although most times Brian came with me. He was good at helping me find myself."

"And now he's gone. So, how do you find the me inside again?"

"Good question. I tried being alone for the last six and a half months."

"Did you find yourself again?" he asked.

The insightfulness of his questions didn't upset her as much as they allowed her to express her thoughts aloud. "Truthfully, I don't know yet. I hope so."

"Last night at the party, you were there physically, but really you were miles away."

"You weren't supposed to notice that."

"It was kind of hard to miss. I'm not saying you snubbed anyone. You were gracious for the most part, but…"

"I was alone in a crowded room," she said.

"Exactly. That can't be good."

"Probably not, but for right now…"

"No. I can't believe you'd give up just like that. I looked in your eyes downstairs when we were cooking and I saw life and joy and happiness. That's the real you. You weren't acting or hiding. You were having fun, and it showed."

"So now you think you know me? Right," she said, feeling defensive.

"No, I don't. How could I, when you won't let me?" he said. He dipped his head, and his eyes pierced deep into her like a hot poker through plastic. "But I'd like to, someday."

She couldn't respond. His request was more than

a plea. It was a promise. He looked at her and saw everything inside. She felt her guard collapse. She stood defenseless. It was a quiet moment. She knew she shouldn't, but she couldn't help herself. She reached up and kissed him. It was spontaneous and impulsive, and as soon as she did she quickly stopped herself. "Sorry," she said.

"For what?" he asked.

"I shouldn't have done that." She stepped back.

"Why not?" he asked, attempting to hold on to her.

"Because starting something like this would be a mistake," she said. He looked at her, obviously puzzled. "Melanie is in the city right now finding someone for you. You want a wife. That's not me." She stepped around him to leave. "I'm sorry."

He touched her arm, turning her gently. He considered telling her the truth, but he knew that he couldn't. Instead he smiled and nodded. "So, I guess this will have to make me sorry, too," he whispered and then took her in his arms and kissed her with an intense passion that instantly consumed them both. Her lips parted, and he delved deep into the recesses of her passion. Her resolve shattered and betrayed her instantly. It felt so good to be in his arms again. There was no other way to put it. Just like before she felt everything all at once: passion, joy, contentment, need, anticipation.

Devon was excitement and passion, and kissing him was like the explosive power of splitting an atom. This, whatever it was, was moving too fast, or was it too slow? She couldn't tell which. Her thoughts were a jumble of the rational and irrational, mixed with raging desire.

All she knew was that she wanted him, and right now he was hers. All she had to do was take him. She didn't care if he would belong to someone else in time. This was her time, her need. Their bodies melted together, and she felt alive for the first time in a long time.

His strong, vicelike arms surrounded her in strength and gentleness. But she gripped him with unimaginable fierceness. Being pressed to his hard body wasn't nearly enough for her. He ravished her mouth and neck. Her heart thundered and her stomach quivered. She couldn't get enough. She needed more. She was hot, on fire, and only he could satisfy her need.

Breathless, she grabbed the front of his shirt and began hastily unfastening the buttons. When she finished them, she opened his shirt and pulled it back over his wide shoulders. She gasped silently, having only imagined what his body looked like beneath the designer clothes and confident swagger. She delighted in the fact that her imaginings didn't nearly do him justice. His chest was magnificent. It was perfect.

She reached up to touch his shoulders. They were wide and strong. Her hands ran down his arms, feeling knotted muscles pull and tense. His broad chest was deliciously magnificent. It was powerful and strong, slimming to his waist with the packed tight shadows of his abs. She continued touching him, delighted and smiling at her private treasure. Then she leaned in and kissed his chest, gently letting her tongue taste and savor the chocolate richness of his body.

She felt his muscles retract and tighten. He was obviously holding tight to his restraint. Suddenly that knowledge gave her a swell of power. She looked up into his hooded eyes. They were dark and focused. She stepped back, then grabbed her sweater and quickly pulled it off. Devon reached out to take it, but she tossed it across the room. She stood in a form-fitted lace camisole. He looked down at her swollen breasts and licked his lips.

His mouth was completely dry. He touched her as she had touched him. Then he kissed her chest and licked as she had done. He was tender and gentle at first. Then it seemed the restraint he'd held thus far cracked. He plunged his face between her breasts and kissed her with a heated passion she'd never experienced before. His fierce power consumed her, and she loved it.

His mouth on her was intoxicating. She couldn't get enough. She arched back and lifted her leg. He grasped her tight, and she let go. He'd literally swept her off her feet. She wrapped her legs around his waist, holding on as he pressed her body against the wall. He lifted her higher and devoured her lace-covered breasts, her shoulder and her neck. His mouth was hot and wanting. A delirious sensation swept through her. His mouth on her skin was like lava. Her body tingled. She moaned deep in her throat. Breathless and panting, she held on tight. She gyrated her hips, grinding against his hardness. She was on the edge of total madness. The almost release felt so good, but still she held back.

Pent up, locked up, held back, constrained, she had been imprisoned by her own pain for so long she dared not release. But being here with Devon awakened something she barely knew existed anymore. It was joy. It was pleasure. She wanted to surrender, to give herself permission to be happy. Maybe just a little, she reasoned.

Then, as wanting him intensified, he kissed her fiercely. Lips pressed hard, his tongue slipped into her mouth and he began to suck. The sensation was unimaginable. She held tight to him, feeling her body and mind release. She let go just a little more, and then everything became a blur. She floated weightlessly in his arms. The kiss had taken her. What she felt, what she knew, what she was had all vanished. The kiss deepened with luscious pursuit. Suddenly he was behind her, on top of her, beside her.

The delirious madness of their kiss had taken her someplace she'd never been before. Her thoughts swam in confusion. She tried to understand. How could a kiss do this to her? Rationally she knew it couldn't, could it? But everything rational began to ease away.

She looked up, seeing the darkened ceiling again, and realized they were lying on his bed. It was both a blessing and not. She knew her legs had wobbled at one point. She just hoped she didn't pass out as they kissed. He leaned away and touched her. "Jazz, are you okay?" he whispered.

She nodded and smiled. "No, yes," she muttered. "What was that?"

"What was what?" he asked, looking down into her eyes with passion and desire still swimming in his.

"That, the kiss," she said.

He smiled again. "Are you okay?" he repeated softly.

She hummed. "Definitely better than okay," she said.

Side by side they lay looking into each other's eyes. The passion that once was had subsided, and this easy, comfortable feeling was calming and patient. The room was dark as they lay on the bed. She knew it was just a lighting trick, but the darkness gave her a bravery that she knew she'd never be able to muster otherwise. She stroked the side of his face tenderly. "Devon, we can't do this."

He nodded. "I know. It's not time yet."

"What do you mean?" she asked.

"You'll see. When you're ready for me, and you want us to happen, I'll be here waiting for you."

"You are so arrogant."

"I know. I get that a lot," he joked.

She smiled. "Devon, I don't need a relationship right now. I can't handle it. Is that okay?"

He nodded. "Do you need a friend?" he offered.

She smiled and nodded. "Yeah, I definitely need a friend."

"Good. Me, too," he said.

"So, friends can talk about anything, right?"

"Oh yeah, definitely anything," he said.

"And they help each other out sometimes, right?"

"Umm-hmm," he agreed.

"And friends can kiss."

He smiled. "Oh, absolutely."

"Good." She kissed him tenderly then reached up and stroked his face again. He closed his eyes, seeming to savor the feel of her touch. She closed her eyes, too, and relaxed back into the feel of his big, comfortable bed. She moved to cuddle closer. He wrapped his arms around her protectively. The moment was perfect.

A few minutes later he heard the calmness of her slumber. He looked down at her body. The form-fitted camisole rose as she inhaled. He focused on the swell of her breasts. He hungered for more, but touching her now was out of the question. He closed his eyes, regaining control of his desire. Jazz was the woman in the back of his mind all his life. She was his dream even before he knew what life was about. He'd idolized her as a kid and worshiped her as a teen. As a man there were numerous distractions, but none could compare to Jazz. Women came and went in his life, but she always stayed. And now he had come full circle. She lay beside him and he wanted so much more than just her body.

An hour later Jazz woke up and looked around. Devon was gone. She sat up and looked around the room. She spotted him standing on the balcony. She watched a moment. He still wore the white shirt, although now it was blowing wildly against the storm's breeze. He seemed to be lost in his thoughts. She got up and walked to the balcony. He turned and leaned back against the rail. He smiled, seeing her standing there in the doorway still in just her camisole and baggy pants. "You fell asleep," he said.

She nodded and then walked over to stand beside him. "I guess I was tired."

"Running away can do that."

She looked at him, knowing that he'd figured her out too well. "Yeah, I guess it can." She turned to the night sky, seeing light flashing through the thickness of the clouds above. A sense of smallness swept over her. "I guess the storm is coming this way now."

"No, it'll pass us by," he said. Just then a fierce rumble of thunder roared in the distance. She tensed and wrapped her arms around her body. "Are you chilly?" he asked.

"No, I'm okay." The thunder roared again, and she shivered.

Devon could plainly see that she wasn't okay. He walked over, stood behind her and wrapped his arms around her securely. She leaned back into his strength. She closed her eyes, hoping to remember this moment for years to come. Lightning flashed, and he instinctively held her tighter. "Do you want to go back inside?"

"No." She turned within his embrace and looked up into his eyes. She could see that passion and desire still raged. She smiled, knowing that he was the release she needed. "I want you to make love to me." His expression didn't change, but she could feel his body's reaction. She touched his chest, then raked her nails down the length, stirring a dull tingle. His body shuddered away. She saw the muscle in his jaw tighten. She circled his nipple with her finger. His hooded eyes quivered.

"Do you know what you're doing?" he asked. His voice was husky and strained.

"Tell me." She kissed and licked his chest as before, knowing that would incite his need further. It did. His body tensed and his arms slackened around her. He grasped then held tight to the rail, trapping her with his body. She caressed his neck, his shoulders and his arms. He shuddered. She kissed his neck then down the thick muscles of his arm. She nibbled and bit, feeling his body quiver and shudder against her. "What am I doing, Devon?" she whispered. Then, using the palms of her hands, she circled his nipples. They hardened instantly. A low guttural groan rumbled through his throat. "Do you like that?"

She continued teasing him, tasting him, touching him and playing the dangerous game she knew would end so pleasurably. "Do you still want me?" she expounded, rocking her hips and stomach to the hardness between his legs.

He opened his eyes and glared at her. "You know I do."

"What do you want? Tell me."

"I want to taste you," he said.

She smiled. "You do, huh?" she asked. He nodded slowly. "Okay, then show me. Taste me right now," she teased. She reached up and wrapped her arms around his neck and pulled him close. She kissed him. His response was explosive. She gasped, not expecting his restraint to release so quickly. He was everywhere, touching her, caressing her, wanting her. His mouth descended down her neck to her shoulder then farther down, down, lower. He was on his knees kissing her stomach, her hips. He unsnapped and unzipped her pants, letting them fall free.

He looked up. She stood in her camisole, panties and heels. His eyes seemed to blaze. He braced his hands on the lace-top bodice and ripped it open savagely. She gasped, surprised, then grabbed his shoulders to steady herself. But before she could react, his mouth took her breast and suckled. He was tasting her, and the pleasure of his mouth and tongue was insanity. His hands held her back, pressing her close to fill his mouth completely. He licked her nipple fast in quick succession then slowed his pace to methodical torture. Her mind was awash with colors and light. She couldn't think straight even if she wanted to. She closed her eyes tight and moaned her pleasure, hearing a rumble of thunder close. It rumbled again. It wasn't until Devon stopped completely and held her waist firm that she realized he'd been asking her something.

"Jazz, listen to me. Do you want me to stop?" he asked a third time. "We can still stop."

She looked down at him and smiled then shook her head. "No, don't stop." He leaned and gently kissed both nipples. Then he covered them with his large hands, letting his thumbs circle and tantalize her pebbled nipples. She licked her lips and bit at her lower lip. His hands were masterful, and his mouth was unbelievable.

He took her one hand and placed it over her other breast. With his hand over hers, he guided her to massage herself. Of course she had touched her body before, but never like this. It was sensual and hot. She looked down, seeing his mouth and his hand on her hand over her breasts. She arched back and he switched positions, taking her other breast into his mouth while she felt the swollen dampness of the other. Her body shook and quivered. She was wet and ready for him now. "Devon, let's go back inside to the bed," she said breathlessly.

He either didn't hear her or didn't want to. He released her one hand and then slowly pulled her panties down. Her legs wobbled. She knew what he was going to do next. He told her. His hand pressed between her legs. He felt her wetness thicken. He lifted her leg to his shoulder and kissed her inner thigh. She held tight to his shoulder and the rail. "Devon," she called out. "Devon."

The first thrust of his fingers made her stomach flip. The second made her body shudder. The third nearly drove her to the edge. He was inside her, but his thumb stroked the tiny place above her nib. She weakened. Her legs gave way. His fingers went deeper, and she nearly shattered. "Do you feel me inside of you?" he asked. Her mouth was open and completely dry. She couldn't speak, so she nodded. "No, say it. Tell me," he instructed.

"Yes, I f-feel you," she stammered, not recognizing her own voice.

"Do you want more?"

She nodded. "Yes, more." She rocked her hips into him, and he continued delving deep into her. The intensity of his touch was beyond her wildest thoughts. He knew exactly what to do, and he was doing it with unrestrained delight.

She moaned and gasped, feeling her arousal rising higher and higher. His mouth took her breast again. His tongue tantalized her nipple. The rhythm of his hand and his mouth synchronized. She surged and pressed against him, meeting his cadence. Then, when her body began to shudder and she neared her climax, he placed her other leg on his shoulder and tasted her. She held to the railing behind her. His tongue replaced his thumb, and her nib replaced her nipple. He suckled until seconds later she exploded.

The intensity of her orgasm was mind-blowing. She was instantly blinded by white lights in the darkness around her. He continued, and she came again. This time the white lights seemed to shatter and rain down on her. She didn't feel her body, only the surging ecstasy swelling and exploding again. She shrieked, this time releasing all her pain and frustrations.

"Yes, yes, Devon, Devon, yes."

He stopped and sat back, releasing her legs. She slumped forward over his shoulder. He stood, placing his arm under her knees and holding her to his body. She closed her eyes and held tight, knowing he was carrying her inside. He placed her down on his bed, removed her heels and then covered her with a soft, cloudlike throw. She closed her eyes and moaned her contentment as the softness covered her like a gentle cloud.

"That couldn't have done much for you," she said, opening her eyes. He was staring down at her. The expression on his face was pure satisfaction.

"On the contrary, I love tasting you," he whispered.

"But…"

"We have plenty of time to satisfy each other later." He took his shirt off and tossed it on the bed. She looked up at him longingly. The look in his eyes told her everything she needed to know. At that moment, she was the only woman in the world. She felt loved, and even if it was just for that one moment, it was enough to last her. "Okay?" he said. She nodded. "I'll be right back." She nodded again.

When he walked away, she suddenly felt the chill of loneliness. She sat up, grabbed his shirt and put her arms through the sleeves. She wrapped her arms around her body. His scent was on the shirt. She inhaled deeply letting the essence of his body seep into her lungs. She still wanted him. He had quenched her desire, but she still wanted more. She wanted to feel him inside of her.

She lay down, seeing the room darken again. The unique lighting effects still fascinated her. She looked up at the ceiling and smiled. It seemed to glow and ripple, probably a reflection from the fish tank. She stretched back and then leaned up on her elbow. Devon walked back into the bedroom.

Seeing her lying on his bed with just his white shirt on stopped him in his tracks. His jaw dropped slowly and a muscle pulled tight. She smiled seductively. "You said that we have plenty of time to satisfy each other later. Well, I was thinking, how about if later is right now?" she whispered.

Chapter 8

INTERIOR—DEVON'S HOME

Devon's eyes focused on Jazz and never veered away. He walked over to the bed and stood just beyond her reach. He looked down the length of her body. Everything about her was arousing. There was no way he could turn away from her this time. He had restrained his desire earlier; he knew she wasn't ready. But now there was no way he could walk away.

She left the shirt open just enough to hint at the prize beneath. The front of the shirt crossed over just below her waist, leaving the sweet swell of her breasts nearly visible. The teasing view almost took his breath away. He immediately thought about taking her into his mouth earlier. The swollen fullness of her breast was the perfect mouthful. "You have no idea how beautiful you are lying there."

She smiled graciously. "Thank you. I'm glad you think so. Want to know what I think?"

"What do you think?" he asked.

"I think you have too many clothes on."

He smiled shyly. "You think so, huh?"

Jazz nodded. "Oh, definitely. As a matter of fact, I think we both do." She climbed onto her knees and knelt in front of him as he stood beside the bed. She placed her hand on his chest. The contrast of her small hand on his broad chest had appealed to her. She ran her hands over his body, feeling his shoulders and arms. Then she ran her hands down his body to his stomach and waist. She unsnapped his jeans then held the zipper. Her hand brushed against his already bulging hardness. She felt him jump and lean away. "You're not afraid of little old me, are you?" she asked, smiling seductively.

"Jazz, you have no idea what you do to me."

She smiled then reached up and touched his lips. The intimate act sparked another surge of desire. He took her hand and kissed her fingers. Then he opened his mouth and licked. She watched, enthralled by the erotic act. He guided her index finger into his mouth. The warmth of being inside of him sent an instant thrill surging through her body.

He began sucking her finger. She opened her mouth to speak, but found herself completely mesmerized by the seduction. Her body shivered involuntarily. If this was his way of enticing her, he was more than succeeding. She held her breath as she watched his intimate act continue. The memory of him sucking other parts of her body came to mind. Her body moistened for him instantly. She was ready for him now.

She slipped her hand from his mouth and ran her moistened finger down the front of her body. She dipped her hand beneath the opening of the white shirt. He watched intently, spellbound by her sensuous actions. His eyes half closed and his jaw muscle tightened again. "Did you know that I like touching your chest?" she whispered then ran her fingers across his chest, raking her nails softly down his body. Her intent of going all the way was obvious.

He shuddered and his eyes flew open. He stilled her hands and looked into her eyes. He leaned in and kissed her long and lingering. He released her hands, and she wrapped her arms around his neck and pulled closer. The kiss ignited even more passion as the hunger of their desire swelled. When the kiss ended, he continued to her neck and shoulders then opened the shirt wide. He looked down at her perfect breasts. They stood full and firm, with nipples already as hard as diamonds.

He leaned over and captured one nipple in his mouth. She gasped as he pulled then gorged himself with her breast. She arched her back with one hand planted firmly on his strong shoulder and the other holding his neck to her body. He held her back, pressing her forward into his mouth. She gasped, twitched and writhed with pleasure. She was breathless as he ravished her. His tongue tantalized each nipple, licking and nibbling one and then the other. Her body was going weak.

He held tight then sat down on the side of the bed and pulled her onto his lap facing him. She straddled his hips. She instantly felt the masterful hardness pressing into her. He placed his large hands over each breast then slowly began circling and massaging, teasing and tempting her with his palms. Her body began to shake and a deep groan rumbled in his throat.

"You have too many clothes on," she muttered, barely coherent. He nodded. "Take them o—" She gasped before she could finish as he reached between her legs and caressed her core. She moaned, knowing already what his talented fingers could do to her. He held her close and kissed her as his hands roamed free. Then he slowly lifted her back onto the bed. He stood and removed his pants and his shorts. She watched with delighted anticipation. Then seeing him naked nearly took her breath away. He was more than magnificent. He was stunning.

He grabbed a condom from the bedside drawer, put it on and then climbed onto the bed beside her. She rolled over to perch on top of him. She sat comfortably mounted with his hardness standing straight up against her stomach. He was amazingly thick and long. She looked into his focused eyes. "We can stop if you want to wait," he offered. She shook her head decidedly. She had no intention of waiting a moment longer. She grasped him firmly and rose up to position herself. Then, without a second's thought, she lowered her body onto him, impaling herself in one quick motion.

The shock of his body entering her nearly made her scream then whimper. She leaned forward, obviously stilled by the act. "Are you okay?" he asked with concern.

The quick pain had startled her, but now the fullness of his penis inside her was incredible. She felt every adoring inch of him. It was amazing. "Jazz, are you okay?" he repeated. She nodded then tightened her inner muscles as he twitched. He felt her. She smiled and began gyrating her hips up and down, in and out.

She rose up and then down again. Devon held tight to her waist as each motion brought them closer and closer to their climax. She leaned forward. He captured her breast in his mouth. Then his rogue tongue licked at each nipple. The tantalizing torture of his mouth on her and his hardness inside of her was mind-blowing. Each pulsating movement caused another ripple, which caused another thrust, which caused another surge.

She rode him harder, quicker, penetrating deeper, grinding her core against his hardness. The climax came in a flash of blinding light. She gasped loudly, exploding and trembling as if every nerve ending in her body had erupted. Breathless, she held tight to him. He reached down behind her and grabbed her buttocks, pressing her closer and deeper. Then he rolled over, taking her with him.

She was beneath him with his hands still on her buttocks. He lifted her up. She wrapped her legs around his waist and grabbed his neck and held tight. She was completely suspended off of the bed. With one hand on her rear and the other on the bed, he was making love to her while she was in midair. The impossibility of their position aroused her even more. The friction of his long, luscious strokes against her pushed her closer and closer to the edge.

She closed her eyes tight as she hovered intimately connected to his body. The fierceness and intensity of their pace quickened. As rapture approached, she held her breath. Each powerful thrust pushed her further and further over the top. Seconds later, she screamed. The blinding orgasm gripped her hard. He thrust into her once more. Every throbbing, quivering inch of her body tensed as she came again. Then, with one final, unrestrained thrust, he went rigid and his body shook as he surrendered his pleasure to her.

He gently placed her back onto the bed then lay down beside her. She rolled to her side. He slipped behind and cuddled close behind her. "I have to go," she said dreamingly.

"No, you have to stay right where you are," he whispered in her ear. He surprised himself. He'd never insisted that a woman stay with him in his bed all night. But everything about Jazz had broken the rules.

"Close your eyes and sleep," he said, but she didn't. And when she knew he was asleep, she moved to the edge of the bed then looked back and smiled. "Good night," she whispered then got up and left.

When she got back to her bedroom at Melanie's house, she grabbed her cell and called her friend Savannah. She answered quickly. "Hey, I called to tell you that I was just lying next to a hunk of man and the two of us just had hot 'n' sweaty butt-naked, scream-his-name-over-and-over-again sex."

Savannah screamed and laughed riotously. "Everything, tell me everything."

"I'll tell you later. I'm whipped. Goodnight." She lay back on the pillows and smiled in the darkness. "YES!"

Chapter 9

EXTERIOR—BEACH

Devon sat on his deck's rail, looking out at the dawn of a new day. The sun had already crept over the horizon and a crispness chilled the morning air. He took a sip of his bottled water then stretched his muscles to prepare for his five-mile run. With most of Sag Harbor still asleep, it was the perfect time of day to run. He stretched his muscles against the wooden rail, preparing and organizing his day, but his thoughts wandered to the night before, to Jazz.

Thinking about Jazz had now become a habit. She had set a new standard he was certain no other woman could ever reach. She was fun and smart and so very sexy. And even her baggy top and pants couldn't hide her lusciousness. He had dreamed about making love to her again. He liked seeing her on top of him. He wanted to look into her eyes as they came together. But when he woke up, she was gone.

He licked his full lips as an easy smile stretched wide. He had really enjoyed their time together. Being with Jazz was better than he imagined. Although she seemed tentative and uncomfortable at first, she soon relaxed and seemed to enjoy herself. She was nothing like he expected, but he liked the contradiction. He expected her to be a Hollywood type. He'd been around enough of them to know their style: high fashion, high drama and high maintenance. But to his surprise Jazz was a thoughtful, funny, intelligent woman. The fact that she was the opposite of everything he thought he knew about her intrigued him.

When he took her to his bedroom he had no intention of stepping a foot past the threshold. But when she kissed him, all he could think about was how much he wanted her. Every teenage fantasy he'd ever had sprang to life. She'd been part of his fantasy for so long, the reality of actually being with her seemed more dreamlike than ever.

He walked back through the house and down to the gym, where he headed to the back door that led to the beach. He keyed in the alarm system, exited, and then reactivated the system. After a few more warm-up stretches to get his body ready for his five-mile run, he unlatched the back gate and walked out onto the sand and down to the water's edge.

After a few deep breaths, he took off running down the stretch of the beach. He ran at an even pace, keeping his heart rate steady. Then after about twenty minutes, he slowly accelerated to a sprinter's top speed. His trainer once told him that the sudden burst of energy would shock his system for the miles ahead. After about forty-five minutes of alternating speeds, he turned and headed back down the beach. Moments later he was joined by another early runner. "You're late," Devon said.

"Actually, you're early," Vincent responded, touching his two fingers to his neck to gauge his pulse rate as he fell into step with Devon.

They talked sporadically, mostly about sports and the upcoming seasons. Then they ran at an even pace for about a mile and a half before either spoke again. "So, has Mel sent you out on another date yet?" Vincent asked.

"Kind of," Devon said.

Vincent glanced over to him. "What does 'kind of' mean?"

"I had dinner plans with Melanie last night. She got stuck in the city, but Jazz came."

"Jazz? And she showed up?" Vincent asked.

"Yeah, I invited them both. I wanted to thank Jazz for helping me out of a tight situation at the party the other night."

"I presume you're talking about the teenyboppers on your tail all night."

"Yep."

"And Jazz helped you out. How'd she do that?"

"Let's just say she ran interference for me."

"Really? I'm surprised she got involved."

Devon glanced over at Vincent, wondering what he meant, but decided not to comment. "Anyway, she came over and we had a nice evening. She's much different than I expected."

"What did you expect?"

"I'm not even sure anymore," he said. Vincent shook

his head. "She's never herself. She plays this part for the world to see. I just want to get to know the real Jazz."

"And what exactly would you do with the real Jazz?"

"What do you mean?" Devon asked.

Vincent slowed, then stopped. He felt his pulse then put his hands on his hips and looked out at the bay. The water was a hazy, murky blue, with ripples of white foam cresting on the shoreline. He took a deep, centering breath then turned to Devon. "Do me a favor," he began, breathing hard to catch his breath.

Devon also slowed, stopped and then walked back to where his friend stood. He looked at him with concern. They didn't usually stop running once they began. "Sure," Devon said. "What is it? What do you need?"

"I need you not to hurt her."

"What?" Devon asked, expecting Vincent to say something totally different.

"Jazz," he said, breathing hard. "Don't hurt her."

"Hurt her?"

"Yeah. If you're looking to have a good time, keep looking."

"Whoa, where's all this coming from?" Devon asked then realized that maybe Vincent and Jazz were more than just friends. "Are you and Jazz together or are you…"

"No, man, she's like another sister to me," Vincent confessed quickly. "I care about her and what happens to her. She's got nobody now. Brian was there all her life. He was like her guardian. He protected her, sometimes from things he couldn't even protect himself from. He was messed up bad at times, but he was always there for Jazz."

"I heard they were close," Devin said.

"Brother and sister close. The media tried to hype it as being something different, but mostly everyone who knew them knew the truth. They adored each other. When he was on top, he watched out for her. When his light faded, she took care of him."

"What do you mean, took care of him?"

"He got paid for everything she did. If she starred in a movie, he was in that same movie. Same with television. She looked out for him. Then when he really started going down, she sent him to rehab. When that didn't work, she'd take him away with her. They'd stay away for months at a time until he got himself together again."

Devon shook his head. "The media always made it sound like they hated each other because of their father."

"Frank was a whole other issue, for both of them. Jazz has a strong passion for life, but she's vulnerable right now. She hasn't been the luckiest when it comes to the men in her life. So do me a favor. Tread lightly."

"First of all, I would never—"

"Yeah, I know you'd never intentionally hurt anyone. I know that. But it still happens. You've been known to leave a trail of broken hearts. And trust me, Jazz can afford to buy her own diamonds, so a consolation prize isn't going to work."

"You make me sound heartless."

"Nah, you're a guy with bank. I get that. Women throw themselves at you. But that only shows how little some women value themselves."

"I agree," Devon said. "But Jazz is different. I care about her, I really do. I didn't expect to, but I do."

"Understandable," Vincent said, seeing Devon's sincerity. "She's had some tough times. Everybody wants a piece of her. In case you haven't learned yet, she's strong. But she also has a heart of gold, and I'd hate to see her hurt, albeit unintentionally."

"I want to get to know her."

"Also understandable. Just know that I'm honor bound to come down hard if you hurt her."

"You? Come down hard? In your dreams," Devon taunted.

"Please, I know you still wake up with nightmares after I warned you about dating my cousin," Vincent said as he started running, backward at first. Then he turned, knowing that Devon would soon catch up. He was right. An instant later Devon was right there by his side.

"First of all, Jessica asked me out. And second, we're talking about a junior high school Sadie Hawkins dance."

"Didn't matter," Vincent said.

"And I would never think about Jess or Ronnie like that."

"I'm just saying, I'd have to hurt you."

"Oh, and you think you can take me?" Devon joked, amused by Vincent's threats.

"See, I was giving you a break, but all bets are off." As soon as he said the last word, he took off like a flash. Devon laughed heartily and within seconds caught up and even passed him.

Vincent lagged behind, then somehow found a burst of energy and caught up. They ran side by side, still trash-talking. "Is that all you got, Mr. Football?" Vincent teased, running even faster and cutting Devon off.

"Mr. Football?" Devon said, bumping Vincent. "Who

you calling Mr. Football?" he said, easily taking the lead again.

"If the helmet fits, wear it," Vincent called out, closing in on him again.

"I got your helmet," Devon said, running past him.

"Hey, remind me again why they gave you that big fat contract? 'Cause it wasn't because of your running. Your sister can outrun you," Vincent yelled over his shoulder.

"Then she must be beating your butt, too, because I'm barely breaking a sweat over here," Devon jeered, beside him again.

"Sweat this," Vincent said as he bumped Devon, knocking him off balance and into the water.

Devon splashed hard and then sat up laughing. He watched Vincent continue running, but at a slower pace. "That's one," he called out after his friend.

"Later, Mr. Football," Vincent said, laughing, and continuing to run down the beach.

Devon sat a moment longer, seeing Vincent turn and head to Melanie's back door. He saw someone standing on the deck, but a second later they were gone. His thoughts instantly went to Jazz, but he couldn't be sure. He stood up and walked back down to the beach to his back door. Once inside, he headed straight to the shower.

Two hours later, showered and shaved, with thoughts of Jazz still running through his mind, Devon sat at his desk to work. Although training camp wasn't for another few weeks, his other business ventures kept him extremely busy year-round.

He'd just read through a major endorsement deal from a recognized vitamin supplement company. The deal was extremely lucrative for all parties concerned, but he just couldn't get behind it. He decided against it since it would create a conflict of interest with most of his other sponsors. He knew his appeal as an athlete and celebrity was mainly with kids and teens, and he didn't want to jeopardize that relationship.

He tossed the proposal aside, mindful that he needed to speak with his attorney. Just as he grabbed the next item, his phone rang. He answered. It was his East Coast assistant, Darcy.

"Good morning. Ready to get started?" she said brightly in her Boston accent.

"Good morning," he replied as he stood and headed to the kitchen for a cup of coffee. "Yeah, what's going on this week?"

"Okay, we just got the testers for the new cologne. Your samples should be delivered today."

"What do you think of it?" he asked, knowing that she'd already sampled it.

"I like it much better than the last scent, and the marketing team said that it tested very well. It's not as spicy as the last fragrance, and it seems richer and fuller, if that makes any sense."

"Sounds good," Devon said, taking his cup out onto the deck. "I can't wait to try it."

"Okay, also if you approve this new scent and logo design, the ad agency wants to go ahead with the holiday season launch. For that they need you in front of the camera as soon as possible."

"When exactly is as soon as possible?" he asked.

"Now, today, tomorrow, basically," she said.

He pressed a few keys on his PDA and connected with his desktop calendar. "Make it the day after tomorrow."

"Okay, I'll set it up. Also, Liam needs you in to

reshoot the jean ad. If you can believe this, the marketing people tested the ads with a focus group and apparently you look too sexy." Devon laughed. "I know, but that's what they said. They need you to tone it down a bit since we're marketing primarily to a younger consumer."

"Reshoot. How does that fit in my schedule?" he asked.

"It doesn't right now. It's going to be tight. But if you can get into the city day after tomorrow for the fragrance shoot then maybe I can schedule the jeans re-shoot then, too. But I'll have to make some calls and work it out."

"Okay, make it happen," he instructed, knowing that Darcy was brilliant at what she did. If anyone could rearrange his and everyone else's schedule, she could. He turned and headed back to the office. "What do I have going on at the end of this week?"

"You have four must-do personal appearances, two here in the city, one in Texas and one in Florida. They're contractual obligations with the sponsors, so you pretty much have to be there. Do you want to drive down and leave out of LaGuardia or hire a private service?"

"LaGuardia is fine," he said, standing in front of the painting Jazz had admired so much the night before. He had considered giving it to her then, but he knew she'd never accept it. So he thought about having another one painted just for her. "Send a car. Have Liam call me this afternoon. I have a couple of projects for him. Do you have anything else for me?" he asked, still thinking about Jazz and the night before.

"Yeah, one more thing. Trina called to get your new cell number," Darcy said.

"Did you give it to her?"

"Devon, I really like my job. What do you think?"

He knew better than to even ask. Darcy was never a

big fan of Trina's. She kept quiet about it, but he knew they didn't care for each other. "Good. She doesn't get it, understood?"

"Fine by me. I'll pass the word along."

"Do that. Anything else?"

"No, not right now. I'll text you in a few with the updates. Anything you need on this end?" she asked.

"No. Wait, yes. I need to arrange for a painting."

"From your artist friend?" she asked.

"Yes."

"I read that he's opening a new show in a gallery in either TriBeCa or SoHo. I think it's in two weeks. Either way I'll arrange for a private showing before it opens."

"Excellent. Talk to you later." He hung up, troubled by the thought that Trina wanted his cell number. Dealing with her was the last thing he needed. He dismissed her request as quickly as she'd dismissed him.

He focused on work again, but thoughts of Jazz continued. He didn't know what time she left, just that it was before the storm hit. It was the lightning that woke him. Seconds later the heavy rumble of thunder made him sit up. He reached out for her, but she was gone. An empty feeling settled inside of him. He never liked losing, never got used to it. He got up and looked for her. She'd left and locked the door behind herself. He considered going after her, but he didn't. He knew she needed her space, and he knew that he'd have plenty of time to see her again. So he let her go.

He went back to his desk, opened the laptop and brought up a file he'd been reading when Darcy called. After reading the same sentence three times, he realized that his thoughts kept wandering to Jazz. He typed her

KIMANI ™ **ROMANCE**

An Important Message from the Publisher

Dear Reader,

Because you've chosen to read one of our fine novels, I'd like to say "thank you"! And, as a special way to say thank you, I'm offering to send you two more Kimani™ Romance novels and two surprise gifts—absolutely FREE! These books will keep it real with true-to-life African American characters that turn up the heat and sizzle with passion.

Please enjoy the free books and gifts with our compliments...

Glenda Howard
For Kimani Press

Peel off Seal and

Place Inside...

FREE GIFTS SEAL
EDITOR'S THANK YOU

(K-ROM-10R2)

W e'd like to send you two free books to introduce you to Kimani™ Romance books. These novels feature strong, sexy women, and African-American heroes that are charming, loving and true. Our authors fill each page with exceptional dialogue, exciting plot twists, and enough sizzling romance to keep you riveted until the very end!

KIMANI ROMANCE...LOVE'S ULTIMATE DESTINATION

Your two books have a combined cover price of $13.98, but are yours **FREE!**

We'll even send you two wonderful surprise gifts. You can't lose!

THE EDITOR'S "THANK YOU" FREE GIFTS INCLUDE:

➢ Two Kimani™ Romance Novels
➢ Two exciting surprise gifts

YES! I have placed my Editor's "thank you" Free Gifts seal in the space provided at right. Please send me 2 FREE books, and my 2 FREE Mystery Gifts. I understand that I am under no obligation to purchase anything further, as explained on the back of this card.

PLACE
FREE GIFTS
SEAL
HERE

About how many NEW paperback fiction books have you purchased in the past 3 months?

❑ 0-2   ❑ 3-6   ❑ 7 or more

E7XY   E5MH   E5MT

168/368 XDL

Please Print

FIRST NAME

LAST NAME

ADDRESS

APT.#   CITY

STATE/PROV.   ZIP/POSTAL CODE

Thank You!

The Reader Service - Here's how it works:

▼ If offer card is missing write to: The Reader Service, P.O. Box 1867, Buffalo, NY 14240-1867 or visit www.ReaderService.com ▼

BUSINESS REPLY MAIL
FIRST-CLASS MAIL   PERMIT NO. 717   BUFFALO, NY

POSTAGE WILL BE PAID BY ADDRESSEE

THE READER SERVICE
PO BOX 1867
BUFFALO NY 14240-9952

NO POSTAGE
NECESSARY
IF MAILED
IN THE
UNITED STATES

name in the search field and clicked on her official Web site.

He smiled instantly. She was stunning, posed on the red carpet with an eager-looking man in a tuxedo beside her. He looked to be of mixed race, with a mass of shoulder-length curls. A spark of jealousy slashed through Devon when he activated the video feed and watched it play. Jazz as she walked the carpet was poised and elegant, but her date was antsy and nervous. He was identified as England's Manchester United soccer superstar, Jeremiah Kent. Devon clicked through more photos, seeing her mother, father and brother. But it was the photos of her that stilled his heart. He was falling. He knew that he cared about her. He also knew that loving Jazz was as easy as breathing.

Chapter 10

EXTERIOR—PATIO

Jazz stood on the deck, watching the two men she thought she recognized. The beach was relatively empty so she spotted them instantly. They ran along the water's edge. They were still pretty far away, but she could see it was definitely Vincent and Devon. After last night she'd know his body anywhere. She smiled, secretly admiring his physique. Both were physically fit, strong, muscular, but Devon was clearly the more defined of the two.

He wore a sleeveless T-shirt with shorts, but she could plainly see the muscled outline of his body. His cinnamon-toned skin glistened against the sun and water. She took a deep breath and shook her head, exhaling slowly. The memory of his arms wrapped around her as they made love sent tingles through her body all over again. Her stomach quivered just thinking about the night before. He was irresistible, and she was insatiable.

His kisses had hooked her instantly. Nobody should be allowed to kiss like that. He'd sucked her tongue. She didn't even know that was possible. The feeling was intense. Her head spun, and the next thing she knew she was lying on the bed beside him. How was it possible to lose herself so completely with a kiss?

Devon was every woman's fantasy. He was athletic, smart, confident, fun to be with and, heaven knew, too, too sexy. But he was an athlete, and she'd been down that road before. Four dates with tennis star Gavin Parks had been blissfully tranquil at first. Then his childish behavior and off-court temper tantrums soon ended their relationship. It turned out all he wanted from her was a celebrity in the stands rooting for him.

After Gavin was a tumultuous year and a half with England's Manchester United soccer superstar, Jeremiah Kent. She should have learned her lesson with Gavin, but she didn't. Jeremiah was fun and unpredictable and challenging. But his constant womanizing, petty jealousy and temper kept them on a roller coaster of emotions. It wasn't until he checked into rehab that she found out he was high throughout most of their relationship. Either way, she'd had it with sports stars.

Dating a celebrity was problematic; dating an athlete was insanity. Their fiercely competitive nature was an asset on the court or the playing field, but in a relationship it was a major obstacle. They all just wanted to have their egos stroked, and they'd use anybody they could to get what they wanted.

She watched as Vincent and Devon stopped and talked awhile. She couldn't see their faces clearly, but whatever it was they were talking about seemed to be serious.

They eventually turned and looked out at the water. Moments later, Vincent began running. Devon soon followed, running faster to catch up. They appeared to be in fierce competition, each running faster and faster, bumping the other to gain the momentary advantage. But it was obvious who was winning: Devon.

Then Vincent bumped him, and Devon lost his balance and fell into the water. Jazz gasped. He went down hard. Seconds later she saw that when he sat up in the water, he was laughing. Jazz shook her head then suddenly realized someone was standing next to her. She was so engrossed in voyeurism she hadn't noticed. "Jess," Jazz said. "Good morning. I didn't realize you were here."

"'Morning," Jessica said, still looking out at the beach. She sipped from a china cup, then smiled. "I have some paperwork to catch up on while Mel's away, so I figured I'd take care of it early and get it out of the way." She chuckled. "Those two are like little kids playing on the beach. They're forever competitive, just like in college."

"Really?" Jazz said curiously.

"Oh yeah. My friends and I used to go to Vincent's college track meets all the time just to see Devon run. The two of them were usually the best runners there. They traded wins. One time Devon would win and the next time Vincent would."

"So Vincent and Devon were good friends in college?" Jazz asked.

"Good friends? Oh, hell, no, definitely not. They were more like bitter rivals. They all but hated each other. They were both incredible runners and super talented. Watching them compete was amazing. They learned to respect each other's talent. After a while they became friends. You know, I used to have such a crush on Devon about a hundred years ago."

"Well, I hear he's looking for a wife," Jazz said, alluding to the fact that he signed with the Platinum Society.

"You mean me and Devon?" she asked. Jazz nodded. "Nah, that ship has long since sailed. He's more of a big brother now. I adore him, but that's it." She turned and walked over to the table. Jazz followed.

"So Devon went into football. Why didn't Vincent?"

"He was supposed to. Vincent won a spot on the Summer Olympics national team. He went and won two gold medals, but in the last race he blew his knee out crossing the finish line. He won, but a few surgeries later he realized he'd never be the same. He stopped running for a long time after that."

"Wow, that's terrible. But he's running now."

"Actually, Devon has everything to do with that. They started hanging out socially and eventually Devon got Vincent back into running. I don't know how he did it, but he did. Vincent was so miserable for a while. Now he's back to being himself. He's not as good as he used to be, and he'll never make the NFL, but he's happy again. That's all that matters."

"I wonder what Devon did or said to help him?"

"I don't know, but whatever it was, it really helped him. Devon's good like that. Oh, he gets the bad-boy press, but he's really a good guy."

"Are you saying that all the articles in the papers about Devon are made up?"

"You would know better than me. How much of what they say about you is true?" Jazz nodded her understanding. Jessica smiled happily. "You like him, don't you?" Jazz nodded. "You should get to know him."

"To what end? He's looking for a relationship. I'm not."

"There are all kinds of relationships," Jessica said.

"Well, more specifically, he's looking to get married. Isn't that why he signed on with the Platinum Society, to settle down and find a wife?" she asked. Jessica didn't respond either way. "I don't want to distract him from that, and I don't want to get emotionally involved just to have him walk away with someone else."

"Why can't you be good friends, then?"

"He asked the same question last night."

"And?" Jessica prompted.

"And," Jazz began then turned away. "I don't know. It's strange with Devon. There's this thing between us. I know it sounds weird, but since the moment he walked into the party, there was this something. He stared at me, I stared at him. It's like a magnetic attraction," Jazz said.

"You mean like a spark, an instant attraction?" Jessica asked. Jazz shrugged and then nodded woefully. "Jazz, you're attracted to each other. That's a good thing."

"No, not for me. I've done the athlete thing with Gavin and Jeremiah. Both were disasters, by the way."

"What do they have to do with Devon?"

"All athletes," Jazz said.

"All three are totally different men," Jessica said. "If you really feel this attraction for Devon, don't you owe it to yourself to find out where it leads?"

Jazz considered her suggestion, but a part of her was still too scared to open up. "Jess, what happens if I open myself up to Devon?"

"You have seven kids, name the first girl after me and then live happily ever after."

"You're such a romantic."

"So are you," Jessica confirmed, "and you know it."

Jazz nodded. Devon was definitely not the man she initially thought he was when they first met.

Moments later, Vincent walked up the path leading to the patio then climbed the stairs to the deck. He smiled as soon as he saw them sitting there at the table talking. "Hey, 'morning, I thought that was you guys standing at the rail," he said breathlessly.

"Good morning," Jazz said, obviously grateful for Vincent's interruption. "You guys look great out there. Of course that competition thing was a bit over the top."

"Actually, that was pretty tame, considering." Jessica smirked.

Vincent laughed and then coughed. "Can't help it—we go way back with that. So, what are you two up to today?"

"Work. I have a million things to take care of in the office," Jessica said.

Vincent nodded and then looked at Jazz for her response. "Nothing, really. I have a few calls to make this morning. Then I'll probably do some reading later on."

"Why don't you go into town and take a look around?" Jessica suggested. "It's the perfect time. It's still early in the season, so the tourists haven't arrived yet. You'll have the whole place to yourself."

"You haven't seen Sag Harbor yet?" Vincent asked.

Jazz shook her head. "No, not yet," Jazz said. "I've been kind of hiding out here."

"You're missing a real treat," Vincent said. "It's beautiful this time of year. The museums alone are worth the trip."

Jazz nodded, considering Jessica's suggestion. "Actually, I've been saying that I was going to have a look around. I just might do that."

"Great. You can use my car," Vincent said. "I won't be using it. I'm headed to the coast for a few days. As a matter of fact, I'd better get showered and changed. My flight's in a few hours. So," he began as he slapped his hands together and looked at them, "who's going to volunteer to drive me to the airport?"

Jessica and Jazz looked at each other, then to Vincent, and then back at each other. They started laughing, knowing exactly what the other was thinking. It was a well-known fact that traffic to and from the airport this time of day was sheer madness. "For real, I can't get a ride?" he asked. Jessica and Jazz laughed again.

"Sorry," Jazz said sympathetically.

Vincent shook his head as Jessica continued laughing. "Ya'll are wrong. I guess it's a good thing I already hired a car to take me. Okay, I'm out. Jazz, the car's in the garage and the keys are on the dash. I'll see you in a few days."

"Thanks, have a good trip," Jazz called out after him.

"See ya," Jessica added then turned to Jazz. "Now, back to our previous conversation…"

"I was hoping you'd let it go," Jazz said.

"Me? Never. How long have we known each other? Seriously, are you interested in Devon?"

"No," Jazz lied with difficulty.

"Why the hell not?" Jessica asked plainly. Jazz looked at her, surprised by the comment. "Look, you're single.

He's single. You're both attractive, intelligent people with a lot to offer. If the attraction you just described to me is half as strong as I think, then—"

"Then what? Throw myself at him and have a sex thing until he finds his one true love, then just walk away? I can't do that."

"Jazz, there are no guarantees in any of this, so why not?"

"The why not is simple—he will surely break my heart, and I don't think I could stand another heartbreak."

Jessica nodded, deciding that pushing Jazz further would be useless. "Okay," she said softly then stood to leave. "We all just want you to be happy. If it's Devon and he makes you happy, fine. If not, that's fine, too. Know that a man by your side won't change who you are or what you feel. But the right one will make those feelings soar. Finding someone so instantly compatible is the greatest feeling in the world. I see it every day, and it makes me forever hopeful."

"The truth is, he scares me," Jazz admitted, then looked up at Jessica. "Of course, not physically, but emotionally. I can see myself getting lost in him, and that's scary. That's what my mom said happened with Frank. It was instant, and she lost herself. Look what happened, the disaster her life became." Saying the words out loud gave her pause. She'd never dared utter what her mother once told her, but she knew she could trust Jessica.

"Jazz, you're not your mother. You know that, and as far as love is concerned, it's a hell of a motivator. It'll make you do all kinds of crazy things. But when it's right, there's nothing like it. It can last a moment or a lifetime. Either way, it's always worth it."

Jazz smiled with hope. "You think so, huh?"

Jessica nodded. "I know so. Are you going to be okay?" she asked. Jazz nodded. "Okay, I'm gonna get started. I'll be in the office the rest of the morning if you need me. But why don't you think about getting out of here for a while? Visit the sights, see the town. There are some really nice boutiques. Try Suzi's Closet. It's a great place to start. Her clothes are incredible."

"I'll think about it," Jazz promised. Jessica nodded and left her alone. Jazz's mind raced. Thinking about Devon led to thoughts of her mother and father and their love, then to her brother, then back to Devon.

To change focus, she glanced at the overnight package her agent had sent her and her laptop. The decision was easy. She quickly opened her laptop. She logged on and checked in with her manager who forwarded her emails. Thankfully she had a service that handled and answered her fan mail. Important e-mails were sent to her manager's office, sorted, then sent to her. It was a daily thing that had become a weekly thing, and was now a monthly thing. She had over a hundred unopened e-mails, all marked urgent. She opened the first one, then went from there.

It was strange getting back to her life. She was alone for the first time in a long time. With her mother and Brian gone, and Savannah away in England, she felt an odd sense of contentment. She had no idea where it came from, she just knew that...

She paused. She remembered a conversation last night about being alone and finding herself. Devon had a way of cutting through her guard of mistrust and pain. He got to her, and she opened up to him. It was scary knowing that someone could see that far into her heart.

Her e-mail beeped. She looked down at the message. It was from Frank. She deleted it without opening.

Instantly another e-mail came. It was from her grandfather. He wasn't computer savvy, but when it came to sending her e-mails, he was an expert. He ended with his usual call-your-grandmother message. She smiled. Of course she'd call. She knew it wasn't just her grandmother who missed her.

She grabbed her cell and called. The conversation lasted over an hour. Jazz adored her grandparents. They had always been the stability in her life. When she was younger and her mother toured, she stayed with them. It was like having a normal family. Then her mother's fame began to fade, and she was at home more. Jazz loved that even more. Soon after, she started in the business professionally. She was five when she got her first modeling contract. Then she did commercials, small guest spots, her own TV show, a recording contract and finally movies. She never looked back. She was everything her mother wanted her to be.

After the phone call, she went back to the remaining e-mails. Another hour passed quickly. She stood and walked back over to the rail and looked out at the beach. Devon had long since gone. Thinking about him was becoming a habit. One she couldn't afford to have. He wasn't for her, and she wasn't sure she'd know what to do with him if he were.

Their lives were so different. Sure they were both in the spotlight, but his was by choice. She only stepped into the limelight to do her job. Once that was over, she wanted nothing more than peace and quiet and the idea of a normal life. Lost in her thoughts, she didn't see him as he approached. "Good morning," he called up.

Jazz looked down, seeing Devon climb the steps

from the beach. Her stomach immediately fluttered. "'Morning," she said softly.

Devon walked over and stood beside her, looking out at the view. He turned to look at her. "You look beautiful this morning."

"Thanks. Did you enjoy your run?"

"With Vincent?" he asked with a smile knowing instantly that she'd seen them. "Yes, it was good. I enjoy running with him."

"Are you okay after falling into the water?"

He chuckled and looked back out to the bay. "You saw that too, huh?" She nodded. "I'm fine. We were just horsing around."

"Tell me something. What did you say to Vincent to get him running again?"

Devon turned to her, surprised that she knew that. "You've been busy, haven't you?" he asked. She smiled. "I told Vincent that since he wouldn't run and we couldn't compete, I'd retire from football."

"But you didn't."

"No, we went out running that same day. Apparently he had a lot of money on me in the upcoming game. He didn't want to lose a fortune." She laughed, knowing that it wasn't true. "So, what are your plans today?" he asked.

"I don't know yet."

"Excellent. It's the perfect day to hang out. I have to go in town, but after that, why don't you come over? I'll even spring for lunch."

"Thanks anyway, but I'm really not up for going out today. Besides, I still have a few things to take care of here," she said, glancing at her laptop that was on the table.

"Okay. Why don't I stop by later, just in case you

change your mind?" he said then walked toward the steps leading back to the beach.

"I won't change my mind," she assured him.

"Just in case," he repeated with a knowing smile. "See you later."

Jazz went back to the table and sat down. Devon hadn't mentioned what happened between them last night and the fact that she'd left his house without a word, and she wasn't about to. As soon as she saw him, her heart jumped for joy, but her mind was putting on the brakes. All she could think about was being hurt like her mother and repeating her mistakes. Being in love with a man who belonged to someone else was the cruelest kind of love. Instant attraction was usually a disaster, and that was the last thing she needed. She picked up her laptop, went back into the house, grabbed her dark sunglasses and hat and headed to the garage. She had no intention of being here when Devon returned.

Chapter 11

EXTERIOR—SAG HARBOR

Blowing Devon off was quick and less painful than she expected; still, he was right about one thing. It was a perfect day to hang out. The weather was a balmy seventy-five degrees. The sky was crystal blue, and the sun was blazing bright. Jazz was excited to see, as Devon had put it, *the beauty of Sag Harbor.* She put the top down on Vincent's car and let the brisk air breeze through her hair. She loved the smell of the day after a storm. The air was refreshed, and everything bad seemed to have washed away.

She drove down Main Street and parked near Monument Park. She got out and walked the south side of town, stopping occasionally to window-shop. She continued passing boutiques, restaurants, coffee houses and even a few small art galleries.

Jazz decided that it was time to treat herself. After being secluded for weeks, she was excited to do a little shopping. With her dark sunglasses and wide-brimmed hat, she eased through town, confident that no one would recognize her. She was right. She blended in easily with the new trickle of early tourists and the locals. There was a constant flow of pedestrian traffic, yet no one bothered to even look in her direction. For that she was grateful.

She checked out the windows of a few boutiques. They seemed to be stocking merchandise for the upcoming season. She stopped at an upscale boutique with an artful window design. She went inside and looked around. As soon as she entered, a woman met her at the door. She had blond hair with punk-rock spikes and magenta tips. She smiled widely showing a neat row of hot-pink rubber-banded braces. "Good morning. Can I show you anything in particular?"

"Actually, I'm just looking around," Jazz said.

"We have some really nice things in this week. If you need help, just let me know."

Jazz nodded and continued browsing. There were other customers in the store, and one of them constantly stared at her. Feeling self-conscious, she eventually purchased a few men's summer-knit sweaters and several hand-painted silk scarves. She paid in cash and waited for the sales clerk to bag her items. The customer finally came up to her. "Excuse me. I'm sure you get this all the time, but you look a little like Jazelle Richardson."

Jazz nodded and smiled as she took her bags. "Yeah, actually I get that a lot. Thanks." She smiled, turned and left.

"Make sure to come back again. We get new shipments daily," the clerk called out as the door closed.

Jazz continued strolling through town. It was still early, and the walk was exactly what she needed to clear her head. Her next stop was the small fashion boutique Jessica had told her about, Suzi's Closet. The instant she stood at the window, she fell in love with the merchandise. It was essentially high-fashion designer clothes with an everyday appeal. It fit her style perfectly. Unfortunately, the store was packed. There were several dozen women mingling around. After being nearly recognized the last time, she decided not to try her luck but wait until the store was less crowded.

She continued walking, then stopped at the bookstore a few doors down. She went in, hoping to find something more interesting than the scripts she'd been reading. She looked around, quickly assessing the main sections. Romance, fiction, travel—she breezed through the stacks, picking up a few books then replacing them, searching for nothing in particular. A few moments passed and she wandered into the sports section. She browsed until a smiling face caught her eye on the end-cap display. It was Devon.

She walked over and picked up the book. It was a sports guide for kids. She flipped through, seeing photos of him with kids and also in his professional life on the field.

"If you're interested in football, we have a small selection of DVDs in the back of the store. Championship games, mostly."

Jazz turned, seeing a store employee standing in the aisle across from her. She smiled. "No thanks. I'm just browsing."

He nodded. "Or if you interested in the L.A. Stallions or Devon Hayes in particular, there's a great article on him in *Sports Illustrated* this month. You know he has a place here."

"Really, but no, I'm not interested, thanks," she said holding on to the book she'd picked up and moving to the next aisle.

Focus had never been difficult for her, but here lately she was struggling to center her attention. No matter where she was or what she was doing, her thoughts seemed to stray to Devon. She turned down the next aisle and the next, moving too quickly to be browsing, but she needed to get as far away from Devon as possible.

"Maybe a movie," she said aloud, and then looked around. There were several patrons in the store, but no one paid her any attention and the store employee was busy helping someone else. She looked at the new movie releases, spotting her last movie instantly. She picked it up, turned it over and smiled, remembering her time on set. Her costars were crazy, and she loved every minute. She always enjoyed the comradery on set. It was like being in a huge family where everyone wanted the same thing.

She replaced the movie and moved to the next section. She picked up another DVD and glanced at it. Before turning it over, she saw a young woman coming towards her. She recognized her instantly, although she looked much younger in her school uniform. She was at Melanie's party. She was the young girl following Devon around all night.

She worried there would be a confrontation, but to her delight the girl merely pardoned herself and kept walking. Jazz moved a few more feet in the opposite direction then stopped curiously. The young girl paused at the new movie display. She grabbed a box. "Hey, over here, I found it," she called out. Two friends, about the same age, came charging down the aisle. Single focused, they never even noticed Jazz. They gathered as the first girl held a DVD in her hands. "What do you think?" she said. "He's not all that cute, though."

"So who cares?"

The other girl nodded. "You should seriously go after him."

"Eww, and he's married," she replied.

"So what? Forget his wife. You should go after him."

"I know, right?" one of the other girls said, giggling. "Seriously, you should definitely go after him. Plus, I read in the tabloids that he just signed this huge contract for the sequel. He's about to seriously blow up."

"Yeah, but the movie was lame."

"Who cares? They're giving him a mint to do another one. As long as the money's coming in, who cares if he's any good?"

"She's right. You gotta take care of yourself. What do you think you're gonna do after high school? Go to college, fall in love with a lawyer and have his kids like your mother? Please. I don't think so. Why settle for sloppy seconds when you can go after filet mignon? Having his kid would definitely set you up for life."

"I know, right?" the same girl repeated. "Definitely."

"This is business, so just do what you have to do and think of the money you'll get in the end."

"I wanted Devon Hayes," the girl from the party pouted.

"Yeah, what happened with that?" one of the girls asked.

"I heard Devon was gonna be there, so I got my dad to take me to the party. He was there, and he was gorgeous. All these other old women were trying to get at him, but I was blocking hard. Then Jazz Richardson showed up. They must have a thing, 'cause they were outside practically doing it right there in front of me. He had her up against the pole humping her. She was screaming his name and everything. I saw the whole thing."

Jazz gasped, knowing the girl was lying about the other night. They had kissed, and that was all. This was how ugly rumors got started.

"You should have used your cell phone and sold the photo."

"I didn't even think about it. I was just so mad. I hate her guts. She thinks she can have anybody, just 'cause she's famous."

Jazz eased farther away and turned down the next aisle. With her large hat on and her head down, it appeared as if she was looking at a CD cover as she stood almost directly across from the girls.

"That's a shame, 'cause Devon Hayes is gorgeous and his pockets are seriously deep. Plus, he's getting that fat contract next season."

"Yeah, but you had to know he was gonna be extra careful after what happened to him. It almost ruined his career. They say he's been off-the-market ever since then."

"Him off-the-market? What a waste. I could sure fix that. Can you imagine being with him?"

"I bet you he's incredible in bed." They giggled.

"I bet you he is huge." They giggled again.

"Imagine riding him all night long. See, I could have had all that. It's all that stupid reporter's fault. She screwed him big-time and made him all suspicious about everyone. I bet he doesn't trust anybody now."

Jazz had to stop herself from looking up. She had no idea what they were talking about, but it sounded serious. All she gathered was that Devon's career took a hit because of a scandal with a reporter.

"It's a shame he made her get rid of the baby, though."

Jazz's jaw dropped. She was stunned.

"Do you really think she was pregnant and it was his?"

"I don't know. I guess we'll never know for sure. They say she lied to trap him, but whatever."

"I heard she was doing like three other guys, but since he had the deepest pockets she went after him. She almost got him good, too."

"Yeah, but her stupid father got greedy."

"See, that's why you should never tell your parents what you plan to do. They always want in on it and mess things up. Come on, we gotta get back to school." They pocketed the DVD and walked out.

Jazz stood stunned, shaking her head. Their audacity was beyond disgusting. How could anybody purposely go after a man in hopes of trapping him with a baby? It was wrong, it was revolting—it was her mother. It didn't take her long to realize she was the answer. Her mother had done the same thing. True love or not, it was still wrong.

Disheartened, she walked to the front of the store to leave. "Excuse me, miss." She turned. "If you'd like to purchase those items, I can take them for you over here."

She looked down, realizing that she was still holding the book and DVD she'd picked up earlier. "Yes, sure, of course," she said. She walked over to the counter and handed the book and DVD over. The cashier began ringing the two items up when she noticed a copy of *Sports Illustrated*. She picked it up and added it to her purchases. The cashier rang everything up, and she paid and left quickly.

She headed back in the direction of the car, but stopped, noticing that the boutique was now almost empty. She went inside. There was a woman paying for her purchase and another woman behind the counter. "Hi, welcome to Suzi's Closet. I'll be right with you."

Jazz nodded and began looking around. She found a number of items she liked. She pulled several from the stands and draped them over her arm. "Hi, I'm Suzi. I'll take these for you." She took the merchandise and hung them by the dressing room. "You have some great selections. Are you looking for any occasion in particular?" Suzi asked.

"No, just shopping in general."

"You're the perfect customer. I have some new pieces against the wall and some original pieces towards the back of the store. There's a royal blue dress that would look sensational on you. I'll get it."

"Thanks," Jazz said, enjoying the personal attention.

Suzi brought the dress over. Jazz was stunned. It was gorgeous, but not for her. Her best friend Savannah would look incredible in it. "That's stunning."

"Would you like to try it on with the others? I'd be happy to alter it to fit you," Suzi said, walking toward the dressing room.

"Actually, it's for a friend of mine. Her birthday's in a few weeks, and she'd look great in that."

"I'll be happy to hold it a few days for her."

"She's in London right now."

"Are the two of you approximately the same size?"

"Approximately. She's a bit bustier."

"No problem. Try it on and I'll fit it to you and leave a bit more room at the top for her."

"Great." Jazz followed Suzi to the dressing room, where she found her other outfits waiting. She tried everything on and loved them. The last piece she tried on was the blue dress. It was much sexier than she'd buy for herself, but there was no denying it was breathtaking. She stepped out of the dressing room and up onto the riser. She looked at herself in the three-way mirror. "Perfect," she said aloud.

"I couldn't agree more."

Chapter 12

EXTERIOR—SAG HARBOR

Jazz looked up at the mirror's reflection then spun around quickly, almost toppling off the stand. "Careful," Devon said, holding her waist securely.

"What are you doing here?" Jazz asked.

Devon smiled easily while holding a bright red dress in his hands. "I told you, I had to go in town. Imagine my surprise seeing you walking out of the dressing room in that." He eyed her from head to toe and smiled, obviously liking what he saw. "If you don't buy it for yourself, I most certainly will."

"It's not for me. I'm considering it for a girlfriend."

"It looks beautiful on you. Why don't you find something else for her?"

Jazz turned back to face the mirror and examined

her reflection again. She observed his reaction in the mirror. He most definitely approved of it.

"Oh, that's perfect. She's going to love that. It's a shame it's not for you. You look great in it," Suzi said, walking over.

"I couldn't agree more," Devon said.

"Here's the dress, Devon. I think it came out exactly as we planned," Suzi said as she held up an emerald-green evening dress with matching jacket. Devon nodded his approval. "I can send it out this afternoon if you like. Excuse me," Suzi said as she went to greet a customer who'd just walked in.

Jazz took the opportunity to change back into her clothes. As soon as she came out of the dressing room, Devon held two dresses up to her.

"What do you think, the red or the green?" he asked Jazz.

"I like them both. Although I think I'd need to see them on you to get the full effect," she joked.

"I'm buying them for my sister. She's been working really hard, and now she's up for a major award. It's a big deal in the advertising world. It's in a few weeks, and I'll be escorting her."

"Right," Jazz said skeptically.

"No, really. I'm serious. I'd never ask your opinion if I were buying something for another woman."

"Okay, fine. I believe you."

"So which one?" he asked.

"What's your sister like?"

"She's ambitious, smart and fun. She owns an advertising agency in San Francisco and works too hard for her own good."

"And these are the two choices, right?"

"She loves the color red, but this is more her style. Either would look great on her."

"Is her personality extravagant or more subdued?"

"She has her moments with both."

Jazz looked at both dresses. They were equally beautiful in different ways. "I'd go with the green. It's an awards event, and chances are a lot of her peers will be there. The red is beautiful, but maybe for a different occasion."

He nodded. "I agree. Thanks. Suzi," he called out, "we're taking the green dress. Could you send it ahead?"

"Sure, I'll get it out this afternoon," she said then turned to Jazz. "Is there anything I can have delivered to you?"

"Yes, I'm going to take this with the alterations we talked about and all of these as well," Jazz said, handing over her black credit card.

"Excellent," Suzi said, walking back to the counter. Jazz and Devon followed. "I'll have everything together for you in about half an hour. I can have them delivered anywhere you'd like. I am very discreet when it comes to my clientele."

"I'm staying at Melanie Harte's home."

"Perfect. I have another delivery going there today."

"Great, thank you," Jazz said, taking back her card.

"No problem. Make sure to come in again."

"I will," Jazz said.

"Devon, Terri should receive the green dress in two days."

"Thanks, Suzi. See you later."

Jazz walked out, and Devon followed. "Are you hungry?"

Jazz realized that she hadn't eaten all day. "Yes. Know any good places to eat around here?"

"I know the perfect place."

They ate at a small outside café. She ordered a salad, and he ordered a steak sandwich. Their meal was interrupted only occasionally by overly exuberant Stallions fans. Some wanted autographs, others photographs. Devon took it in stride. Jazz made certain to keep her head lowered and looked away during most of the conversations. When they did have time to themselves they talked mostly about her career both in music and movies.

"I've always wondered about one thing," Devon began.

Jazz sipped her soda and tried to keep control of her pleasant smile. But the idea of being asked about her life always gave her pause. "What's that?"

"After the sitcom went off the air, you disappeared for a while. I always wondered what happened to you."

"Nothing. The sitcom was great, but by the fifth season I was getting tired of it. I needed a break. Remember I'd been working nearly all my life. I started modeling baby clothes for magazines before I was one year old. I continued modeling, doing commercials and the TV show up through my teens. I needed to get out of sight and stay under the radar for a while. I did some off-Broadway shows, but mainly I went to school."

"College?"

She nodded. "I cut and dyed my hair, used my first initial and mother's last name and had a very successful college career as J. Brooks. It was great. No one knew who I was. And those who did know didn't care and didn't bother me about it."

"I think you like total anonymity."

"Yeah, I do. Sometimes my life gets too sensationalized. People forget that I'm just a normal person."

"Not exactly. You're a movie star."

"Don't you ever get tired of the craziness and just think about chucking it all and disappearing?"

Devon smiled brightly. "No, never. There are kids all over this country dreaming about someday doing what I do. I love my job. Few people can actually say that."

"You're lucky."

"Are you saying that you don't enjoy what you do?"

"Actually, I do. It's the other stuff that I can live without. The crazy tabloid stories, for instance."

"Yeah, I can commiserate there."

"Sometimes they get pretty mean."

"You can't let them get to you."

"I don't usually, but sometimes it's harder than others."

"Like when your brother died," he offered.

She nodded. "Yeah, they were really brutal."

"What was your brother like?"

"Brian." She smiled, looked up and seemed to drift away into her memories. "He was supercool. He was gentle, kind, fiercely protective, fearless and unafraid." He smiled, seemingly amused. She looked at him questioningly. "What, you don't believe me?" she asked, slightly disturbed.

"On the contrary, that description sounds a lot like you."

"I wish. No, Brian had the cool of Billy Dee and

Denzel, the wild fun side of Depp and Hendrix and the intellect of President Obama. He was so loving and loyal. He was dark and passionate, with a brilliant zest for life that was unimaginable. I know it sounds strange to say that he loved life but then committed suicide, but that's how he was. Always conflicted.

"We first met on the set of one of his movies. Talk about awkward. His mother, Elizabeth Rotherchild, was there, and my mother was there. They looked at each other and all hell broke loose. I was young, maybe ten years old, and I had no idea what was going on. I mean, I knew that Frank was my dad and it was okay that I never got to see him much. But learning that I had a big brother was major."

"What happened?"

"Once again our screwed-up family drama made the headlines. Elizabeth wanted me off the film. She threatened to pull Brian out and get Frank involved if I stayed. Of course, my mom was adamant about me keeping the part and them honoring the contract. The bottom line was that the studio caved. I lost the part, and they sent me a check that helped pay for my college education."

Devon chuckled. "Wow, that's amazing. So how did you and Brian eventually become as close as you were?"

"E-mails and text messages, mostly. He e-mailed me to apologize for everything, and that started it all. If his mother had any idea how long we'd been friends, she probably would have strangled both of us years ago."

"He didn't tell her?"

"Oh, no way." She chuckled. "Elizabeth Rothchild, soap opera queen, was known for being melodramatic, but that was nothing compared to her temper tantrums.

You can't just tell her things like that and expect her not to freak out."

"She must have hated that fact that the two of you became close."

"She did, and actually my mom did, too. She wasn't Brian's biggest fan at first, either. After a while they both knew there was no way they were going to break us up. We admitted that we kept in close contact at first just to spite them, but that didn't last long. Brian and I have so much in common." She stopped, took a deep breath and corrected herself. "*Had* so much in common."

"He sounds like he was an amazing man."

"He was," she said then seemed to quickly regroup. "Okay, that's it. Enough about me. Tell me about you."

"Come on. You know my life. Everybody does," he said.

"Contrary to popular belief, I don't. Sure, I've seen the commercials and the endorsements. But that's it. You're a football player. What position?"

"I'm the quarterback for the Los Angeles Stallions."

"Why aren't you playing now? Are you hurt?"

He chuckled. "You really don't know sports, do you?"

"I've been kind of busy the last twenty-five-plus years."

He nodded. "Okay, I'll accept that. So I'll tell you what. Why don't you stop by this evening and I'll show you some game films? I'll order pizza and pop some popcorn. We'll watch football all night."

"Sounds tempting, but I can't."

"Can't or won't?"

"I'm busy this evening."

A sudden hot streak of jealousy shot through him. "Anybody I know?" he asked jokingly.

"None of your business," she said, smiling.

"Come over afterward."

"Persistent, aren't you?" she joked. He nodded. She shook her head. "Wait a minute. You keep footage of yourself playing ball?" she asked.

"Yes. It's not like an ego trip or anything like that. As a professional athlete, I learn from them. What I did right and what I did wrong. It's like when you see your movies on the screen…."

She shook her head. "Not quite. I've never seen one of my movies on screen."

"Never?" he said, louder than he expected, and then lowered his voice. "That's really surprising. I thought all movie stars saw their pictures."

"I've seen the daily rushes and final cuts after edits, but to actually go to the movies and see myself up on screen in theaters? No thanks."

"Why not?" he asked.

"I'd be mortified, for one thing. Another is that I'd see all of my flaws and imperfections. There's no way I want to see that on an IMAX megascreen. That's why I enjoy theater performing in front of a live audience. I go onstage, do my show and never have to think about that performance again."

"You have to be joking. You're tremendously talented and beautiful. Well, maybe not today with that getup on," he joked. She playfully swung at him as they laughed. "But seriously, I've seen your movies. You're flawless."

She looked away, slightly embarrassed by the compliment. "I wasn't fishing for a compliment, but still, thank you."

"You're welcome," he said then reached across the small table and held her hand. "But it wasn't a compliment. It was the truth."

She looked into his eyes. She saw total sincerity. She also saw something else. Her stomach flinched and her hand shook. The attraction she'd first felt for Devon was getting stronger. Thankfully she still wore her dark sunglasses, because there was no way she wanted him reading her eyes right now. "How did this conversation get back around to me again? I want to hear about you."

"Okay, fair enough. What do you want to know? Ask me anything."

"Anything?" she asked. He nodded. "And you'll answer honestly?"

He nodded again. "Ask away," he confirmed effortlessly.

"Okay, you asked for it. What scares you most?"

"Failure."

"What was your favorite present?"

"A football at age seven. I still have it."

"What do you treasure?"

"My freedom."

"What do you miss most from your childhood?"

"It's a tossup—two-stick orange popsicles and recess."

"Who ended your last relationship, you or her?"

"Me, definitely," he said emphatically.

Jazz noted the instant narrowing of his eyes and the tightened muscle in his jaw. She'd hit a nerve. There was obviously something more than just a parting of the ways. She wondered if it had something to do with what the girls in the bookstore were talking about. "Who do you most not want to be like?"

"My father." His eyes narrowed and his jaw tightened again.

"Okay, who do you call when you're in trouble?"

"My grandfather."

"What can't you live without?"

"You."

She ignored that. "What's the best time you ever had?"

"Today, this moment, right now here with you."

The second unexpected answer took her off guard. Jazz shook her head. "Devon, what you think you feel…"

Devon smiled. "My feelings aren't as transient as you seem to think."

"How can you say that?"

"Because it's true," he said simply.

"Devon, whatever you think is going on between us because of the other night isn't. It was just sex, a physical release."

"Are you sure about that?" he asked.

She nodded. "Positive," she said quickly. They both knew she was lying. "No."

He nodded. "Very aptly put."

"You are so bad for me," she declared.

"And you are so very good for me."

"What am I doing here with you? I can't do this again."

"Do what? I'd never hurt you, Jazz," he assured her.

"We both know that this could go in any direction."

"Let's hope so."

"You're not playing fair," she said.

"I never promised to. I promised to answer honestly."

She opened her mouth to speak, but no words came out. The look in his eyes softened her heart instantly. His eyes focused and held sincerity. She looked away. "Jazz," he said softly, seeing her struggle, "look at me." After a few seconds, she turned back to him. He reached out and removed her dark sunglasses. "I didn't expect this, and I didn't exactly plan it this way. But it's happening. You feel it, and so do I. When we made love last night..."

"Yes, about what happened between us last night. I shouldn't have let it go that far."

"But it did, and it was perfect," he said. She shook her head. "Yes, it was. For both of us. You needed a friend, and I was there," he said quickly, not giving her the opportunity to express more regrets.

"Friends don't usually cross that line."

"Friends comfort friends. You needed comfort. I was there."

"Is that all it was? Comfort?" she asked, looking at him directly. He smiled, but didn't reply. "And you, what did you need last night?"

"I needed to be there with you."

"Please don't tell me that this was some kind of macho thing."

"You really don't trust anyone, do you?"

"It gets kind of difficult after a while. Everybody wants something from me. So, Devon, tell me, what do you want from me?"

"To be a friend. You once told me that you needed one."

"You're going to be married soon. Melanie's out right now seeing to that. So all this is pretty much a moot point. Because believe me, your new wife will not appreciate your having me as a friend."

Devon nodded slowly. He saw the concern and

apprehension in her eyes. Suddenly she was all too clear. "What are you afraid of, Jazz?" She didn't respond. He continued. "Being loved for the wrong reasons or being loved for the right reasons?"

"One night together doesn't mean you know me," she said.

"You're right," he confirmed then paused to look away. "You know, seeing you at the party the other night brought back some great memories. I never told anyone this, but you were my first love."

The words hit her like a javelin through the heart. Jeremiah and Gavin had said the exact same thing. It was something she'd always heard, and it always meant the same thing: trouble. "This was such a huge mistake."

"Why does it have to be a mistake?"

"I shouldn't have gone to your house last night." She gathered her sunglasses and put them on quickly.

"I'm glad you did," he said softly, "although I was disappointed you left so early." She looked around anxiously. "Jazz, we have an attraction, and you can't deny it."

"Yes, we do. It's a sexual attraction that can be handled."

"I think it's a bit more than just sexual."

"Devon, I can't keep playing at this game. I won't be your next toy. We both know this attraction will pass, has to pass," she said. He smiled without responding. "And when it does—"

"And when it doesn't," he interrupted before she finished.

"It will. This would be a disaster, and I've had enough relationship disasters to last me a lifetime. So whatever you think you're feeling…"

"I know exactly what I'm feeling," he assured her.

"Actually, you don't. Memories, childhood memories, are a strange thing. They cling to you, staying with you forever. And even when you've grown up and think you've put them behind you, they're still there. You saw me the other night at the party, and I was the kid from television, the teenager from stage. But that's not me anymore."

"You think I don't know that? I know exactly who you are."

"Oh, so you read minds, too, huh?"

"I don't have to."

She shook her head. "You don't have a clue. I am the perfect vehicle. Men see me and want to use me to relive some past fantasy. Do you have any idea how many dates I've been on where the man tells me that I was his first love?" she asked. He shook his head slowly. "Well, I do. I don't want to be used by somebody anymore."

"It's a little late to re-create who you were."

"What?"

"You don't want people to recognize you, so you run and hide behind dark sunglasses and a big hat. Jazz, you can't hide from who you were any more than you can run from who you are. You were a child star and a teen idol. The same kids that watched you on television and bought your CDs have grown up, too. You created the product. We all bought into it. Now you want everyone to forget everything. It doesn't work that way. You can't turn celebrity on and off. I'm the perfect example of that.

"I've played football nearly all my life. Kids watch me and want to do what I do and have what I have. Do you know how many men would love to have four different women hand them the key to their hotel room every night? I'm not bragging—it's just a fact. I get that constantly. It's the nature of the business. But it's the business that we chose…. Yes, perks, drama and all. You say that people, men, see you and want to relive a childhood fantasy. People see me and want to live their present. It's what we do. It's what we chose to do, and now you use that as an excuse to justify your fears."

"What fears?"

"You're afraid of being loved, or rather that no one will love you for who you really are. That's why you pretend to be someone else and never yourself."

"You don't know me," she said defensively.

"I think I do. I answered the questions you asked. That's what you wanted. I can't help it if you're not ready to hear the answer. You've hidden all your life, and now there's nobody to hide behind. Your mother and brother are both gone."

Her heart slammed against her chest. Her pulse raced and her eyes narrowed. She glared at him furiously. "You don't know what you're talking about," she said between clenched teeth.

"You're standing on your own now, and you're scared. Scared of the future, scared of the past, scared of yourself. But most of all you're scared of being like your mother."

Jazz glared at him furiously. She'd had enough. Making a scene in public was one of her worst nightmares. Jazz knew that she couldn't go there, so she quickly changed the subject. She glanced at her watch. "It's getting late. I need to head back to the house." She stood up quickly. People sitting nearby looked at them.

"I didn't mean to upset you," he said, seeing her distress.

"I'm not upset," she lied less than artfully.

"Jazz, I get that you're a good actress, but anybody can see that maybe I was a bit too honest. I'm sorry."

"Devon, your opinion of me, however biased and erroneous it might be, doesn't affect me." He nodded. "Now if you'll excuse me, I need to get out of here."

"I'll walk you to the car." He stood, too.

"No, that's fine. I can manage alone. Yeah, that's right, all by myself. I'm not scared of the big bad wolf or anything." She smirked then lowered the brim of her hat and adjusted the dark sunglasses. Her hands shook nervously.

"Jazz, let me walk you. I insist," he said, taking her shaking hand and holding it still. She looked at him, but didn't pull away. "I can see that you're angry. You can't drive like this. I didn't mean to upset you."

"No, not at all," she lied slightly more convincingly, but she knew that he still saw right through her. "I'm fine. I'm used to running and hiding, remember?"

"Jazz," he began.

"Devon, don't. The next time you want to review someone's life I suggest you take a nice hard look at your own. Get your own house in order before you start throwing stones at mine."

He looked at her suspiciously. It was obvious she knew something. "What do you mean?"

She smiled. "You know exactly what I mean. You're not exactly a choir boy, are you? You do your dirt and use women then walk away, don't you? Well, not this one. You held my life up to me with a microscope, I think it's only fitting that you look at your own life the same way. Do me a favor—lose my name and number." He looked furious. She smiled, having hit her target.

Devon opened his mouth to respond, but just then a young kid recognized him and called out. He ran over with a pen and paper. His mother followed. He asked for Devon's photo and autograph. Jazz slipped her hand from his. Devon turned to her and knew this was the excuse she needed to walk away. He smiled and posed for the photo. Afterward he looked to see that Jazz was still there. She was. The kid asked him a question. Devon answered while still looking at Jazz.

The young boy handed him a piece of paper and said that he wanted to be a teacher when he grew up. As Devon signed, a couple more kids came over. They took photos and began asking him questions about an injury and whether it would hinder his new contract or his ability to play in the upcoming season. He assured them that he was in perfect condition. They took photos with their cell phones as the conversation continued.

Jazz stepped back, and then moved farther away as a few more kids came over to him. Devon joked and laughed, encouraging the kids to stay in school and study hard. Then the moment took on a life of its own. Soon he was lecturing on grades and responsibility. Jazz watched the ease of his commitment to the kids. This was his element. She moved farther back, then turned and walked away. She headed to her car, got in and drove off. Their last conversation still stayed with her.

It was as if he knew her whole life in one glance. Everything he said about her was accurate, and that scared her. She was afraid of being loved.

Devon called twice. Each time he left a number for her to return the call. She didn't. She didn't have anything to say to him. Having gone from one famed disastrous relationship to another, she'd learned early on that her finding love was at best impossible.

She anchored her cell phone on the car-speaker jack and called her best friend to tell her about the strained conversation she'd just had. "I actually thought he was going to be different. He pretended to be sweet and charming. I was wrong. He crossed the line."

"Why, because he saw right through you? In that case, he sounds perfect," Savannah said.

"Not funny."

"I'm serious. He obviously sees past your insecurities and defenses. I'd say that's a solid point in his favor. Let's face it. Most men are intimidated by you. He's not. That's definitely another point in his favor."

"Actually, Savannah, you're missing the point."

"What's the point? The man sounds like he cares for you."

"I must be crazy to get myself involved in something like this again," Jazz said.

"You're not crazy, but it does sound like, despite your protests to the opposite, you really like him."

"Savannah, focus. We're not passing notes in study hall. It's not about whether or not I like him. It's about the fact that I know how it's going to end and I can't do this again."

"How is it going to end?"

"Drama, headlines, heartbreak, same as always, or my personal favorite—I won't live up to his perfect idea of what Jazelle Richardson should be. I'm not setting myself up to get hurt again," she vowed. "No, not again."

"So what are you saying—you'll never get close to anyone?"

"If that's what it takes, yes."

"And you'll live the rest of your life happily alone?"

"My mother did it, and she was just fine."

"Jazz, stop it," Savannah said hotly. "You can lie to

everyone else. But you can't lie to me, and you can't lie to yourself." There was a pronounced silence. Neither said anything for a few seconds. Then Savannah continued. "You're assuming that this won't last. What if it does? What if the woman he's looking to be with turns out to be you? The man obviously figured you out in record time, and now you're essentially too scared to admit that he's right."

"I'm not scared to admit anything."

"Aren't you?" Savannah said. "You can't lie to me. I know you too well. Don't throw away something that might just be what you're looking for. Don't you think you deserve a little happiness? You said yourself you thought he was sweet and charming, right? Well, girl, you definitely need that right now. After everything that's happened in the past two years, you need a little kindness in your life. Also, it sounds like he understands a lot more than you think. And if and when Melanie returns with this mysterious perfect woman, deal with it then. You can walk away having had a great experience."

"What if I can't walk away? My mother certainly didn't."

"You're not your mother, Jazz, not even close. You've never done the other-woman thing, and you never will," Savannah said adamantly. "So as you can see, there's a difference. Frank was married at the time your mom hooked up with him. They both knew it. Devon isn't married. He's not even close to being married. There's only this abstract notion that Melanie is looking for someone for him. What does that even mean? I'll tell you—nothing. So don't get this all twisted. You're not having an affair with a married man like your mom. Not even close. So what are you going to do?"

"What I have to do. I can't get hurt again."

"Are you sure that's what you want?"

"Savannah, the man makes my stomach jump a mile high. When he touches me I melt like hot lava. When he looks at me my heart does summersaults and backward flips."

Savannah chuckled. "You're falling for him."

"Whose side are you on?" Jazz asked.

"You know that there's nothing he said to you that we haven't already talked about."

"I don't care." Jazz pouted childishly.

"You're definitely being stubborn today, aren't you?"

"No more than usual," Jazz said then sighed. "I've gotta admit, he's got a good heart. You should have seen him with those kids outside the café."

"He's got a good heart. That's an excellent start."

"They loved him, and he seemed to love being with them."

"So what's there to talk about? He's obviously attracted to you and you to him. I say enjoy the moment."

"Even if he breaks my heart?" Jazz said.

"Jazz, listen to me. Stop looking at the forest when the trees are right there in front of you."

"What is that supposed to mean?"

"It means enjoy life as it is right here, right now, and stop worrying about tomorrow and the day after."

Jazz sighed, again shaking her head. The quick memory of them making love distracted her and nearly took her off the road. A driver coming up beside her blew his horn and sped past with an angry expression. Jazz adjusted, grabbed the steering wheel tighter and focused. "Okay, I can't do this right now. I need to focus."

"What was that noise—a car horn?" Savannah asked.

"Nothing," Jazz said, tossing her hat and sunglasses on the seat beside her. "I wonder what this scandal with him last year was all about."

"Look it up. You know nothing ever disappears once it's been on the Internet. And if it was a scandal, it was most definitely on the Internet."

Jazz considered it. "Yeah, you're right. So, you think I should just enjoy the moment even though—"

"No. There is no 'even though.' There's enjoying and living in the moment. When are you going to see him again?"

"He mentioned that he wanted to show me some films of him playing football tonight. I told him I was busy."

"Go."

"But what if—"

"No. There is no 'what-if' in life, remember?"

Jazz nodded. Savannah was right. There was no "what-if." It was a pact they'd made years ago—no regrets, no remorse and no "what-if." Life was too short. "You're right. No 'what-ifs.'"

Chapter 13

EXTERIOR—SAG HARBOR

The growing circle of fans around Devon had finally begun to disperse. He said his goodbyes, high-fived and fist-bumped fans after accepting their good-luck wishes and accolades. When the fans first came up to him, he made sure to keep an eye on Jazz, knowing that she would probably step back out of the way. He caught her eye a few times and nodded. She seemed genuinely relieved by the high-energy fans. Then another throng of teens got out of a car, and Devon knew Jazz had slipped away even before he started looking around for her. He looked down the street both ways; she was nowhere in sight. A few minutes later he was surrounded all over again. School had obviously gotten out.

"Yo, Bolt, looks like you need your offensive line."

Devon turned, seeing his friend Armand driving up

in a pimped-out SUV. With the window down he hung out, smiling as usual. Devon waved then crossed the street. They shook hands. "Hey, how are you feeling? I tried calling you."

"I'm fine. Damn tree grew up overnight."

"Yeah, I hear they do that a lot," Devon joked. "But you're doing good?"

"Oh, yeah. Scotch and pain relievers don't mix. Lesson learned," he said happily. "Thanks for stopping by the other night. I appreciate it."

"I got your back. Nice ride. What you up to?"

"Chilling," Armand said then glanced around Devon, seeing the small throng of fans still calling out and waving.

Devon turned and waved to them. "Ya'll take care," he said graciously. "See you at the games." They cheered and talked excitedly as they moved on.

"See, now that's what I'm talking about. I want that again."

Devon ignored the remark. "So, where are you going?"

"I'm just getting back from training and conditioning. I swear that guy's a demon. He costs a small fortune and enjoys inflicting torture. My body's screaming. But he says I look just as good as I did coming out of Penn State twenty years ago."

"Who is this guy?" Devon asked, immediately concerned that his friend was being dangerously conned.

"Nah, man, get your own miracle worker. I got this one," Armand said, laughing. Then he winced.

Devon noticed instantly. "You okay?"

"Yeah. I might have overdone it this morning. But hell, it'll be worth it come next month." Somebody driving by blew their car horn and cheered for Devon. "See that? That's what I'm talking about."

"Armand, you know that's not real."

"It sounds pretty real to me. I need that again. I know that's why Shelia married me, 'cause I played football."

"Are you sure about that? Weren't you two in college together long before the NFL contracts?"

"Yeah, but she saw it coming. That's why we hooked up."

"Are you saying that she didn't love you when you married?"

"Yeah, maybe, I don't know, probably. It didn't matter at the time, 'cause I wanted her. But she definitely knew I had a career coming."

"Armand, man, when I was a rookie and you were my NFL sponsor and I hung out with you, Shelia and the kids, it was like the perfect family. I could tell she loved and adored you. You had the perfect life, but you walked away."

Armand shook his head. "I know. I let someone else…" He paused and looked away angrily. "She turned my head, and I let her. I divorced Shelia and married her, and she ran through my money like it was air. I was damn near broke when she left me. And even then she tried to take what I had left. Shelia told me to get a prenup at our divorce table. I did. I can't believe I listened to her. That's the only thing that saved me."

"Sounds like Shelia still cared about you," Devon said.

He nodded. "Yeah, I know. She did love me, but I messed it up. All the women I had while we were married. She never said a word. She never complained. I got stupid and full of myself. I walked out on the best thing in my life. So I'm starting at the beginning, back on the line. It'll be like it was before. Shelia will come back to me."

"I don't think it was ever about football with Shelia. I think it was about you."

"Nah, she wanted a football player, and I'm going to give her that again."

"All right, man, I wish you luck with all that. I'll dance at your wedding," Devon said, hoping his friend knew what he was doing.

"That's a bet," Armand said. They shook hands. "Later."

Moments later, Devon walked back to his car. He waved occasionally as he passed fans and people he knew. He got in and headed home but then decided to head into Eastville first. Devon pulled up to his grandparents' driveway a few minutes later. He got out and smelled the smoke instantly. Instead of going to the front door, he opened the side gate and walked around back.

The smell of food cooking got even stronger as thick, flavored smoke billowed into the air. His mouth watered just thinking about his grandfather's grilling. "Hey, now, look who it is. You were right—you told me that he'd be showing up as soon as I got to cooking," Claymont Everett said, seeing Devon round the side of the house. He fanned smoke and closed the grill lid as he smiled wide.

Pearl, Devon's grandmother, chuckled. She nodded her head and opened her arms wide. Devon went right straight for her and engulfed her tiny frame in his embrace. "Hi, honey child, what took you so long? I expected you an hour ago."

"How could you have expected me an hour ago

when I didn't even know I was coming here until a few minutes ago?"

"Never ask the ways of a woman. They have their own rules, and we love them for it," Clayton said reverently, without doubt.

"You just might be right about that," Devon said, thinking about Jazz and hoping that he hadn't completely messed things up between them.

Pearl looked at him intensely. "It looks like she's got your heart already. That's good. It's time." Devon looked at her. There was never any hiding the truth from his grandmother.

"Who?" Clayton said.

Pearl smiled. "The woman he was with in town earlier. She's not just any woman, either, is she? I guess Melanie Harte found you someone really special." Devon didn't answer. Thankfully the phone rang inside the house, and Pearl excused herself to get it.

"You want to talk about it?" Clayton asked, setting a plate of food down on the table. He took a seat across from Devon and waited for his grandson to talk. "Who is she?"

"Jazelle Richardson."

"Yelena's daughter?" he asked. Devon nodded. "You know we knew Yelena. She even came over for dinner a couple of times. She was good people. So, you're with her daughter," he said, nodding his approval.

"Not anymore," Devon said then looked away, troubled. It wasn't just about what his grandmother had said. It was about what his heart was feeling. Jazz was special. His heart had locked on to her and wasn't letting go. "Melanie warned me to go slow, but I didn't listen. I thought I was helping her." He looked back to his grandfather and shook his head. "I can't stop thinking about her," he said quietly. "She's everywhere. I feel her all the time. I even dream about her. When I'm not with her, I think of her. I've never felt like this before with anyone. I want her in my life."

"So what are you doing here? Go get her."

"It's not that easy. I said things—"

"Son, listen to an old man with many, many years of wooing behind him. If you feel this strongly about her, then do something about it. It doesn't matter what you said or what she said. Don't just let this go and wallow in regrets later. And believe me, no other woman will ever measure up once you've been touched. Recognize the truth. Melanie Harte's found your heart's choice."

"No, Granddad, this wasn't Melanie."

"Where'd you meet Jazelle?"

"At Melanie's party the other night, but she didn't even set this up."

Clayton did his cockeyed smile and shook his head. "You think just because Melanie didn't present this woman to you in some formal introduction that she didn't orchestrate this?"

"Either way, it doesn't matter, because it's not going any further. She made that clear. She doesn't want anything to do with me."

"Change her mind."

"I can't. She's blocking me out."

"You're a big, strong football player. Go around."

"I don't know if I have it in me to even try. How can I trust my feelings about anyone anymore? I loved Trina and Tasha and look what happened with them. They used me."

"Jazelle has nothing to do with them, so don't confuse her with them. Trina and that girl Tasha happened last year. After them, you changed. Your grandmother and

I sat by watching you become exactly what you always detested—a user." Devon looked at his grandfather sternly. The disappointment in his eyes showed. He knew he was referring to the player his father was. It's what he hated about his father. "Well, I'm not going to sit by idly and let it happen. Enough is enough. Ever since that Tasha woman tried to trap you into marriage, you've been going out with all these fake, shallow women. You know exactly who and what they are, so that justifies your assumption that women are all alike and should be treated as such."

"I gave them exactly what they wanted. I never used them anymore than they used me, and I never treated them badly. I was always up front and told them the deal."

"Don't go back down that path. That bad-boy image they painted in the newspapers isn't you, and you know it. Do what you need to do to be happy. Take some time. Allow tempers to settle. Then go to Jazelle and tell her how you feel."

"I'll think about it."

"Good."

"I'm going to be out of town for a few days," Devon said. "Tell Grandmom that I'll catch up with her later. See you, Granddad." Devon got up and walked away. Twenty-five minutes later he pulled into his driveway but didn't get out of the car. He turned off the engine and just sat there a moment.

He was thinking about what his grandfather had said. He didn't actually come out and say that he was disappointed, but he knew it was implied. When it came to his grandfather, it was the empty silences and the words he didn't say that screamed the loudest. He glanced up in the rearview mirror. He looked at his reflection hard. He was the same man he was a year ago, a month ago, a week ago. He looked the same and he dressed the same. Nothing had really changed on the outside. But on the inside he was different. Trina and Tasha had changed him. Then, the first moment he'd looked across the room and seen Jazz, he'd changed again.

He knew that he could very well live the rest of his life without Jazz and probably be happy, but he didn't want to. His grandfather was right. She was his heart's choice. He considered going to her now, but his grandfather's words stopped him. He'd give her some time. A few minutes later Devon put the car in reverse and drove away.

Jazz finished the project she'd been working on, changed clothes and came downstairs feeling better than she had earlier. Her vacillations and hesitations had passed. There was no rational reason why she shouldn't enjoy her life. It's what her mother had wanted, what Brian had requested. She knew what she wanted. She wanted Devon Hayes, and, hopefully, he still wanted her. So she intended to do exactly as Savannah suggested— enjoy the moment.

"Hey, you look happy," Jessica said.

"Actually, I'm feeling pretty good. That trip into town was just what I needed to help clear the cobwebs in my head. I thought a nice long walk on the beach might just clear away the rest."

"Good idea and perfect timing. Oh, cool, what's that?" she asked.

Jazz placed the folded paper in Jessica's hand. "It's a little something I've been working on. It's origami."

Jessica examined the folded paper in amazement. "This is so cool. I love it." She handed it back.

"Thanks. So, what's perfect timing?"

"Oh, I was just about to come get you. You have a visitor waiting out on the patio."

Jazz smiled, thinking that it was Devon. "Excellent."

"I'm headed out. Melanie is on her way home. Oh, before I forget, this package is for you, too."

"Thanks," Jazz said, seeing the package on the foyer table. "See you later," she said just as Jessica's cell rang. She waved as she headed out.

Jazz grabbed the package and headed to the patio expecting to see Devon. It wasn't Devon. She stopped instantly and glared at the man standing there. He had his back to her, but she knew exactly who it was. She hadn't seen him since Brian's funeral; the last time before then had been just after her mother's funeral. It seemed just like always. He only came around when things were bad.

Growing up, all she ever wanted was a relationship with him like normal kids. But he was never around. He had his own family, and that didn't include her. She knew who he was, of course. Her mother confirmed that when she saw her photograph on the cover of a tabloid in a supermarket. It was kind of hard to deny after seeing that kind of proof. So she was the daughter of a big Hollywood movie star and director. So what? She turned to leave.

"Hello, Jazelle."

Jazz stopped instantly. She knew that voice too well. She turned, seeing her father standing there. He walked over and opened his arms. She stared at him without speaking. He lowered his eyes and grimaced, knowing that the relationship with his daughter would never be one for which he'd been proud. He had turned his back on her since she was a child. Then, when she was a teen, he was too busy with his own life to deal with her. Only recently had he attempted some kind of reconciliation. But by now it was too late.

"Aren't you going to at least acknowledge me?"

"Do you mean like you acknowledged me years ago?"

"Jazelle, please. You're my daughter. I've always acknowledged you."

"What do you want, Frank?"

"Jazelle," he said as if he needed to say more.

She stared at him menacingly. Only one man in her life ever called her by her full name—her father, or rather, her biological father. "Frank. What are you doing here?" she asked.

"Can't a father stop by and see his daughter?"

"It's a little late for the paternal nurturing, don't you think?"

"Jazelle, please. When are you going to stop punishing me?"

She shook her head. "I'm not punishing you. Maybe it's your conscience, but it's not me. I've heard turning your back on people who once loved you can do that."

"Jazelle, I've said it a million times. I loved your mother fiercely, and she loved me. The circumstances prevented us being together. But what we shared those few months together is what keeps me going even now. I—"

"Please, Frank, I really don't want to hear your declarations of adoration and devotion to my mom. So if that's why you're here, then you can leave now."

"No. I came here to ask you a favor."

She laughed. "You're kidding, right? You want me to do you a favor?" She shook her head, still chuckling. "Oh, this is too rich. Who says there's no Karma in the universe? So, what is it?"

"Read a script. Agree to star in the film."

"Oh, is that all?" She laughed again and turned away.

"Jazelle, enough torturing me," he said, raising his voice slightly. "This isn't about me."

"It's always about you, Frank."

He nodded, acknowledging the truth and knowing her pain ran too deep to protest it any further. They'd played this scene so many times that once more would be meaningless. She was right about this, about everything. It was time to come clean and tell her the truth. "Yes, it is about me. You're right. I admit it. It's always about me and my career. It always has been. I once had the chance of a lifetime to be with the woman I truly loved, but I chose my career instead. I walked away then and I've regretted it all my life. I can't take that back, Jazelle, any more that I can take back Brian's death. All I can do now is fulfill their wishes."

She turned around. "What wishes?"

He looked down, seeing the package he'd brought in her hands. She looked down, realizing what he meant. "This?" she asked. He nodded. "This is from Brian?"

"Yes. He gave it to me the night he—" he paused, walked over to the rail and lowered his head "—the night he died." His voice cracked, and he buried his face in his hands remorsefully. She could see that he was barely holding himself together. A moment later, he gathered his composure and cleared his throat. "You had just gotten back from doing that last film. He came to me."

"What are you saying? Brian gave you this?"

"Open it."

She did and pulled out a manuscript. "What is this?" she asked needlessly, knowing exactly what it was. It was what Brian told her he'd been working on for years. It was his script, his life's work. "He gave this to you? His manuscript?" she asked, looking to him. He nodded. "Why?"

"He wanted me to direct and produce it."

"Brian told me you turned him down repeatedly."

"Have you ever read it?" Frank asked.

"No, he didn't want me to. Not until it was finished."

"I did, four separate times. Each time he brought it back to me it had gotten better and better. The last time he came to me, I read it and told him that it was a great piece of work. I told him I was proud of him and that I'd be honored to take it to the studio. Your brother was a brilliant writer. The script is exceptional. I told him that. I remember he smiled like I'd just given him a billion dollars. I had no idea that was the last time I'd ever talk to him," he said, obviously choking up again. "Read it, please. Not for me. For Brian."

She held the pages close to her heart as if holding her brother's memory close to her. She nodded that she would.

"Thank you," he said then walked away.

Jazz stood a moment then started wondering about the other wish he had mentioned. She went after him. "Frank, wait," she said, calling to him before he opened the front door. He stopped and turned. "You said 'their wishes.' This is Brian's wish. What was my mother's?"

"It doesn't matter right now."

"Maybe it does to me," she said firmly.

He looked at her and finally nodded. "She wanted you to be happy. She wanted me to make sure that you were happy," he said quietly.

Jazz nodded, knowing there was more that he wasn't saying, but she gave him the rest of his secret to keep. After all, it was between them. "Thank you," she said. He nodded, opened the door and left.

Jazz took a deep breath then released it slowly. Her heart still trembled and her hands shook while still holding tight to the script. Seeing her father always left her with the uneasy feeling that she'd just been sent to the principal's office for misbehaving. It was never anything he said or did; it was just him. He was larger than life. There were so many stories about him and his career. He was a legend in the business. He acted, produced, wrote and directed, all with masterfully brilliant results. He had Oscars, Golden Globes and hundreds of other equally notable awards. Highly respected and formidable, he was every actor's dream or nightmare according to the power he wielded.

She sat, slowly gripping the envelope then laid it on her lap. She unclasped the seal, opened it and pulled out the manuscript. She ran her hand lovingly over the crisp white pages. The moment stilled. She couldn't help but feel that these were her brother's last words. She gingerly turned the first page and read the title. She smiled. This was Brian, of course. It was entitled *Untitled Life*. A laugh unexpectedly escaped. Even now, he brought joy to her world.

The opening scene was set in a small apartment near the edge of an unnamed city. She read the direction notes and then cringed when the title character put a forty-five revolver to his head and pulled the trigger. The script took place the instant the bullet left the barrel. It was flashback on what led him to this point. The pages shook and blurred as tears trembled down Jazz's face. She closed the draft quickly and put it back into the envelope. She took a deep breath, but couldn't release it. She kept inhaling, sucking air in. Finally she collapsed backwards, holding the script to her heart. There was no way she could read this now, maybe ever.

Jazz stayed in the large living room a few minutes longer. She looked around. Frank was long gone, of course, but his presence lingered. It always did. He had a way of sucking all the air out of a room and creating an emptiness. It was silly, but that's how she always felt. She stood, turned toward the patio door leading outside, suddenly feeling the need of fresh air sweep over her. She walked back outside onto the patio and didn't stop until she hit the beach.

She walked and ran nearly a half mile before stopping to catch her breath. She turned to look at the bay. The view was familiar. She turned back to the beach and looked up at the house. It was Devon's. She would have recognized the second-floor balcony anywhere. She walked around to the front of the house and knocked. Moments later the door opened. A woman answered. "Umm, hi, I'm looking for Devon Hayes," Jazz said.

"Are you a friend of his?" the woman asked.

"Yes, umm, kind of." She hedged too long and knew by the expression on the woman's face that she didn't believe her. "I'm staying a few doors down the beach with Melanie Harte."

"And?" The woman pried further.

"And I was hoping Devon had gotten back from town," she said. The woman looked at her without responding. Jazz knew a gatekeeper when she saw one.

The woman was young and pretty. She assumed that she was either the estate manager or an assistant. "You know what? That's okay. Never mind." Jazz shook her head and stepped back.

"He's not here," the woman finally said. "I don't know when he'll be back. Probably not for a while. He's away on business. Do you want to leave your name or a message or something?"

"No, that's okay, thanks," Jazz said then turned to leave. She took a few steps, stopped and turned back. "Um, could you leave this for him?" she said. "He'll know who it's from."

The woman nodded and held the fragile origami sculpture gently. "Sure." She looked it over carefully. "Did you make this?"

Jazz nodded. "Yes, I thought he'd appreciate it. It's a…"

"…stallion," the woman said.

"Yes, that's right."

"It's very clever. I'm sure he's going to love this."

"Thanks, I hope so," Jazz said then turned and walked away, knowing that she must have hurt him more than she had thought. Whatever scandal he had been mixed up in must have really gotten to him, and she'd just poured salt into the open wound. She walked back to the house just as Jessica was leaving.

"Hey, I thought you'd already left," Jazz said.

"I did. I forget something, had to come back."

"Jessica, got a minute?"

"Sure what's up?"

"I heard in town that Devon was in some big scandal. What happened?"

"Girl, it was a hot mess," Jessica began. "He'd been dating Trina Preston, some socialite wannabe, for about three years. They got engaged, and everything seemed cool. Then, a few months later, right before one of his games, she goes to him and breaks it off. She said that she was in love with someone else and they were getting married that day in Vegas."

"She said that just as he was going to play football?"

"Yeah, can you believe that? Anyway, he broke his wrist and blew out his knee in that same game. The injury knocked him out for the rest of the season. His team did horribly after that. I think he still blames himself. But the thing is, when a professional football player's out on injured reserves, there's less money. Thankfully he had endorsements. That's why this new contract is so important."

"He needs a new contract?"

"Yes. They're negotiating now, but I hear it isn't going well. A lot of that has to do with what happened."

"I didn't know that."

"Anyway, a few weeks after he got hurt, he met this reporter. She was supposed to be doing a story on one of his children's foundations. They got close, and next thing she wrote this Internet article saying he dumped her because she was pregnant and refused to get rid of their baby. Later her father got into the act and made things even worse. He portrayed Devon as the bad guy."

"What?"

"It was huge news. This was last year. I'm surprised you didn't hear about it."

"If it was last year, then that's right after Brian died. I was traveling abroad and never read a newspaper. I didn't even have a laptop at that time."

"So, after that, sponsors threatened to pull out of his foundation programs and the team owners were furious. His reputation took a serious hit. Then it came out that she does this fake reporting scam all the time. She wasn't even a real reporter, just an Internet blogger. Other athletes and businessmen came forward and told their stories."

"That's insane. What happened to her?"

"She scammed all those other guys, but claimed she fell for Devon. She wanted him to marry her. That was the different part. She never did that with the other men. Last I heard she was keeping a low profile. Her father still insists she was wronged. They had their fifteen minutes, so nobody pays attention anymore. I heard she was writing a book about it, but couldn't get a publisher. Anyway, I have to get going. See you tomorrow."

Jazz stood in the driveway speechless. She was wrong.

Chapter 14

EXTERIOR—SAG HARBOR

Days later Jazz still hadn't seen or heard anything from Devon. She hadn't really expected to at this point, but she had hoped. The conversation with Jessica that day brought everything to light. She was wrong about him, about everything. She attacked him when all he was trying to do was help her. But none of that mattered now. He was gone.

Actually, he wasn't. He was doing some kind of publicity tour. He was everywhere. She watched him on television, read about him in the newspapers and magazines and even watched a podcast on the Internet. He was doing a teen motivational talk about focusing on your dreams and not being detoured by anything. It was pretty good. And it was obvious that his speech was coming from a place of very personal experience.

Afterward she watched a podcast of an interview. He was honest and forthright, even when someone asked him about the scandal. He simply answered the question and moved on. She knew the tactic well. He was rebuilding his reputation. When scandals hit, the formula was simple: ride it out in seclusion for a few months, then reinvent yourself with the help of professionals. It looked as if he was doing a great job.

Jazz watched his commercials and listened to his interviews with an intimate pleasure. She had no idea how she never really saw him before. Lost in her own crystal box, she seldom looked out on others. Brian always told her that her world was a lot bigger than her four surrounding walls. Now she understood what he meant.

But still, seeing Devon was like everything that happened between them was just a dream. But it was real. She knew it. She walked by his house again a few days later. She stopped and looked up. There was no sign that anyone was at home or had been home. She didn't bother to knock or ring the bell. She knew that she'd hurt him. But where his words had been trustful and honest, she'd been just plain mean.

Nothing he said to her that afternoon outside the café was anything she hadn't already known and said to herself a thousand times before. Savannah was right. It was just hard to hear the words coming from him. He was a stranger. And it scared her to know that a stranger could see so far into her soul so quickly.

It was late morning when Jazz came downstairs. Melanie and the office staff, minus Vincent, were already hard at work. Jazz popped her head into the office to say good morning. "Good morning," they said in unison.

"Hey, I'm headed into town. Does anyone want anything?"

Veronica and Jessica declined. But Melanie said that she needed something. She stood and walked into the living room. Jazz followed. She grabbed her purse and began looking through it for something. "You've been quiet the last few days. I hope everything's okay."

"I'm doing okay, better. I've been getting out and seeing some of the local sights. I really like this area. I'm actually thinking of having a home here."

"Really? That's marvelous. I remember how your mother used to love to come here. She and I would sit out on the veranda in the evenings and talk for hours."

"Where was I?"

"This was just a few years ago. I think you were probably on location at the time. This was right after you no longer needed my matchmaking services."

"So that's when you and mom became friends."

Melanie nodded. "She was a special lady. When she visited she sang around the house all the time. It was like having a private concert."

Jazz nodded. "I remember she used to do the same thing when I was growing up. We lived in this small apartment in New York when I was about eight or nine years old. This was right before I got the television series. I was doing commercials and a few modeling jobs, but nothing major. Mom was doing an off-Broadway musical, and she'd practice her songs at home. The neighbors would applaud like crazy when she sang. It was great. They loved her. You know, a few of them even wrote me when she died."

"She was a very special lady," Melanie said. Jazz nodded. "So, you've been busy, getting out. That's good. I'm glad to hear it."

"Yeah, a little bit. Also, my agent has been sending me scripts to read."

"Wonderful. Anything look promising?"

"A few of them are pretty good. But I haven't decided on anything," she said.

She smiled. "You'll find something. Jess told me that Frank stopped by a few days ago. I'm sorry I missed him."

"I'm sorry I didn't," Jazz quipped dryly.

"You know he loves you very much."

"His love isn't exactly consistent. He loved my mother, too. That didn't exactly work out for either of them, did it?"

"Jazz, you don't know everything that went on between your parents. Nobody does. They made whatever decision they did for a reason."

"You're right."

"So, where are you off to today?" Melanie asked.

"I'm headed to the old lighthouse. I saw online last night that there's a lecture and walking tour today. It sounds really interesting. The guide is a retired engineer who's lived here all his life. He's apparently an expert when it comes to early Sag Harbor history. He gives the lecture and tour twice a month. The article said that it was a unique experience."

"It is. Clayton Everett is the guide, and he's awesome."

"Yes, that's him. You know him?"

"Yes. His lectures, or chats as he calls them, are truly fascinating. You'll probably also meet his wife, Pearl. She's a sweetheart."

"I'm looking forward to it."

"One thing. You might consider introducing yourself to them after the lecture."

"You think?"

Melanie nodded. "Definitely. Clayton and Pearl adored your mother. I'm sure they'd be pleased to meet you."

"Okay, sure. So, what do you need me to pick up for you?"

"A gift," Melanie said, handing her a store business card.

"Oh, okay, I can do that. What kind of gift, for whom?"

"It's for Devon Hayes."

"Devon?" Jazz remarked.

"Yes. It's already wrapped and ready to be picked up."

"How's the search for his match going?"

"Not well. I'm afraid I'm having a difficult time. He's being very patient, and I appreciate it."

"Why are you having such a hard time?" Jazz asked.

"I want the best for him, and sometimes that takes a little extra time. I'll phone the store and let them know that you'll be in later. Thanks again for taking care of that for me. That's one thing off my list. Okay, I'll get back to work." Melanie headed back to the office, then stopped and turned. "Oh, before I forget, I'll be attending a party this evening at the Legends Golf Club. You're more than welcome to come along. It starts early evening, around five o'clock, and goes to all hours of the night and into the early morning. I think you'll enjoy it, and it might do you good to get out some more."

"No, that's okay. Thanks anyway."

"Are you sure?" Melanie asked. Jazz nodded and smiled happily. "Okay, but if you change your mind about going just let me know," Melanie said then headed back to the office.

"Melanie, question—what if you can't find anyone for Devon? What happens then?" Jazz asked.

"I have a feeling Devon is going to be very happy very soon. The perfect woman is waiting for him—she just doesn't quite know it yet. But she will. Don't forget to give my best to Clayton and Pearl."

"I will," Jazz said. She headed to the front door, thinking about what Melanie said. She hadn't yet found anyone for Devon. That meant he was still available. The idea made her smile. But the problem was he wasn't here, and if he was he was probably still furious with her. She thought about Savannah's words of encouragement. What did she have to lose?

Jazz drove Vincent's car into town. Everything about it seemed different. The tourist season had obviously begun in earnest. Already the once-sleepy town she had grown to love was bombarded with tourists. There were cars parked everywhere. People lined the streets, laughing and talking for whatever reason suited them. She recognized a few famous faces. And then there were the wannabe famous and the no-hope-of-being-famous faces. All were giddy at being in celebrated Sag Harbor.

Jazz continued to the Chamber of Commerce windmill on Main Street near the Long Wharf. The tour group was beginning to assemble. She parked and walked over, joining in inconspicuously. Some of the sightseers introduced themselves, while others kept mostly to themselves. Jazz fell into the latter group. It was heavily overcast but not rainy, so she didn't wear her wide-brimmed hat and dark sunglasses. Instead, she wore a baseball cap and tinted wire frames.

She stayed as far away from the rest of the group as she could. When they went on the walking portion of the lecture, she hung to the rear and lagged at the very end. A few people looked at her and then took a second look, but she was certain no one really recognized her. With her dark hair, cap and glasses, she was the total opposite of how she appeared on screen and stage.

Clayton Everett mingled through the crowd, talking and laughing with some of the assembled. Soon he gathered everyone together, and they boarded a small tour bus. She sat in the back. He started by introducing himself and his wife, Pearl. He spoke briefly about himself and his background, and then began the tour. It lasted almost two hours. The small group walked the streets of Sag Harbor as Clayton described what might have been seen during its earlier days. He pointed out sights of interest, and they ended the tour at the old church.

Jazz really enjoyed the lecture. Actually, it was more like a friendly chat. Clayton was joyous and lively. He had quips and told jokes interspersed with the very serious.

She lingered at the back of the small one-room church as a crowd of sightseers and other tourists laughed and talked with Clayton Everett up front. Melanie was right. Clayton and Pearl were wonderful. The tour was delightful, and the history was truly enlightening.

She glanced up and looked around the small closed-in area in awe. This was a remarkable building. The history that filled it was heartwarming. She couldn't even imagine what it must have been like to arrive here after such a long, tortuous journey and be hidden beneath the pews in the dark for as long as it took the slave hunters to go away. The frozen winters must have been agonizing and brutal, and the hot, airless summers insufferable.

Jazz wondered how anyone survived. But they did, and they also thrived to start new lives. Through devastation, death and loss, they kept going. Torn away from family, and hunted, they traveled hundreds of miles on the Underground Railroad to finally come to this place. They hid and kept their faith that in the end they would honor their family and ancestors by surviving.

She thought about her own family's losses. Her mother was the center of her world. She taught her everything about life and the business. When her own career soared, she made sure to hold tight to her daughter's hand and pull her up right alongside. Then, when her career was overshadowed by her daughter's, she cheered and supported from the wings. They were each other's biggest fans. When she died, a part of Jazz died, too.

Then, when Brian died, she was completely lost. It was just like what Devon said—for the first time in her life, she stood alone. But instead of honoring their memory and surviving, she ran and hid. Just like the escaped slaves of yesteryear. And just like them, she needed to emerge free and take her life back. They did it. She would, too. Finding her strength, she took a deep breath, trying to release and wash away the hurtful past. She needed to honor her family and herself.

"Did you enjoy the tour?"

Jazz turned, startled by a woman's soft-spoken voice. She smiled, seeing Pearl Everett standing beside her. "Yes, I did, definitely. It was wonderful. You and your husband are amazing."

"Why, thank you. That's so sweet. We need to have you around here all the time, but don't tell Clayton that.

It'll just go to his head." She chuckled. Jazz smiled at her humor. "So, are you a summer tourist or just up sightseeing for the day?"

"Actually, I'm staying with a friend for a few weeks."

Pearl nodded. "Sag Harbor was uniquely historical, and being located along Long Island's East End makes it the perfect retreat. Sometimes we all just need a little space to spread our wings or just tuck back and lick our wounds." Jazz realized Pearl understood more than she said.

"Historically it was first a port of entry, then a whaling town, then a factory community and finally the popular tourist retreat we know now. We have everything—beaches, sailing, boutiques, museums, galleries—but along with the newer activities, there's its remarkable history."

"I had no idea that free African-Americans lived and prospered here before and during the American Revolution and the Civil War. The fact that they built this place and even used it as part of the Underground Railroad is astonishing."

Pearl looked around and smiled. "Indeed it is. If these walls could only speak, we would be honored with tremendous tales of struggle, endurance, heartache, pain and, yes, even triumph. The many lives that have walked through these doors over a century have been, and are still, a testament to the human spirit. My husband does his best to tell these stories, their stories, using the information we have."

Jazz nodded, swept up in her words. "I can see that."

"This church is the oldest in Sag Harbor. It still stands on the original site. Of course this building has just been thoroughly restored, and we're extremely proud of the work. It's listed in the official registry as a national landmark, and its historical significance and reverence is fully noted. This place was the beginning of so many lives."

"It was built in 1839, correct?" Jazz asked.

"Yes, by members of the First Presbyterian Church. It was also known as the Old Whaler's Church. The church roster and manifest list the builders under 'Colored.' This was a large Quaker community, and the very first pastor was an abolitionist. As I mentioned earlier during the tour, the church and others aided escaping slaves. They hid in area homes and also right here beneath the floor."

"Did most stay when the danger passed?"

"Some were smuggled to Canada in ships. Others traveled west, looking for a new start. And then others stayed and started a new life right here."

"A new life. That sounds encouraging."

"You know, you look just like—" Pearl began but Jazz cut her off.

"Mrs. Everett, I'm Jazelle Richardson. It's nice to meet you."

"Please call me Pearl. I thought that's who you were, but you look so different. You darkened your hair and let it grow longer." Jazz instinctively reached up and touched her hair. "It looks perfect on you. I'm so glad you came to visit us today. Oh, Clayton is going to be thrilled."

"Thrilled about what?" Clayton said, walking over to where the two women stood talking. Jazz turned and smiled. "Hi, I noticed you earlier. You know, you look just like—"

"Clayton, this is Jazelle Richardson," Pearl said proudly.

He chuckled and smiled wide. "Well, now, I'll be. It's good to meet you. Who would have guessed that we'd have a movie star taking the tour today?"

"It's good to meet you, Mr. Everett. The tour and lecture were wonderful. You are an amazing storyteller. You should be onstage."

"Oh no, that's all he needs to hear," Pearl joked. "They're be no peace living with him now that you've said that." They all laughed.

"I just wanted to say that you are amazing. I really enjoyed your talk. It was fun, encouraging and very inspirational. I'm not sure if that was your intent, but that's what I got," Jazz said.

"Then you got exactly what you needed," Pearl said.

"It seems everyone gets something different," Clayton added. "We're just delighted you came."

"You mentioned that you're staying with a friend," Pearl said.

"Yes, I'm staying with Melanie Harte. As a matter of fact, she suggested that I introduce myself to you."

"Well, we're glad you did."

"She said you knew my mother."

"Yelena was a good woman. She adored you," Pearl said.

Clayton nodded. "She talked about you all the time. She was so proud of your success." Pearl nodded in agreement. "She is certainly missed."

"Thank you," Jazz said quietly.

"So, how about I take you two lovely ladies out for a late lunch? I'm starved, and there's a wonderful café right down the street," Clayton said.

"Good idea. You'll join us, won't you?" Pearl asked Jazz.

"Maybe another time. I have a few things to take care of still. But it was really nice meeting you both. You're truly inspiring."

"Thank you. It was a pleasure meeting you, too," Pearl said. Then, when Jazz left, Pearl turned to Clayton. "That was a wonderful surprise, wasn't it? I had no idea Jazelle Richardson was staying with Melanie all this time. I wonder if she met Devon. They live right down the road from each other. You know, they would make a really nice couple, don't you think?" Clayton didn't respond. Pearl looked at him suspiciously. "What? You know something I don't?" She smiled hopefully. "What is it?"

"I need to make a phone call first," he said.

Devon's days and nights seemed longer than usual. He traveled and stayed in the city taking care of business, but the pleasure of work wasn't the single-focused distraction he expected. He posed for photographs, did interviews and went on location. It was business as usual; that was what he told himself. Believing it was another thing altogether.

Ultimately he stayed away longer than he expected. But he needed the break. Traveling and keeping busy had always worked in the past when he was overly focused on something. Granted, he had never been this focused on a woman like Jazz before. That was probably why his strategy didn't work. The longer he was apart from her, the more he thought about her. She was in his dreams. He thought about her constantly. He heard her music, saw her photographs and smelled her perfume. At one point, while at a boy's club in Philadelphia, he even thought that he'd seen her in the crowd.

He followed a woman to the other side of the building,

thinking it was Jazz. Of course, it wasn't her, but that didn't matter. It only served to confirm what he already knew. Jazz was in his system. And no amount of time or length of separation was going to end what he was feeling. His grandfather was right: Melanie had found his heart's choice.

He walked into his agent's building and took the elevator up to the management team's floors. As soon as he stepped out of the elevator, heads turned. He was used to it. People always stared. Reed's personal assistant met him midway and escorted him to Reed's corner office. Reed was on the phone and waved for him to sit. Devon walked to the large window instead.

He looked out at the vast, unending landscape that was New York City. From Reed's lofty office, looking down was like looking over a monopoly game board. Tiny cars and boxlike buildings surrounded them on every side. He thought about what his grandfather used to always say in warning: *Don't let your stature rise above who you really are. The trip up the ladder is a lot easier than the trip down.*

"Devon, thanks for stopping by," Reed said, walking over to stand at the window beside him. Devon turned. They shook hands and bumped shoulders in greeting.

"No problem. What's the word?"

"Did my assistant offer you something to eat or drink?"

"Yes, I'm fine. So, what's happening?"

Reed took a deep breath and sighed. "I'm not going to lie to you, Devon. They're holding all the cards. Nothing looks good right now. The negotiations are slowing down again."

Devon shook his head. He had been afraid of this. "What happened?"

"Apparently, someone had a brainstorm. Craig Anthony out of Florida A&M happened. He's had an awesome junior year, and, barring any unforeseen circumstances, it looks like he'll be an easy win for the Heisman in December. I think they're dragging their feet because they want to pick him up in a trade."

"What?" Devon's heart lurched. The word "trade" had a way of sending chills down any football player's spine.

"Devon, he's young. He's twenty-one years old, and he can run the length of a field in less than—"

"Yeah, yeah, I heard. I know all that. What exactly are they saying?"

"They want you, but they want him, too. They know they can't offer both of you deep contracts. Since he's the future…"

"…and I'm the past." Devon completed his sentence. He turned to stare back out the window.

"That's not what they said," Reed emphasized emphatically.

"No, but that's what they meant. They want me to lay the groundwork," Devon said.

"Exactly, teach him the ropes."

"Then?" Devon questioned.

"Then they want you in the front office. Management, coaching, you name it, your ticket, whatever you want."

"Yeah, right. For what? Two seasons tops?" Devon said, knowing the games team owners played in order to appease franchise players and fans. There was no way he could just disappear off the roster. Devon filled the stadium. His speed and agility on the field excited the fans, and they loved him. They couldn't just trade him or let him go. The media and fans would eat them up. No, they needed him around a little while longer anyway.

"I'm headed back to the table next week. What do you want to do?"

"Give me a few days to think about it. I'll call you," he said then looked down at the monopoly game board again. "It's a long way down, isn't it?" Devon said, thinking about his grandfather's words again.

"I wouldn't worry about that. You're gonna be riding the clouds for a long time to come. And actually, there was an interesting side comment made after the meeting broke. So, tell me about you and Jazelle Richardson."

Devon turned to him, questioning. It always amazed him how Reed, once an obscure agent in a small sports agency, seemed to know everything about everyone. "I'm not even going to ask you how you know that."

Reed smiled and chuckled. "A celebrity having a personal life isn't what it used to be. Especially now since half the population is blogging or twittering or whatever the next new social gimmick is going to be. You'd be surprised how quickly word gets around in this business about any and everything."

"I probably would be," Devon said. "How did you know?"

"My assistant brought it to my attention. She reads the entertainment blogs. There was something about Jazelle Richardson and a football player, Devon Hayes, at a matchmaker party in Sag Harbor."

Devon instantly thought about the kiss he and Jazz shared out at the gazebo. "What did it say?"

"It was more of a teaser, so there was nothing really substantial. It alluded to more, but stopped short of saying much. But what it basically said was that the two of you looked pretty cozy having an intimate conversation. It also alluded to the possibility the two of you were a lot closer."

Devon smiled and shook his head. "Jazz and I hung out a little bit while I was in Sag Harbor. I enjoyed her company. That's all there is. No big secret."

Reed nodded. "I'm not the only one interested. As I said, a couple of the owners have expressed interest."

Devon was surprised by the comment. "Let me guess—they want me to distance myself?"

"You got it. They see another publicity disaster coming."

"What if I don't?" Devon asked. Reed didn't answer. He didn't have to. "My contract's on the line, right?"

"Think about it. In the meantime, I'll see what I can do."

Devon shook his head and walked to the door. He needed this contract, but he wanted Jazz. They were giving him a choice. "I'll talk to you in a few days."

He got in the elevator and pressed the button to the ground floor. He looked up at the digital display. The floors clicked by, and it seemed that his confusion clarified as they did. He looked at his reflection in the mirrored siding. His eyes told the story. He was in love. He made his choice.

On the way to his car, his cell phone rang. He looked at the caller ID. It was his grandfather. "Hi, Granddad, what's up?"

"Guess who your grandmother and I just met?" Clayton said.

Devon didn't have to guess; he knew exactly who it was. "I have a quick stop to make, then I'm on my way back now."

Chapter 15

EXTERIOR—MELANIE'S HOME

As soon as Jazz returned to Melanie's home that day, she'd made her decision. The notion had rambled in her thoughts for the last few days. There was nothing and nobody keeping her here any longer. Melanie had been a godsend when she needed her. But now it was time to leave. She needed to get back to her life and put the pieces back together. Her mother and Brian were gone, and nothing she could do would change that. So now she needed to do exactly what those who hid beneath the old church pews did. She needed to make a new life for herself and put the past behind her. There was no need to delay any longer; the sooner, the better.

Melanie was the first person she told about her plans. She would be leaving to head back to New York the following day. Soon after that, she intended to go back home to L.A.

"You know you don't have to leave. Having you here has been a delight. You're more than welcome to stay as long as you need."

"Melanie, you are so good to me. I don't know what I would have done without you. But I need to get back. I've been hiding under the church pews long enough."

"Hiding under the pews?" Melanie asked. Jazz explained the reference to Clayton and Pearl's tour of the old church. Melanie nodded her understanding. "As long as you're sure," she added.

"I am," Jazz said.

Jazz spent the rest of the afternoon packing, making phone calls, first to Savannah, then to her attorney, her agent and her manager. They were all delighted to hear she was ready to come back to work. Savannah was, of course, the most delighted. Since she was returning to the States shortly as well, they had planned on getting together in New York as soon as she arrived.

By early evening, Jazz had finished packing and sent most of her belongings to her apartment. She contacted her assistant and told her that she was coming back. Her record producer was the last to hear the news. He called just as she changed into her bathing suit and headed to the pool. "I hope this phone call means that your self-imposed hiatus from the music world is over and you're ready to record."

Jazz chuckled. DJ Moss was the best when it came to music careers. He'd been her record producer since the beginning. He was pompous, temperamental and truthful to the point of being rude, but he was also the best in the business. "Let's just say that I'm turning a corner. I want to do a CD."

"Man, I thought I'd never hear you say those words again. That's like music to my ears."

"Wait, but first I want to do an EP to test the waters."

"An extended play, six to ten songs. Okay, that sounds good. When can we get together? I can tell you right now that I have about three dozen songs with your name on them. I can contact the label. They'd gnaw their right arm off to get you back into the studio."

"Whoa, not so fast. I have a project I'd like to do first. I was thinking something more specialized."

"Whatever it is, fine. We'll work it out. Why don't we set up a meet and talk about it?"

"Okay, that sounds good. I'll be heading back to New York tomorrow. I'll get out to the Coast by the end of the week. Where are you now?" she asked him.

"Atlanta, headed to L.A. the day after tomorrow."

"Okay. Why don't I call you when I get to L.A.?"

"Jazz, it's good to have you back."

"Thanks, Moss. It's good to be back."

Jazz closed her cell phone and smiled. It felt good to have a purpose again, to see a future again. She looked over at the sealed envelope sitting on the table beside her. She knew what she had to do. She took a deep breath and picked it up. She opened the seal and pulled out the script. Turning to the first page, she started reading. She didn't stop until she'd read the entire manuscript. She laughed, she cried, but most of all she was deliriously happy. She held the papers close to her heart as she picked up her cell. This was one call she'd never thought she'd make. Frank picked up on the second ring. "Jazelle?"

"Yes, it's me," she said evenly.

"Is everything all right? Are you okay?" The strained worry and concern in his voice was evident.

"I'm fine," she said, putting his fears at ease.

"I assume you read it?" he asked cautiously.

"Yes."

"And?" he asked.

"You were right. It's perfect. I want to be part of it."

Frank openly sighed on the other end. It sounded as if he'd been holding his breath for years. "Thank you," he said quietly, seemingly more to himself than to her. "When can we get together and talk?"

"I'll be back in New York tomorrow. I don't expect to be heading back to the Coast until the end of the week."

"Fine. I'll meet you either in L.A. or New York, whenever, wherever you say. Just call me when you're ready. I'll be there."

She nodded. "Okay. Thank you."

"No—thank you. I'll see you then, and, Jazelle, thank you for calling me."

"You're welcome. I'll see you in a few days." She closed her cell and smiled. Conversations with her father didn't come easy. They were usually aggressive, argumentative or downright hostile. This was a first. They were actually civil. There was no guarantee that any of this would work. The studio might hate the idea of them working together. It was a well-known fact that she and her father didn't get along. But for Brian, she would do anything.

"Jazz, I'm headed out," Melanie called from the patio doorway.

Jazz got up, wrapped the sari around her hips and headed into the house. She smiled as soon as she saw

Melanie standing in the foyer. "Wow, Mel, you look sensational," Jazz said admiringly.

"Thanks."

Jazz walked Melanie to the front door. They talked about the evening's festivities and Melanie's sponsorship of several of the charity events that evening. "Have a great time."

Melanie flashed a bright white smile. "I always do. Now, are you sure you don't want to come along? It's one of those events that starts early and ends whenever, and it's always a lot of fun. I'll be happy to wait while you change or have the car come back and pick you up."

"No, I'm fine. I have some last-minute details to take care of, and then I'm going to take a nice long swim and relax the rest of the evening. I have a feeling it's going to be a long time before I'll be able to just chill and veg-out again."

"I'm certainly going to miss having you here."

"I'm going to miss being here," Jazz said as they hugged. "Okay, have a great time for me, too." Melanie nodded and walked to her waiting car. Jazz waved as the car drove off. She closed the door and turned back to the empty house. She headed back out to the pool area. The blue water sparkled fresh and crystal clear. She walked around to the deepest end of the pool, removed her wrap and dove into the sparkling water. She swam a half-dozen laps then lay on her back, breathless, floating in sheer exhaustion.

It felt good to push herself. She raised her arm slowly and stroked backward to the far edge of the pool, then rested a moment, letting the late afternoon sun warm her face. She heard her cell ringing. She pulled herself out of the water and hurried over to the lounge chair. Just as she opened her cell, it stopped ringing. She checked caller ID, finding that it was an unknown caller. She grabbed a towel and dried her face then walked back over to the pool and dove in.

She swam several more laps before realizing that someone was watching her. She stopped and grabbed hold of the pool's edge at the far end and looked behind her. She recognized the silhouette immediately. It was Devon. He stood, staring at her just inside the patio's open doorway. Her heart soared at seeing him there. Breathless, she wiped her face with her hand and smoothed her wet hair back. She smiled inwardly. He was back.

Devon didn't expect the welcome sight he received. His mouth went dry instantly. Seeing Jazz in the pool was one thing; seeing her wet, walking around so freely in her scant bikini, was his undoing. Every seething impulse in his body wanted to grab her up and make love to her right then and there. By the pool, on the lounge, on the grass; it didn't matter—he just wanted her. But he held tight to his desire. He closed his eyes and took a deep long breath, exhaling slowly. The forced tightening in his jeans made standing uncomfortable. Walking, he surmised, would be nearly impossible.

He told himself that it was solely his grandfather's phone call that brought him back, but he knew better. It was Jazz. Not seeing her or being with her the last few days had left him empty. Sure, he'd done everything he needed to do; he completed his business transactions, did the interviews, posed for photos, sponsored events, but the luster and enjoyment that was usually always there was missing. It seemed crazy to want and need someone so much, so quickly, but the fact was, he did want and need her.

In reality they'd only just met, but in the short time they shared, something inside of him had changed. It was as if they'd known each other forever. Now he stood in the shadows, watching her. There was nothing more perfect than seeing her again. He knew right then that his life would never be the same without her. She was the one, the real one, the only one.

Still unnoticed, he watched as she dove into the water. It didn't matter about form or style or the amount of splash she made. She was undoubtedly a perfect ten in every respect. She swam a few laps before stopping. She grabbed hold of the pool's edge and turned to him. He licked his lips and, as casually as humanly possible, strolled over. Midway, Jazz released the edge and swam over to meet him at the ladder near where he waited. He stood looking down at her with his back to the setting sun, allowing her to look up at him without being blinded.

"Hi," she said, still breathless from swimming laps.

"Hi," he said, barely smiling as he looked down at her beauty. Seeing her again confirmed what he already knew: he was completely in love with her. He also saw that she was her old self again and not the cold, disheartened person from the café.

"You're back," she said. "I didn't know if you were ever—"

"Coming back?" he asked, finishing her thought.

She nodded. "When did you get in?"

"Just now. A few minutes ago," he said.

"Wait, how did you get in here?" she added, looking back at the house. The front door was locked; she was sure of it.

"I got home and found this sitting on my desk. I was

on my way over when I passed Melanie on the road. She had her driver turn the car around. She let me in." Jazz recognized the gift immediately. She glanced behind him, expecting to see Melanie. "Melanie continued on to the party."

"Would you hand me a towel, please?" she said then heaved herself out of the pool. He reached down to help her stand. She pulled up and bumped against him. "Sorry. I got you wet."

"Believe me, I don't mind." He grabbed the towel from the lounge chair and handed it to her. She dried off quickly, then wrapped the sari around her hips.

"So, you're back. I guess you're going to that party at the country club? I hear just about everybody else in Sag Harbor's going."

"No, actually I thought I might stay at home tonight. I'm not particularly feeling in a party mood. By the way, thank you for this. It's beautiful."

"I'm glad you got it," she said, glancing down at the folded paper in his hand.

"My mother told me that a mysterious fan dropped something off to me at the house. I had no idea she meant you. Why didn't you tell her who you were?"

"She was your mother? I had no idea. She looks so young."

He smiled. "She loves hearing people say that."

They paused a moment. "Anyway, it's beautiful, amazing." He held the origami black stallion up gingerly. "Thank you."

"It was supposed to be a peace offering for the other day. But you'd already left. I wanted to apologize for what I said. I was wrong. I attacked without thinking and accused you of something vile and ugly. I overheard some things, and I jumped to conclusions. I shouldn't have repeated it when I didn't know the whole truth."

"Do you think you know the whole truth now?" he asked.

"Probably not all of it," she said.

"She wanted marriage. She threatened to go to the team owners and pressure them with bad publicity if they didn't force the issue."

"Did she?"

"Yes."

"Threats, blackmail, extortion—it seems like an interesting way to start a new life together. How did she think it was going to end, the two of you blissfully happily ever after?"

"I don't know. But it didn't turn out like she wanted. Now everybody knows her for what she is."

"I'm glad about that."

"Me, too. But still, it was a distraction last season. The team didn't do as well as expected. I'm not saying that the team's losses were all on me, but as one of the team captains and a franchise player, I can't let anything like that happen again. I can't let a personal situation distract me like that." His cell phone rang.

"No, of course not." Jazz glanced away. His last comment felt as if it had cut right through her. She knew what he was saying. Her defenses went up instantly. "That would be selfish."

"I have a contract in negotiation. The team owners are pressing me to keep focused. My personal life and my business life have been conflicted for a while now. I need a balance. That's why I went to Melanie. She found the perfect woman for me."

"Sure, I understand." His phone rang twice again.

Devon saw the change in her eyes when she looked

back at him. She was putting on the façade she used to keep people away from her. "Jazz." His cell rang again.

"Devon, you don't have to say anything. I understand. Your career is paramount, as it should be. You need to get this contract. And I need to go. I have some work to do and phone calls to the West Coast to make. It's good to see you again. Welcome back."

"Jazz, that's not what I'm saying." His cell rang a fourth time. He looked at the caller ID. It was his agent's number. "I have to get this." He turned. "Reed, what is it?"

"Devon, it's Trina, your agent's switchboard put me through to you. I think we should—"

He closed his cell. He didn't need this right now. He turned, seeing that Jazz had grabbed the towel off of the lounge chair and gone back into the house.

Jazz closed and locked the patio door and didn't stop until she was in her room with the door closed behind her. She leaned back against the frame and thought about what had just happened.

She had actually fallen for Devon and fearfully pushed him away. Now it was over. They both knew it. He had made it abundantly clear. Her rival was a football contract. She looked at her suitcases already packed for her trip back to New York tomorrow. It was perfect timing. All she had to do was call a car service and go.

She went into the bathroom and turned the water on full force. She got into the shower and let the warm water pour over her face and down her body. She intended to wash away everything she felt for Devon. But she didn't; she couldn't. And she knew right then that running away this time would lead her back to where she was before: alone.

Devon was the first man to make her feel like she was alive. Whereas other men cautiously tip-toed around her feelings, he didn't. He spoke up and told her the truth, whether she wanted to hear it or not. He seemed to know and understand her, even when she didn't want him to. Savannah was right. He had figured her out, and it had scared her. Everything she ever wanted in a man was there in him.

She felt a loss of what could have been. In all actuality, she was tired of being alone and tired of running away. After the shower, she put on her robe and lay across the bed. A few minutes later, she fell asleep. She dreamt about Devon.

Just like she remembered their first night together, a storm raged. Thunder rolled and lightning flashed in the distance. Jazz awoke and sat up, seeing Devon lying beside her. He was asleep. He had come to be with her sometime as she slept. She looked down the length of his naked body admiringly. She instantly wanted him. All she had to do was enjoy him.

She reached out and touched his body. He was hot. She ran her hand across his shoulders, over his chest and down to his stomach. The strong muscles tightened beneath her hands as his eyes opened. He smiled at her. She leaned in and kissed him. He wrapped his arms around her body and pulled her close as his tongue delved into her mouth. He pulled, releasing her tied belt, and ran his hand down the center of her body. He caressed her breasts, rounding his palms on her nipples. She moaned with lustful longing. He pressed between her legs, opening them to him. Her body quivered. Her stomach fluttered, and every nerve ending spiked. She was dizzy with desire.

He rolled and slid on top of her. Her legs wrapped around his body, and in an instant he was inside of her. She closed her eyes and smiled as their dance began. The motion of their bodies moved like a pulsating wave as their passion swelled. Faster and faster they stroked. She could feel her body soaring higher and higher on sensuous waves of ecstasy. He was taking her there. Higher and higher, faster and faster, she felt the pinnacle coming.

When she woke up moments later, the room was dark. She looked at the clock. She'd been asleep for two hours. She lay there, alone, with the memory of the dream fresh in her mind. The wild, wanton intensity was still so vivid. She began thinking about Devon and everything he'd said. She knew it was over, but she wanted to be with him just once more.

She got up, slipped on a dress and went downstairs. Melanie wasn't back yet. She went outside and looked around. Devon was obviously gone. She walked down to the beach. The night sky was clear, and a million stars sparkled above. She began walking. Farther down the beach she saw a spark of light flash in the distance. She walked toward it. As she got closer she saw that the spark of light was actually a small pit fire just a few feet away from a house—Devon's house. It seemed to beckon her closer. She walked toward it like a moth to a flame.

As she neared, she saw Devon sitting there in silence. He had his shirt open. His body was breathtaking against the fire's blazing colors. He held a drink in his

hands as the fire crackled and sparked against his skin.
She walked over and looked down at the man who had
captured her heart. He looked up.

Chapter 16

EXTERIOR—BEACH

Knowing it was over was hard to accept, but knowing that he had hurt Jazz and she hadn't forgiven him was devastating. Devon sat and watched the blaze erupt as he tossed another log onto the fire. The flames shot up high as cinders shattered and scattered into the night air. He watched them drift upward then slowly dissipate into the darkness. He stared into the luminous glow from the outdoor fire pit, looking for his answer. It didn't come.

He took a sip of his drink. The amber bourbon burned down his throat and settled in his gut. It was the only thing he felt, and even that was numbing. The fire crackled as flames shot up again. He looked into the blaze, then just beyond. Jazz appeared out of the darkness. At first he thought she was a vision, but he knew she wasn't. She was dressed in a long white fitted dress. She walked around the fire and stood beside him. Devon looked up at her. His prayers had been answered. Neither spoke for a few moments. They just stared at the fire. "May I join you?" she asked.

"Of course," he said.

She sat down beside him and reached for the glass in his hand. She took it, smelled it and then took a deep sip. She shuddered instantly as the bourbon burned her throat. She took another sip and then gave the glass back to him.

"I thought you didn't drink."

"I didn't say I didn't drink. I said that I seldom drink. There's a difference."

He nodded. "Jazz, you have every right to hate me right now. I understand," he said quietly. "I hate myself."

"Thanks for the permission, but I don't really need it."

"Please, let me finish. I was wrong, and what I said at the café wasn't true. I know that now. You're an incredible woman, a very brave woman."

"No, everything you said at the café was true. It was just hard hearing it from you. It's scary to know that you could see me as I am. How can you know me so well and just have met me?"

"Melanie chose you for me, and I chose you for me. When I was away, you were all I thought about. My agent told me I had a choice to make—my contract or you." She looked at him questioningly.

"Can they do that?"

He smiled and nodded. "Sure, they can release me right now if they want. They just have to sign the papers and it's over. But there's no contest. You're my heart's choice. It's you, always you, forever you."

"Devon, don't. This is too much responsibility. What if we don't work out? You'll have nothing—no contract, no endorsements. What happens then?"

"You need to live in the moment," he whispered. "Don't worry about tomorrow."

"But this is your life."

"No, Jazz, you are my life."

"I don't know what I'm doing here. I just know that I can't run away anymore. I want to be with you."

He smiled and nodded. "That's good, 'cause I want to be with you for a long, long time. I love you."

"When you said that you…" She paused.

"…that I love you," he finished for her.

"Yes, you do know that we don't even know each other, really. We've never even been out on a real date before."

"That's just it. My heart knows everything there is to know about you. I know what makes you happy and angry. I know what hurts you. I know what makes you laugh, and I know what makes you cry."

"Are you sure you're not confusing sex with love?"

"Jazz, this is love. It's not about making love to you, which is something I intend to do for the rest of our lives. But what I feel in my heart, in my soul, for you isn't about some kiddie infatuation or some leftover teenage crush. It's about a man seeing a woman across the room and knowing in that instant that she was his. Now, I don't know about rainbows and fireworks and all that other stuff that love is supposed to be. I just know that the moment I saw you, I knew you were the one for me." He wrapped his arms around her and pulled her close. She rested her head on his shoulder, then touched his face gently and smiled.

"Okay, so where does all this leave us?" she asked. "Where do we go from here?"

He looked up at her with hopeful eyes. "We start over from the beginning."

"The beginning?" she asked.

"Yes, the beginning. Jazelle Richardson, would you do me the honor of going out with me? There's a place I'd like to take you. It will be perfect for our first date."

She smiled wide. "Hmm, let me think about it," Jazz joked.

"You're gonna make me suffer, aren't you?" he asked.

"Oh, definitely," she promised, chuckling quietly.

He smiled and nodded. "I'm looking forward to that." Knowing that she was able to joke, even at his expense, was a huge relief off his mind. He stared into her promising eyes. She would always be his heart's choice. They fell into an easy silence as each turned back and looked at the fire. It had begun to die back. The flames weren't as bright, and the sparks were subdued. After a while, Devon spoke.

"My father was a professional football player. He was good, very good. He met my mother in college, and he said it was love at first sight. She got pregnant. They got married and had two kids. I'm the oldest. I have a younger sister. She lives in San Francisco and owns a small ad agency. My mother and father divorced when I was about twelve years old. They were having problems. His career had really taken off, and the offers were pouring in. Women were always calling the house looking for him. He loved the attention. My mother didn't. She left him, and he filed for divorce the next day, citing desertion. I remember my mother was devastated. They didn't have a prenup, so, angry and hurt, she took half of everything he had. We moved back here to Sag Harbor to live near my grandparents.

"A week after the divorce was final, my father remarried. Peggy, my first stepmother, was only ten years older than me. They'd been practically living together for two years. Shortly after their nuptials, my father got hurt on the field. It was a career-ending hit. His contract was dissolved. At the time no other team would pick him up.

"The marriage lasted about a month after that. He had a prenup, but in the span of four months Peggy nearly bought him into bankruptcy. He got some of it back—the houses, cars and jewels—but not everything. Dawn, wife number three, whom he was seeing while with Peggy, lasted a year. He tried to make a comeback, get another contract, but it never worked out. He coached for a while. His heart was always out on the field."

"What about your mother? What happened to her?"

"My mom remarried a nice guy. She and Gordon, my stepfather, own a real-estate company here in Sag Harbor. They have a daughter, my younger sister. She's in college now. They buy, sell and flip houses. They're the ones who were able to get this property back in the family. It originally belonged to my mother's family decades ago."

"Is your father still coaching?"

"No, he's a man of leisure now. He married a very wealthy woman who loves having an ex-football player on her arm. I guess its poetic justice that he became the trophy spouse he always wanted to have."

"How your father's life turned out—that's why you want this new contract, isn't it?" He nodded. The honesty of his answer surprised her. "Are you afraid of turning into him?"

"Yes." The pain and sadness in his eyes pierced right to her heart.

She chuckled to herself. "Aren't we a pair? You're afraid of turning into your father, and I'm afraid of turning into my mother."

"Yeah, how about that."

"So I suggest we stop it."

"Us, being together?" he asked cautiously.

"No, being afraid. I'm not my mother, and I never will be. You're not your father, and you never will be. The sum of our experiences led us on a different path than them. We need to stop being concerned about being like them and just focus on being who we really are."

He smiled. "You know, you're pretty smart."

She smiled brightly. "I'm not just a pretty face."

"No, you're so much more," he said softly. She reached out and stroked his face. Then she leaned in and kissed him. Passion from the dream, from her heart, from her soul, exploded. She wrapped her arms around him and climbed onto his lap. He held her tight. The kiss was perfect. It was sweet and tender and promising all at the same time. When it ended, she smiled and leaned back. He held her in place, still on his lap. She ran her palms over his chest then touched his nipples. His body bucked impulsively. She smiled and touched him again, just seconds before he grabbed her hands to still them. "What was that?" she asked knowingly.

"Nothing," he said.

She nodded, then reached up and started unbuttoning the front of her dress. She worked her way slowly down to her navel. It was obvious by then that she had nothing on underneath. Devon leaned in, kissed and nuzzled her neck. "I think we need to go inside."

"I think you're right," she whispered back, having felt the thick hardness of his erection against her thigh.

Devon picked her up and carried her inside. He closed and locked the doors behind them, then took her up to his bedroom. He gently sat her down beside the bed. "Now, where were we?" she teased. "Oh, right, I remember now." She pushed him down on the side of the bed, then climbed onto his lap again. She sat facing him with a smile that could only be considered seductively menacing. "Right about here," she leaned in and whispered close to his ear. Then she continued unbuttoning her dress. Devon watched attentively. Nothing could tear his eyes from her at that moment. When she finished, she opened the dress wide.

Devon's mouth went dry as he gazed lovingly over her naked body. She was perfectly, deliciously curvaceous in all the right places. His eyes roamed freely, taking in everything she offered. Greed excited him. He wanted all of her, everything all at once, her flat stomach, her firm hips, her narrow waist, her rounded rear and her lip-licking legs. But it was her taut breasts that drew him first and foremost. They were the perfect mouthful, and he so enjoyed gorging himself. He encircled her waist and brought her forward as he leaned in. He kissed her neck, her shoulders and each pebbled nipple. Then he feasted.

Jazz held tight to his shoulders as he caressed, stroked, licked, teased, tasted and tantalized her body. She gasped and shuddered. Her desire soared as his passion and hunger devoured her. The fierceness of his mouth and hands made her dizzy with anticipation. She wanted more.

She leaned back, stood and removed the dress completely. Devon's jaw tightened and his heart pounded thunderously. His devout admiration intensified a hundredfold. "You are so beautiful," he whispered.

"And one of us is entirely overdressed," she whispered back. Devon immediately slipped out of his sweats and sat down. The firm hardness of his erection didn't. Jazz smiled and slowly turned around, allowing him to see every inch of her. The strained tightness of his swollen erection was consuming him more and more. His breath quickened, body throbbing with unrestrained need.

Jazz saw the arousal and the wanton desire in his eyes, but she still wanted more. She walked over to the night table where she'd seen him get condoms before. She opened the drawer and pulled out several. She tossed three onto the bed, then opened one. She eased it out of the pack and blew into it, then tied it off. She caressed it, handling and holding it as if it were him. She touched it to her body. The sight was erotic and sensuous and seductive.

She tipped the latex nib to her full lips and kissed it. Then she lowered it to her nipples and traced it around her breasts, then down across her abdomen. She trailed it to her waist and hips, then lower still. She touched it on her thighs, then turned, slowly stroking it over her rear and between her cheeks. She turned around again and moved closer to her attentive audience.

Devon had followed the condom's mesmerizing trail over her body. His protruding erection ached and begged to be satisfied. He grabbed a condom from the bed and covered himself. His body tensed and shook in readiness.

"Tell me what you want, Devon," she said. "Tell me what's your heart's choice."

There was no thinking or considering, no decision to make. He knew there was, is, and would only ever be one heart's choice for him. "You," he said decisively, without an instant's wavering. "You, only you, forever you and solely you, Jazelle. You are my heart's choice." He took her hand and pulled her closer between his legs. She raised her leg to straddle him, but he stopped her. He intended to first show her exactly what he meant.

Jazz closed her eyes as she stood and reveled in the pleasure of his mouth and hands on her body. The feel always excited her. His mouth was hot and searing, and his torturous tongue bedeviled her in every way. His hands were large and not quite rough, but manly and possessively strong. And when he licked, sucked, tasted and touched her, she burned. And right now, she was a blazing inferno.

He turned her around, placed his hands on her shoulders and slowly, lovingly went lower. He touched and caressed her back, her waist and her rear. His hands and mouth were everywhere. She gasped and moaned in mind-numbing delight. He drew her closer to lean back against him. She looked down, seeing his hands covering her breasts. He teased her nipples with one hand as the other went lower.

She laid her head back against him as he brought her down to sit on his lap again. She looked down. His erection stood up between her legs. The sight, the knowing and anticipating that this was for her, was exciting her even more. Her body tingled. She began moving her hips and gyrating her body.

Devon kissed her shoulders and back gently as his hands stroked her body. Her lustful hunger abounded.

She couldn't get enough of him. Maybe it was the dream she'd had earlier, or maybe it was their talk. Whatever it was, she knew that she wanted him now. She quickly reversed herself, facing and straddling him. Her hunger in wanting him was insatiable and apparently so was his.

She leaned down and kissed him. They devoured each other. After a while she sat up and looked down at his perfection. His dark pebbled nipples took her interest. She leaned over and circled her palms on his nipples. His body tensed. She tweaked them, and he bucked impulsively. She smiled knowingly and reached down between their bodies. She found her treasure. She held tight, placing him where she needed him to be. She raised her hips to impale herself as he surged forward. They met in the first of many explosive thrusts.

The intensity of their joining eclipsed everything around them. Strength for strength, power for power, passion on top of passion, they made love. She sat up, reaching back, keeping her balance by holding on to his thighs. She gyrated, grinding into him. The easy flow of her body met his in the rhythmic dance of passion. He held her waist, looking up and loving the sight of her on top.

She leaned forward, placing her hands on his chest. She tweaked his nipples, remembering his sensitivity. He instantly trembled and lurched upward deeper into her. She tweaked again. He bucked. The correlation was obvious. The more she stimulated his nipples, the harder he thrust. She found that she liked this new power over him. She tweaked more, and he gave her exactly what she wanted. Fast and furious, she held tight for the ride of her life. Then, in one blinding, breath-stealing, mind-dizzying, thrusting instance, she climaxed.

Her body shuddered and shook. He smiled. He liked the sight of her climaxing. He thrust his hips upward. His hard arousal stimulated the one spot that could make her scream his name. She came again, breathless and shrieking, holding tight as her body trembled weakly. He thrust into her once more. She came again in a spasm that made her scream his name. That was what he wanted to hear. He sat up and held her tight. Still shaky, she wrapped her arms around his neck and waited, wondering if her heart would ever be hers again.

Moments later, still connected, they continued. She sat up then plunged down onto his hardness. Over and over, deeper and deeper onto him she propelled her body, then faster and faster until they were both beyond the point of no return. They exploded. Writhing, sated and breathless, they held each other in passion, in pleasure, and then later in sleep.

Shortly before dawn, Devon awoke and reached out to an empty bed. Jazz was gone. He sat up and looked around. The room was lit up. Jazz was gone, again. He got up and wrapped an elaborately designed sarong low around his hips. He walked through the house, hoping that she hadn't left him like the last time. He noticed the kitchen sliding door was slightly ajar. He stepped outside onto the deck. She wasn't there. Then, just as he turned to go back inside, he saw her standing on the beach at the water's edge.

He walked down the steps and over to her. He stood just behind her as dawn approached. Not wanting to interrupt her moment of serenity, he just stood there silently. Then it occurred to him that she might want to be alone. He took a step back and turned to leave.

Jazz knew he was there even though he didn't say a word. She turned and saw him turning away. "No, don't go," she whispered. "Please, I want you to stay with me."

He stopped and turned back to her. "I saw you standing out here. I came out, and then it occurred to me that you might prefer to be alone."

"I think I've been alone too much." She reached out her hand to him. He grasped it, tucking her easily into his strong embrace, wrapping his arms around her body and holding her tight. She leaned back against his strength, feeling her own power increase. Being embraced within Devon's arms always made her feel stronger. They stood in silence, watching the new day approach.

"I've seen you out here before," Devon said softly. "I didn't know it was you."

She nodded. "Sunrise is very special to me. It's a new chance, a start of something, a new beginning. A brand-new day that I can change and make of it what I want."

"I like that idea—a new beginning."

"Me, too," she said, turning to him. She smiled, looking up into his warm eyes. His tenderness soothed her troubled heart. They kissed softly. Then she laid her head on his shoulder as his strong arms held her tight. This was where she wanted to be, now and forever.

"Would you be my beginning?" he asked, nuzzling her close.

She smiled. "Yes, I will be your beginning."

For Devon the seemingly lighthearted comment was more than just words. He wanted Jazz to be his beginning today and every day for the rest of his life. He loved her, and even though she hadn't said it, he knew that she loved him, too.

Just then her wayward dog came up to her. "Hey,

where have you been lately?" she looked down and asked. The dog barked once and sat down, raising his paw as his tail wagged nonstop.

"Who's this? A friend of yours?" Devon asked.

"I don't really know, I guess so. He hangs out on the beach with me sometimes in the mornings when I walk. He comes and goes. I don't know where he belongs or who he belongs to."

"Probably a stray. I don't see any tags on him," he said. The dog stood up again, wagging his tail. He rubbed his face up against Jazz's leg happily. "It looks like he really likes you." Just then someone whistled down the beach and the dog took off running.

"Fickle. So much for liking me. I think I have that effect on a lot of men. They love me then leave me."

"Not this one," Devon promised, holding her again.

After a while she answered him. "Yes, Devon, I'd like to go on a date with you. You can pick me up at my apartment. I'm leaving for New York today."

Chapter 17

INTERIOR—NEW YORK

After the initial shock of hearing that Jazz was leaving Sag Harbor, Devon quickly regrouped. He planned an amazing evening out in New York City. He picked her up at nine at her SoHo apartment and headed to one of the hottest restaurants and night clubs in the city.

"So, where are we going tonight?" Jazz asked, marveling at the city lights all over again. She never got enough of New York City.

"You'll see," Devon said, easily maneuvering the streets.

"A surprise, huh? Okay, I like surprises."

Devon glanced over at her and smiled. "Really, I'll have to remember that. So, now that you're back in New York, what are your plans?"

"Actually, New York is just a pit stop. I need to go home."

"Los Angeles," he said.

"Yes, I haven't been back in almost a year. I left right after Brian died."

"When are you going back?"

"Soon—day after tomorrow. I have something to finish and some meetings to attend. Plus, I need to catch up with my producer and my father."

"Your producer, as in music producer? Are you thinking about making a CD?" She nodded. "What about your career as an actress?"

"It's still there. I have no doubt that my father made sure of that. Brian wrote a script. Frank has it. It's brilliant. He's talking to the studio about it now. He's going to produce and direct, and Brian requested that I star in it."

"That's fantastic. When does all this start?"

"It already has."

"And your father? I've always heard that the two of you don't get along."

"That's a long, crazy story." She took a deep breath and slowly began. "Frank and I never had a father-daughter relationship. We never got along. Well, that's not completely true. I adored him when I was young. He'd come over to the house or we'd meet him someplace, and it was like heaven. He'd buy me anything, everything. Then I grew up. I found out my family history, and that was the end of that. Ultimately, my mother sacrificed everything to keep me and give him what he needed."

"Which was?"

"His career."

"But how did that alienate the two of you?"

"He had a chance to make it right, but he didn't. Years

ago a book came out. It was the unofficial biography of my father's life. I read it. It claimed that my mother seduced him and tried to destroy his family. I knew she didn't, but it was still so hurtful and vicious. The details were perfect. It was like the writer knew exactly what was going on in our lives. Anyway, that pretty much ruined my mother's career. On the other hand, my father's career exploded."

"And you thought he had something to do with it?"

"No, he would never do that to her. If anyone, it was Brian's mother who fed them the lies about what happened. She's a real work of art. Brian used to tell me all these things about her—her prescription drug abuse, her wild partying. So it was suspicious that the book made her look like a Mother Theresa. She was the wronged wife, and after a while she took on that role and became Mrs. Perfection. When my father finally divorced her, she did what she did before and went public to make herself look good. A second book came out. This time it wasn't as flattering as the first. Her career went down fast. The soap opera queen was finally dethroned. I can't say that I was all that heartbroken when I heard."

"So you didn't blame your father the first time?"

"No, not really. Our relationship was already pretty bad. The book just put a different face on it. It is what it is."

"So then why all the animosity toward him now?" he asked.

"He could have stopped it. All of his friends knew that he loved my mom, but nobody ever said a word. He never told the truth and stood up for her. I always figured that's what being in love was supposed to be about. Stepping up and protecting the one you love.

That's what my mom did. She stepped aside to let Frank have his dream."

"She gave up everything for him," Devon said.

Jazz nodded. "Everything except me. That's what she always taught me—love and sacrifice. But in the end it wasn't enough. She loved and protected what they had all her life." She lapsed into silence then decided not to let this spoil their evening. "Okay, enough of that. So tell me—what's happening with your contract?"

"Nope, no football talk tonight. Tonight is solely for us."

"Hmm," she said, "I think I like the sound of that."

Moments later Devon drove up to the valet stand and all heads turned in his direction. The Spotlight NYC, owned by his cousin, was a well-known hangout for celebrities, so photographers and paparazzi were there in full force. There was an instant trample of pushing and shoving as each cameraman was eager to get that perfect shot, hopefully one as scandalous as possible.

Before getting out, Devon took Jazz's hand and looked into her eyes. "Are you ready for this?" he asked. She nodded and smiled. "We can go someplace less conspicuous."

"No, this is perfect."

He nodded, then got out as the cameras started. Near blinded, he smiled with ease and strolled to the passenger side of the car. He reached his hand down, and Jazz grasped it, and just like that, she stepped back into the spotlight. The camera flashes went wild, and questions peppered them like a raining downpour. She answered a few as they walked into the restaurant's foyer. They were immediately escorted to a private booth.

The evening was magical. Dinner and entertainment

were sensational. Jazz met the owner of Spotlight NYC, Devon's cousin, Dennis Hayes. He sent over a bottle of wine and a full dessert tray to top off the evening. Later, well after the restaurant had closed to the public, Jazz went onstage and was introduced to the local singer who was the night's entertainment. She was young and her voice was pitch-perfect. Her name was Phoenix, and she was thrilled to meet Jazz. They talked about performing and careers. She wanted desperately to get signed, so Jazz took her information and promised to pass it on to her producer.

After everyone had gone, Jazz and Devon hung around with Dennis as he finished up for the night. Jazz sat at the piano onstage and played. Her voice was as pure and perfect as always. She played and sang some of her mother's music and then some of her own. Devon stood at the bar in the empty dining area enjoying the private concert. Dennis walked over and stood next to him.

"Man, she is incredible. I forget how amazing her voice is. It's gotten even better over the years. She's got that old-school sound going on now. I tell you, if she ever wants to book a small venue, I'm putting my bid in right now. She'd pack this place to the rafters."

Devon was just as amazed. Jazz had never sung in front of him before. He knew she could sing, of course. He had her CDs and remembered her singing as a teen sensation, but her voice was richer and fuller now. The tone was sultry and seductive. "Yes, she is most definitely incredible."

"Yeah, I know that she's a great actress and all, but she really needs to perform again. She'd blow this place out." They continued listening in silence to the next selection. When it ended, Dennis turned to his cousin.

"So, you and Jazelle Richardson," he said rather than asked. Devon nodded as he smiled adoringly at Jazz. "Is it serious?" Dennis asked.

Devon nodded again. "Very. I love her."

"That part is very obvious. You haven't taken your eyes off of her since you walked in the front door. I don't know how you drove here tonight," Dennis said, chuckling.

"She's exactly the woman I want in my life."

"I'm happy for you, man. I wish you the best." They shook hands and bumped shoulders. Jazz walked over, smiling. She thanked Dennis for a wonderful evening as they prepared to leave.

When they left, the street was empty. All signs of cameras and photographers had long gone. They said their good-nights to Dennis and headed home. Several streets were blocked with road repair, so they cut through Central Park. On a whim, Devon parked his car and they walked down Fifth Avenue.

It was early morning, and the streets were mostly empty. They strolled and window-shopped, stopping first at FAO Schwarz, and then continuing to Bergdorf Goodman and other fashionable stores along the avenue. When they came to the crown or, rather, tiara of Fifth Avenue, they stopped. Tiffany & Co.'s window wasn't particularly stylish or chic, but everything it represented was. It was old money and old glamour.

Jazz looked over the sparking jewels secured behind the thick glass. Her eyes instantly went to the center display of one window. It was a single diamond cut into a star, and it was breathtaking. She smiled, remembering her first star.

"I love this place," she said dreamily. "My mother brought me here when I was a kid. She'd just gotten her first paycheck from some off-Broadway production she was doing. She bought me a star earring. It was my first diamond anything. I was ten. I still wear it."

Devon stood behind her and held her close. "So, if you had to choose one of these, which one do you like the best?" he asked of the stunning display of diamond pendants in the side window.

"That's impossible. It would be like choosing your favorite star in the night sky. They're all equally stunning," she said, looking longingly at the center display while easily avoiding his question.

"No, they're not. You outshine them all," he said, taking her waist and turning her around to face him. He leaned down and kissed her tenderly, then pulled a light blue ribbon attached to a stunning diamond pendant from his pocket. Jazz gasped. It was the center display, and it was huge. It shined and sparkled brilliantly beneath the street lights.

"You're kidding. You bought this?"

"No, I bought this for you," he said.

"Devon, no, I can't accept this."

"You have to," he said, unfastening the clasp and putting it around her neck. "I tore up the receipt." He secured the latch and took a step back. It was just as he imagined—stunning.

She touched her earring and then her pendant, then leaned up and kissed him. "This is the best breakfast at Tiffany's ever. It's perfect, thank you."

"You're welcome."

She touched the diamond again. "I love it. I love you."

"I love you, too." He wrapped his arms around her as they walked a bit farther then crossed the street and headed back to the car. They went back to her apartment just as dawn broke over the city. They were totally exhausted after a wonderful day and night together. Devon stayed over. They made long-lasting love before falling asleep in each other's arms.

A few hours later, Jazz woke up to a gentle kiss. Devon was dressed and sitting on the side of the bed, smiling down at her. She touched her neckline, feeling the diamond star still there. She never slept in jewelry, but it seemed perfect that it was the only thing she wore when they made love the night before. "You're dressed," she said sleepily.

"I have to go. My agent called earlier. There's craziness going on with the contract. I have to get there as soon as possible."

"There's a problem?" she asked. "What is it?"

"I don't know. He didn't say. Front office wants me now."

"What did he say exactly? What happened?"

"I'll take care of it."

"Is there anything I can do?" she asked.

"No, it's on the West Coast. I shouldn't be long."

"Wait. I'll go with you," she said eagerly.

"No, stay here. I'll be in meetings all day. I'll call you when I'm on my way back," he said. "Whatever it is, I'll take care of it and be back later this evening, so be rested and ready for me when I get here." He leered.

Jazz instinctively knew that something was going on. She also had a feeling Devon knew more than he was saying. "But maybe I can help," she said, sitting up quickly. The sheet dropped, exposing her breasts. Devon looked down at her body longingly. He licked his lips and closed his eyes to focus on what he needed to do. But right now all he could think about was their night of passion and making love to her again right now.

"Jazz," he said, looking at her perky breasts and tender nipples again. "You're killing me."

She smiled and shook her head. "What, you mean two times last night just wasn't enough for you? You want more?" she teased, lowering the sheet to her hips.

"Don't tempt me, woman," he nearly growled. "There's a private jet and a neurotic agent waiting for me to meet him in L.A. right now."

"Newsflash, mister—I'm waiting for you, too," she sassed, knowing that he wouldn't do anything. After all, he didn't have time. But she was very, very wrong.

In the blink of an eye, he pinned her hands down over her head and kissed her hard. Then he trailed intense kisses and tiny bites down her neck and across her shoulders to her chest. He licked her nipples, causing her surprised gasp to turn into a deep, throaty moan. He secured both her wrists with one hand and felt his way down her body with the other. She twitched and writhed beneath his skillful hands, followed closely by his equally masterful mouth.

Then, as he'd done their first night together on the balcony at his place, he went down lower and lower until he found what he treasured. Gently and purposefully he feasted like a condemned man. Dipping deep and enjoying the lusciousness of her giving body. She came hard the first time, and then begged her surrender after the second time. She lay breathless with her eyes closed tightly. Her body was a liquid mass of tingling nerves. She felt Devon's kisses on her body again. He trailed back up her body, kissing the diamond star tossed near her shoulder.

She opened her eyes, seeing him straighten the pendant around her neck, purposely brushing each nipple. "Know that I always want you. Place and lack of time will never make a difference, so never tempt me."

She nodded and closed her eyes again. She must have fallen right to sleep, because she woke up two hours later to her cell phone ringing. She grabbed it quickly, thinking it was Devon. "Hello."

"Hey, you ready to shop 'til we drop?" Savannah said brightly.

"Are you here?" Jazz asked excitedly.

"Yep, I got in late yesterday. I intended to call you last night, but jet lag had me staggering into walls. So, come on out—it's time to play."

"Give me an hour. I'll meet you at our regular spot."

Devon's flight landed on time. Reed met him as the hatch opened as soon as the jet engines stopped. "Welcome to L.A.," Reed said happily.

Devon got into the waiting car, and the driver headed to the Stallions main office. "You look happy."

"I am happy."

"Okay, I'm here. So, what's going on?"

"Looks like your little secret is out. You're all over the Internet. It seems Jazelle Richardson has been tempting you to the East Coast, or so some say. Check this out." Reed handed him his PDA. There was a photo of him and Jazz standing at Tiffany's window, kissing. The caption read that he'd just proposed and she'd accepted.

"It's not true—at least not yet, anyway," Devon said.

"It doesn't matter. I got that gem from the Stallions front office. They want to know what's going on. You ate dinner at the same restaurant at the same time that

New York's head coach was there with a few of the owners of the franchise. Coincidence, perhaps, but the Stallions' owners don't think so."

Devon laughed. "Are you joking? I didn't even know they were there. Dennis Hayes is my cousin. He owns the place. The President of the United States could have been there last night and I wouldn't have known," Devon said honestly.

Reed chuckled joyfully. "Again, it doesn't matter. They think the rumors are true. It's no secret that New York wants you. By all accounts it looks as if they're secretly courting you. And to add a cherry on top of this, your new girlfriend's father, Frank Richardson, is a part-owner of the New York franchise."

"What? How did all this come out?"

Reed was almost giddy. "My assistant found out that little gem. She's got a best friend at Simon Wells's office, who just happens to be Jazelle Richardson's agent. They hatched this little infofest. A blog here, a photo there—we might as well have the rumors working to our advantage for a while."

"But it's all just coincidence and circumstantial," Devon declared. "Jazz never even mentioned her father's affiliation."

"Call it whatever you want. The Stallions are hungry to sign you at your price, and that's all that matters." Reed laughed heartily as the driver pulled up in front of the office building housing the Stallions franchise.

Devon's phone rang just as they entered the building. "Hey, what's going on?" he said, knowing it was his sister, and continued walking to the bank of elevators.

"Don't ask. Where are you?" Terri asked.

"I'm in L.A. What up?"

"What's up is that you're supposed to be here this

evening escorting me to this banquet. You remember. The one you talked me into attending and even sent a gorgeous green evening dress for me to wear."

"Oh no, Terri. I completely forgot all about it. Okay, I'll get there as soon as I can. I promise." He closed his cell as the elevator doors opened.

"Here, take this," Reed said, handing him a brand-new Montblanc pen. "You're gonna need it."

Chapter 18

EXTERIOR—NEW YORK

Jazz and Savannah laughed, talked, shopped, ate and shopped some more. They spent the whole day together catching up. Jazz told Savannah all about Devon and their time together, especially their first real date the night before. She spared most of the juicy details, much to Savannah's dismay. Savannah smiled, delighted by the news. "No wonder you look so fabulously elated," she said. "Seriously, you're like glowing over there."

Jazz laughed joyfully. "Am I that bad?"

"Yeah, you haven't walked on the ground all day. But that's a really good thing. Jazz, I'm so happy for you, girl. It's about time you found yourself a winner. It's definitely your time to be happy."

"You know what? I'm happy for me, too. I've never felt so incredibly loved. It's like what my mom said. I'm just so happy inside. I feel like I'm about to explode with joy." She giggled. "Savannah, he loves me, and I actually know it. I feel it. The way he looks at me makes me feel like I own the world. It's like colors around us are brighter or something. I know it sounds crazy strange, but that's how it feels."

"Honey, it doesn't sound crazy strange at all. It sounds perfectly divine. He loves you. Well, what about you? Do you love him, too?"

Jazz nodded joyfully and smiled wide before nearly crying with heartfelt joy. "Yeah, I do. I love him. I feel it all over. When he's away I miss him, and when he's with me I can't get enough of him."

"Now, that's what I'm talking about. That's love. Girl, look at you," Savannah said. "You're damn near giddy." Both Jazz and Savannah giggled and laughed happily. "Come on, we need to celebrate some more."

By early evening they'd gone to all of their regular boutiques and even popped into a few newer ones. All purchases were being sent directly to their respective homes in L.A. Jazz was overjoyed to be back and happy to have her best friend with her. "Are you sure you bought enough shoes?" she asked Savannah, a self-proclaimed shoe fanatic.

"A woman can never have enough shoes," she said as they walked through the fashion district one last time. "Look, what about that one?" Savannah asked, stopping to look in the boutique window. A sexy violet dress caught her eye. Jazz stopped to check out the dress in the window. She considered getting it, but decided it wasn't quite what she was looking for.

"No, I want something really spectacular. When Devon comes home tonight, I want his jaw on the floor when he sees me."

"Whoa, what's that?" Savannah asked, seeing the reflection of the newsstand behind them in the glass window. She turned, walked over and picked up the paper. Jazz and Devon were smiling as they headed into Spotlight NYC. "Looks like the tabloids didn't waste any time on you two. Can you believe this crap?"

Jazz walked over and looked over Savannah's shoulder. She went cold, and her heart sank instantly as she read the headline Jazz Temps Bolt to the Big Apple. She grabbed the newspaper from Savannah. The attendant looked up at them and frowned. Jazz kept reading as Savannah tossed him payment for the paper. Jazz, hands shaking, hungrily read the article. She was stunned. It was like reading that her fairy tale had turn into a nightmare. "I can't believe this," she whispered.

"What's it say?"

"It says that I got Devon to leave L.A. and sign to play here in New York. The Stallions are cutting him."

"That's ridiculous. It's all just lies to sell newspapers."

"No, it's not," she said too calmly. "It makes perfect sense. That's why Devon's agent called and wanted him in L.A. as soon as possible. They're cutting him because of me, because of this."

"What are you talking about?"

"The article says that Frank is a part-owner of the New York football team and through me is negotiating with Devon. The Stallions team owners walked away from negotiations. Devon lost his contract because of me."

"No," Savannah said emphatically, "you know that's not true. And even if it is, which I seriously doubt, he lost it because of this trash, not you. What happens with his contract has nothing to do with you."

"It has everything to do with me. He knew something this morning, but he just didn't say it. I need to go," Jazz said, then immediately stepped out into the street and raised her arm for a cab. "I can't be responsible for him losing his contract and ending his career."

"What? Where are you going?"

"L.A.," she said, shaking her arm impatiently as several cabs sped by. "This is why he didn't want me to go with him this morning. His contract is in trouble, and he knew that it was my fault."

"Jazz, listen to yourself. You're sounding paranoid. You're so afraid of repeating your mom's life that you're jumping at the slightest boo. Since when do you take this trash seriously?"

"Since Devon left this morning." A cab driver pulled up, and they climbed in and gave her address. Jazz dialed Devon's cell phone, but no one answered. "He's not answering. His flight landed hours ago."

"Don't panic. I'm sure everything's fine. Nobody pays any attention to these rags, certainly not the owners of a professional football team all the way in L.A."

"Savannah, everything in here is true enough to make sense. If he loses his contract and gets cut, it means that he won't be playing football anymore anywhere. He loves that game. I can't be the one to take it from him. He'd hate me the rest of his life."

Just then the cab driver's sports-talk radio station started talking about Devon. They announced that Devon's contract was stalled in negotiations and that dating her was probably a good idea since he was going to need the money. They talked about his recent drama and the team's interest in a much younger college player.

"Excuse me, would you change the station, please?"

Savannah said, seeing Jazz's distress. The cabbie reached over and turned to a reggae station. "Thank you. Okay, listen to me. First of all, you're not sure about any of this. The newspaper, the radio station—it's all publicity talk for ratings. You know that."

"Savannah, I know that his agent called early this morning, telling him to get out there as soon as possible. He sent a private plane for him. What else could it be?" They arrived at Jazz's apartment. She headed right to the bedroom and started packing.

Savannah sat on the bed, frustrated by the day's turn of events. She watched her friend whip quickly around the room, gathering her essentials for a quick flight. "You can't just leave like this. What are you going to do?"

"Talk to the team owners. Tell them it's not true. If it means they want me out of his life, I'll do it."

"You'd give up love for his career?"

Jazz stopped and looked at Savannah. Suddenly, it was all so clear. This is what her mother had done years ago. She had walked away from her father to save his career. "Yeah, I would. I love him that much."

Savannah nodded and smiled. "Let's do this."

"There's a standard flight out of LaGuardia in about two and a half hours. Book me on it."

"Yes, fine, I'll book it for us," Savannah said. Jazz looked at her. "What, did you think I wasn't going, too? I know that it's the anniversary of Brian's death, one year ago tomorrow. You're not going alone. Besides, it'll give me at least three hours to talk you out of this craziness." She walked over to the desk and opened the laptop. A few minutes later, she booked the flight. Jazz finished her packing and turned just as Savannah closed the computer. "Okay, you're set. There was only one seat available. I'm booked on the next flight, four hours later."

"Thanks, Savannah. Well, I guess I'll see you in L.A."

Savannah nodded. "Jazz, don't do anything rash."

"Do I ever?" Jazz said, hugging her friend.

"All the time," Savannah said, hugging back. "See you soon."

Devon stood and applauded wildly as Terri walked to the stage and held her much-deserved award in her hands. She thanked the other talented nominees, her staff and associates and, of course, her family. Devon smiled proudly. It was a thrilling moment, and he was delighted he could share it with her.

There were drinks and dancing afterward but neither Terri nor Devon wanted to stay. "It looks like they're going to party all night long. Are you sure you didn't want to stay and celebrate your win?" he asked as they stepped outside the hotel and he motioned to the limo driver he had hired to take them to the awards banquet.

"Positive. It was fun, but I'm exhausted and I have a million things to do tomorrow. Let's just go home. You're staying over, right?"

"No. I need to get back to New York tonight."

She looked at him skeptically and then at the fog's thickness around them. She could barely see across the street. "I don't think so. It looks like it's too foggy to fly out."

"I hope not," he said.

Just then a couple walked by. They overheard the end of their conversation. They'd apparently just left the airport and were complaining that all flights had been grounded.

"Devon, there's this thing called reality check, and the reality of this situation is that when the fog rolls in this thick, all flights are canceled and planes are grounded. The best you can hope for is maybe a flight tomorrow morning."

"That's not going to happen."

"Yes, it is," she said.

"No, it's not," he asserted.

"You are so stubborn," she insisted.

"And you are so pessimistic," he joked.

They glared at each other and then started laughing as only brother and sister could. She slapped him on the arm, barely disturbing his tuxedo jacket. They laughed again. Just then two women walked up and asked Devon for his autograph and a photo together. He grabbed his sister's hand and pulled her next to him. Appeased but disappointed, the women walked off smiling still. "That's not the photo they wanted," Terri said.

"But that's the only one they're getting tonight. I'm here to celebrate you, not me."

"Actually, we should both be celebrating—my award and your new contract," Terri said as the limo driver pulled up. They settled in the backseat as the driver got back in and pulled away from the curb.

Devon chuckled. "I still can't believe they wanted to give me the five years I asked for. Even Reed was shocked by that."

"Yeah, but what I can't believe is that you didn't accept it. You actually turned them down. I never thought I'd hear of that happening—you retiring."

"Well, not quite yet. In two years."

"It sounded like they were handing you the sun, the moon and the stars. It was everything you always wanted. The perfect five-year contract," she said, softening her voice so that only he could hear her. "I'm stunned you turned it down."

Devon nodded. "I realized that playing football and the perfect contract weren't everything. If they gave me what I wanted, they could never have signed Craig Anthony to play for the team. I couldn't be selfish like that. He deserves his chance just like I got mine years ago. He's a good quarterback, and I want to do my part to help him and the team. Armand helped me when I was rookie—it's time I passed on that tradition. It's all about balance."

"I talked to Grandmom. She told me about you and Jazelle. You know you'd make my life a lot easier if you proposed. I could get to sign her for the national cosmetic campaign I was telling you about."

"Then by all means consider your life made easier."

Terri continued talking without really hearing what Devon had said. "I mean as my sister-in-law, I could probably get her to do a dozen or so commercials. I'd have clients coming out of the woodwork. I read up on her after we talked that night. Did you know her best friend is Savannah? Is that the coolest thing or what? Savannah's mother owns the hottest modeling agency in Europe. And with Jazz's father being who he is, I'm talking product placement on TV and in films. I'd have a monopoly, and I'd—" She stopped and looked over at him. "Wait. What did you just say?" she asked hopefully.

"Do you ever stop talking business?" he asked as he dialed Jazz's cell-phone number for the thirtieth time that day. Her phone was still turned off.

"So, wait, go back. You said for me to consider my life easier, right? So that means what?" she questioned anxiously. "What are you saying?"

"I'm saying this." He reached into his tuxedo jacket and pulled out a stunning diamond ring.

Terri's jaw nearly dropped to her lap. "Oh my God." She started laughing. "It's beautiful. You proposed. Wait, no, you still have the ring."

"I picked it up today."

"Devon, I'm so happy for you." She reached out and hugged her brother, then squealed and hugged him again. "I'm so happy for you both. Oh my God, I'm so happy for me. I have one foot in the sports world and one in the entertainment world. This is fantastic. I have the serious hookup now. I've got about a million calls to make first thing tomorrow morning."

"Whoa, hold up. Don't you think I should possibly propose and give her the ring before you plan her entire life as a campaign spokesperson?"

"So what are you doing here? Go find her and propose."

"Actually, I've been trying to call her all day and all night. Her phone's turned off. I don't know what's going on. I have a red-eye flight out tonight. As soon as I drop you off, I'm headed out."

Terri picked up the small phone in the back of the limo. "Driver, could you please take us to San Francisco International Airport?"

"I'm sorry, ma'am. It's fogged in. There are no flights in or out, but I can definitely drive by just in case."

"Yes, do that," Terri said. He agreed. She hung up the phone. "Okay, big brother, hopefully it'll be clear enough so that you can take care of your business. Make sure to call me and let me know."

"I will. Thanks, little sister." Moments later they arrived at the airport. The wide-open space made it seem even foggier. It was just as the driver said. There were no flights in or out that night.

Chapter 19

INTERIOR—LOS ANGELES

When it came to having a breaking point, Devon didn't have one. When it came to giving up on something or someone, he couldn't fathom it. He didn't surrender, and he didn't give up. When he wanted something, he focused on getting it and went after it full force. So when it came to wanting Jazelle Richardson in his life, he was adamant. He smiled victoriously, knowing that everything in his life was finally balanced. Still, the frustration of not being able to fly out or contact her ate at him all night. He barely slept.

He showered, changed and went downstairs. The smell of coffee hit him instantly. He went to the kitchen, seeing Terri sitting at the table with a mug in her hand. She wore one of his jerseys and sweats along with her reading glasses. She was so focused on what she was doing on the computer that she didn't even realize he was standing in the doorway. "Good morning," he said.

She jumped and grabbed her hand to her heart, nearly spilling her coffee on the laptop's keyboard. "What, are you nuts? Don't do that," she chastised hotly. "You nearly scared me to death."

"Don't tell me you forgot I was in the house," he said, walking over to the coffeepot. A twelve-cup carafe, it was already over half empty. He poured a mug and walked over to the table. "So, what are you doing at six in the morning?"

"I couldn't sleep, and I needed to answer e-mails and make changes to my Web site, plus I had to send out some advance letters and notices. Then I needed to blog about last night and…"

"Never mind," Devon said, chuckling at his sister's crazy-busy life. "Sorry I asked. You seriously need to take some time off or take a vacation or something," he suggested.

"Yeah, I know," she said, absently focused back on the monitor again. "I'm going to take one right after my nervous breakdown."

"Terri," he said, looking down at her seriously. She hmmed without looking up. "Terri," he said again. She looked up, grimacing, but continuing to type. "Stop," he said. She stopped. "Is it the money? Do you need money?"

"No, I'm fine," she said.

"Then don't do this to yourself. Look at you. You barely slept last night, and I'm sure this wasn't the first time. You can't keep burning the candle at both ends."

"Look who's talking. You're the most focused person I know, besides Dad, of course. You've never let anything stop you from getting what you wanted. Your career is the perfect testament to that. You've always gone after your goals full force, no stopping."

"Yes, and look what it's gotten me."

"Houses, cars, tons of money, notoriety, fame, celebrity—let me know when I can stop."

"Stop," he said. "You didn't say love."

She smiled. "You have love."

"Now, yes. But look at all this wasted time focusing on what really wasn't important. I'm thirty-two. Don't let your life pass you by chasing something that's not real."

She sat back and looked up at him. "You really are happy, aren't you?" He nodded. "And the contract you signed—you're happy about that, too?" He nodded again.

"It's time for us to slow down, Terri. If it means that you need to hire three or four more people, do it. You can't keep going like this. I won't let you. I was headed for a rewind of Dad. It wasn't pretty. Don't follow in my footsteps like this. I want better for you. You deserve it."

She nodded. "Our little sister has been bugging me about taking her on vacation. I think our big brother needs to send us someplace warm and sandy with lots and lots of drinking, shopping and half-naked gorgeous men."

"Okay, that's way too much information, but you got it. Let me know when and where."

"Deal. In the meantime, I need to finish this, so shut up and cook me some breakfast before your flight out of here." Devon laughed. Terri was without doubt the worst cook on the planet. "Nope, you're on your own," he said with a chuckle.

"Oh, listen—two things. I saw on the Internet this morning. Your friend Armand is in the hospital."

"What? What happened?"

"I read the article, but it really doesn't say much. Apparently he got hit really badly at some football camp, and he has some broken bones, a cracked rib and a really bad concussion. That's all they're saying."

Devon shook his head woefully. He had been afraid something like this was going to happen. "Where is he?"

"L.A., in the hospital. Also, Devon, they're talking steroids, the really bad kind."

"All right, I'm headed down there."

She nodded as she stood to follow him to the front door. "I'll drive you to the airport. Everything's back on schedule."

"Good, what's the other thing?"

Terri sighed heavily. "Trina e-mailed me this morning with congratulations. She wants to have a chat."

Devon shook his head. "I can't deal with her drama right now. Come on, let's go."

Two and a half hours later, Devon arrived at the L.A. Medical Center. He saw Armand's ex-wife Shelia sitting in the waiting room. She looked up as soon as he walked over. She stood and crumbled into his arms. "What was he thinking?"

"I don't know," Devon lied.

"Yes, you do," she said, leaning back and walking away. "It's this obsession with the game. You all have it. You can't let go. He wanted back. Do you know that I hated football? I always have. I never liked it, ever. It's brutal and savage, and it destroyed my marriage."

"Shelia…"

"Don't Shelia me. You know exactly what I'm talking

about. Look at your mother and father. It ruined their marriage, too. It never fails. What made him think that he could go back? Why, what was he thinking?"

"He was thinking about you," Devon confessed.

She looked up at him, deeply hurt and confused. "What?"

"I talked to Armand in Sag Harbor. He was there in training. He wanted to get back into football because he wanted you back in his life. He thought you'd come back to him if he made everything the way it was before." She instantly broke down and cried. Devon hurried over to embrace her and sat down. "He loves you still. He was just trying to win you back the only way he thought he could."

"I love him. I always have and always will. It wasn't about what he did for a living. How could he even think that?" She looked up at Devon and shook her head. "Don't let that game destroy your life. There's so much more than a hundred yards and a couple of goal posts. You used to listen to me when you were a rookie. Listen to me now. Know when enough is enough. Let it go and walk away."

"I already have," he promised her.

A nurse walked over, smiled and nodded. "We're done. You can see him now."

Both Devon and Shelia thanked her and stood. "You go. Tell him that I stopped by, and I'll be back later."

"Are you sure? I know he'd want to see you."

Devon shook his head. "Shelia, he wants to see you. Trust me." She nodded and walked down the hall to Armand's room. Devon watched until she disappeared from sight. He turned, seeing Trina standing behind him waiting. She smiled as if nothing had ever happened between them.

"Hi, sweetheart. You're a hard man to find."

It was all he could do not to laugh. "Trina."

"Devon, I'm so sorry about Armand. I know how much you adore him. Is there anything I can do?"

"No, nothing," he said, walking past her.

"Devon, can we talk?"

He stopped and turned to her. "Talk?"

"Yes, I have so much to tell you. But not here—tonight. We can maybe meet someplace, or I can have dinner cooked for you. I just need to see you."

"To what end?"

"I still love you, Devon. I always have. I made a mistake. I'm so sorry I hurt you. I just want us to be like we were before this thing happened. Please, tonight."

"I'm busy."

"I know you're angry with me. I understand. But I can make this right. Just give me a chance."

"That's not going to happen."

"Because of your movie star?" She flashed her true colors.

"No, Trina, because of you." He turned and walked on.

"Devon, I can make you forget her. Give me another chance."

He turned. She stood smiling sympathetically. "Trina," he said, "you could never be the woman Jazz is. And as for forgetting her, it would never happen. Thanks for the closure. Have a nice life."

He walked back to his car and called Jazz. As her cell rang, he knew that he'd done the right thing. Shelia was right—football wasn't everything. He was just happy he'd learned that lesson from Jazz a while ago.

* * *

"Vincent, what on earth are you doing here?" Jazz said, surprised to see him standing and chatting with a woman in the lobby of a record company.

"Hey, Jazz, long time no see," he said then introduced the two women. Each recognized the other and proclaimed herself to be a big fan of the other. After a quick conversation, Jazz and Vincent stood talking alone.

"She's fantastic. Is she your…"

"No, she's a new client," Vincent said quietly.

"Impressive."

"You're back."

"Not completely, but I'll keep you posted."

"Rumor has it that you and Devon are together."

"Is that what the rumors are now?" she hedged. "So, are you coming or going?" she asked, changing the subject and looking around the lobby as people rushed in and out.

"Coming. I have an appointment upstairs."

"Interested in a singing career?" Jazz joked.

He laughed hardily. "Trust me, that you don't want to hear. No, we have a new client. I'm doing the first contact."

"Wow, sounds like the Platinum Society is everywhere."

"We certainly are," he agreed then glanced at his watch. "I gotta go, but let me know when I need to press my tux." He kissed her cheek and winked.

Jazz shook her head, watching him hurry to the bank of elevators. She turned to leave as her cell rang. She answered, assuming that it was Savannah telling her she'd arrived.

"Jazz," Devon said.

"Devon, hi, where are you?"

"I'm still in L.A. I was up in San Francisco last night and got fogged in. Then I found out this morning that a friend of mine is in the hospital. I'm catching a flight out this evening."

"I'm in L.A.," she said.

"What? When did you get here? Where are you?"

"I came in on the red-eye this morning. I had some business to take care of."

"Where are you now?" he asked.

"I'm on my way to the studio to meet my father."

"Great. I'll meet you at the studio afterward. We need to talk."

"No, I have another stop to make after that. Why don't I meet you later? Stop by the house. We'll talk then." She gave him her address and hung up quickly. A few minutes later, her cell rang again. This time she looked at caller ID. It was Savannah. "Hey, are you here?" she asked.

"Yep, I just got in. I'm at my house. What happened?"

"I couldn't get a meeting with the owners. Apparently they're out for the rest of the day."

"And that means what?"

"I don't know. Devon's meeting me at my house later. I'm headed to the studio to meet with Frank and the new studio head."

"I have to change and do some running around. I'll meet you at your house later. We'll go together."

"Savannah…"

"Unless you're going to tell me that you've changed your mind about ending this with Devon, I don't want to hear it. I'm going with you this evening, end of conversation. I'll be at your house at eight. That's plenty of time before sunset." She hung up.

Jazz walked to her car, shaking her head. Savannah was her best friend and had been most of her life, but sometimes she was a huge, pushy pain. At other times she was the perfect friend. But this was something she needed to do alone. It was her final goodbye to her brother.

She drove to the studio to meet with her father. He'd put her name on the drive-on list, so she entered the gates easily and found his office. As soon as she pulled up, she saw him waiting at the door for her.

"Welcome," he said, smiling cautiously.

She walked up to him, and, for the first time in nearly two decades, she hugged him. He went still, and then he embraced her with all the love and emotion pent up in his heart. "Thank you," he said proudly, still holding tight. They stayed like that awhile until someone cleared his throat. They looked back. The studio head stood smiling in the doorway.

"Right, let's get going on this. Jazelle, I'd like you to meet your new boss, Clark Keaton, head of the studio."

"Ms. Richardson, Jazelle, it's an honor to finally meet you. We're all excited about this new project. Having you and your father connected is going to shoot this film through the roof."

The three went inside and got down to business. Two hours later, most of the logistics had been ironed out. The next step was getting agents and lawyers involved and actually sealing the deal and signing contracts.

After the meeting was over, Jazz and Frank sat in his office and talked. For the first time in a long time, it was a comfortable conversation. "So, why didn't we meet in Clark's office? I'm sure that was the accepted way, right?"

"He's really excited to have you on board. He's a huge fan, and I'm not just talking Hollywood talk. He's for real. When I brought the project to him, he nearly choked saying yes. So, to answer your question, I told him that I wanted this first meeting to be comfortable for you. I didn't want your first time here to be overwhelming, especially not today." She nodded, knowing that of course he'd remember. "What are your plans for later?" he asked.

"I'm going to the bridge at sunset."

"Good, I'm glad. So, what's this I hear about you and some football player that I'm supposed to have convinced to play with the New York team?"

"I guess I should ask you. Was New York ever interested in Devon?"

"Yes, very interested, but not through me," he said. "They knew that our relationship wasn't, shall we say, cordial. Any suggestion to you from me would have resulted in him never considering an offer from them. No, not me. It was just sensationalized reporting for the sake of selling papers."

"Since when do you own a football team?"

"I don't. I'm an investor. That makes me a part-owner, a very small part-owner. There's a major difference on the tax forms, trust me. Hadn't you heard? Your father's a very wealthy man. So was your brother. He left everything to you."

"He what?" she asked, surprised. "But I thought his will was still being contested by his mother."

"The judge ruled a few days ago. The will is probated. Brian left everything to you, including the stock in

Elizabeth's online-shopping company. At fifty percent, you're half-owner."

"You've got to be kidding." Jazz chuckled and shook her head. She knew it was her brother's last practical joke. He connected her to his mother, forcing her to finally deal with Jazz. Something she'd always refused to do. "Well, I can tell you that the first board meeting ought to be extremely interesting. What exactly am I supposed to do with half of her company?"

Frank chuckled, waving his hands. "No, no, don't look at me, I'm out of it. They're your shares, fifty-fifty. But I wouldn't worry too much about it. I have a feeling you're gonna be hearing from Elizabeth's attorneys soon to offer you a quick buyout."

"I guess refusing the offer would be spiteful," Jazz said, smiling mischievously.

Frank just shook his head. "Now you sound just like your mother. I'm sure Yelena and Brian are up there cracking up."

Jazz laughed, and just as quickly the humor left her eyes. "When Mom left and you went back to your career and your life with Elizabeth, what did you think? Did you despise her for leaving you?"

"Despise your mother? No, I could never despise her. I knew exactly what and why she did what she did. She wanted me to be happy. But what she didn't know was that I was happy with her. She knew that I loved acting, that much was true, but I loved her more. She could never see that. We were only together for a short time, but in that time we fell in love for life."

"But when she left with me, you went back with Elizabeth."

"Only because Yelena asked me to," he said.

"She wanted you to go back to her?"

"In Yelena's eyes, it was best for my career. At the time, Elizabeth was a very popular soap-opera star. America adored her, and she used that to her advantage. She wanted me back, and she intended to make Yelena's life difficult if I didn't go back to her."

"So you went back for appearance's sake."

He nodded. "I can see now that it was wrong. Everyone suffered in the end, especially you and Brian." He stopped talking and looked away.

"Brian and I were just fine. He was a great brother. I don't know what I would have done without him."

"We were all blessed."

"I need to go," Jazz said hesitantly. "Are you going to be okay?" she asked as she stood and walked to the door.

"Yes, I'll be just fine now," he said, walking her to the office door and back to her car. He waved as she drove off.

Jazz looked in the rearview mirror, seeing the man she loved to hate. All of the old loving feelings were back again. It was what her mother had always wanted, and she knew that she approved. She turned out of the studio gate and headed to her last stop.

Chapter 20

EXTERIOR—BRIDGE

Devon drove over to Jazz's house less than an hour after their phone conversation. She'd told him she had a studio meeting, but he couldn't stay away, on the off chance she was possibly returning early. He traversed the Hollywood hills with ease, passing several gated communities until he came to hers. He stopped at the guard's station. Of course the guard was a Stallions fan. He allowed Devon in with hardly a second glance.

Devon found Jazz's home and pulled up to her gate. He rang the buzzer. No one answered. He tried twice more but still got no answer. He drove off, troubled. Jazz seemed different, and that bothered him.

He drove back into the city and stopped at Reed's West Coast office. He needed to take care of the last-minute contract details and approve the official press release. The team owners were about to release the news about his future. Afterward, he headed back to the hospital to see his friend. Shelia had stepped out, giving them the opportunity to talk. "Hey, this is getting to be a habit."

"Don't make me laugh. I cracked two ribs. I guess you were right. Some of those rookies were pumping iron since birth. I didn't even see him coming. I can't do this."

Devon nodded. "I'm out in two."

"The contract?"

"They gave me five years. I dropped it down to two. They can bring in the next crew."

"You gave back three years. Man, you're nuts."

"Nah, I'm smart."

Armand nodded. "Did you find your love?"

"She was there all along. Jazelle Richardson."

"Get out—for real?"

Devon pulled out the ring and showed him, just as Shelia walked back in. "For real."

"Good Lord, please don't tell me you're marrying her."

"Jazelle?" Devon and Armand said in unison.

"No, I thought this was for Trina. She's been hanging around here all afternoon, asking when you were coming back. I finally had to get the nurse to shoo her away. What Jazelle Richardson? So, what they're saying is true? You're going to New York?"

"No, I'm here for another two years, then I'm out."

"Devon, this is stunning. She's going to love this. When are you proposing?"

"Tonight," Devon said.

"Good luck," Shelia said, hugging him.

"Hey, stop that. She's my lady. Go get your own."

Devon looked at Armand, then at Shelia. "Your lady?"

"We're gonna try this again. Remarry."

"Congratulations," Devon said, hugging Shelia again.

"A'ight now," Armand said. They laughed and talked about their future plans. By the time Devon left the hospital, it was much later. He assumed Jazz was home by now, so he drove back to her house. He rang her gate's buzzer, and this time she answered. The gate opened, and he drove up the driveway. He got out and hurried to the front door. It opened wide, but it wasn't Jazz standing there.

"Nice painting. Yours?"

"No, it's a gift for Jazz."

"No, the big bow gave the gift part away. Did you paint it?"

"Oh, no, I didn't."

"Devon Hayes, I presume," Savannah said, smiling. "Jazz was right—you are gorgeous." Devon looked at the dark black-haired crystal blue-eyed beauty with his mouth wide open. "Better close your mouth and come on in, darling. The neighbors talk, and paparazzi are everywhere." She crinkled her nose and winked as she turned and sashayed away, leaving him to enter and close the door behind him. "Can I get you a drink?"

"No, thanks."

She walked over to the small wet bar in the living room and began pouring herself a glass of wine. "I'm Savannah, by the way. Jazz and I go way back. We share everything," she said, then looked up at him pointedly, "and I do mean *everything*."

Devon smirked and shook his head. He understood instantly. He'd been in this situation dozens of times.

Women liked the idea of sharing him with their close friends, often at the same time. But there was no way he was going there. He wanted only Jazz, and he wanted her exclusively. "Look, I don't know what you think might be going on here, but it's not. Jazz is the one and only woman for me, now and forever. So if you think that this is some kind of…"

Savannah chuckled and nodded. "Very good, I'm glad to hear that. You'd be surprised how often the response to that line turns out differently."

"I'm with Jazz *exclusively*. No one else," he said emphatically, taking no chance of her misunderstanding him completely. "I'm sure you're a nice person, but no thanks."

"I have to say, Devon, that's got to be about the nicest refusal I've ever gotten."

"You were testing me?"

"Call it a best friend's prerogative," she said casually. Devon shook his head. "Don't be too offended. Jazz is like a sister to me. But as I was saying, she told me about you, *everything* about you."

"Everything? That can't be good," Devon said, seeing in her eyes that she knew everything.

"On the contrary, that's very good. I'm rooting for you."

"Is Jazz here?"

"No, sunrise to sunset. It's almost sunset—she's probably just about there by now."

"What do you mean, there where?"

"Today is the first anniversary of Brian death's on the bridge."

"I know. I wanted to be with her today. That's why I was trying so hard to get back to New York. But she's here. Do you know where I can find her?"

"Sure. You should go to her. She needs you more than you know."

Moments later, Devon was in his car driving to the bridge where Brian had driven off. He didn't waste any time. He parked, seeing a woman standing midway on the bridge looking out at the approaching sunset. He hurried to reach her, and then stood behind her, waiting respectfully.

Jazz smiled. She didn't even have to turn around to know Devon was with her. She closed her eyes and pressed the play button on her cell phone. She saw it as clearly as if it were written in a script—every action, every movement, outlined precisely as it was to be played.

ACTION.

FADE IN—SCENE ONE:

1. INTERIOR DARK BEDROOM—MOMENTS BEFORE SUNSET

Asleep in her bed, Jazelle Richardson wakes up, hearing the phone ring. She rolls over, covering her head, ignoring it. The answering machine picks up. She hears Brian Richardson's voice. "Jazze." She reaches out and grabs the phone.

JAZELLE:

(yawning)

Brian, we wrapped today. I've been on set for thirty-two hours. I finally get to sleep in my own bed and not in a trailer.

2. EXTERIOR BRIDGE—MOMENTS BEFORE SUNSET

Brian Richardson sits in his idling car, waiting on the bridge between their two homes. From his vantage point all he can see is the clear horizon as the sun lowers. He's smoking a cigarette and sipping bottled water.

BRIAN:

(gazing across the skyline)

It's almost sunset. I just called to say goodbye.

JAZELLE:

Where are you going, back east?

BRIAN:

(pauses)

Nah. Not this time.

Jazelle:

(hearing something in his silence, she gets a sudden chill)

Brian, what did you take, pills, drugs, alcohol?

BRIAN:

Nah, not this time, I'm stone-cold sober.

Jazelle:

(chuckle)

You, sober?

BRIAN:

(laughter)

I know, right? Imagine that.

JAZELLE:

(sitting up in bed)

What's going on? What's wrong?

BRIAN:

(heavy sigh)

It's almost sunset. I just wanted to say…

JAZELLE:

(starts getting dressed quickly)

Hey, I gotta idea. We just wrapped production a few hours ago. Let's go to Tahiti again, just you and me, like the last time. I'll come pick you up right now. We'll fly out tonight and take a few months off to just chill and veg out. My next film is on location in Prague. You'll love it. There's a nice juicy part they developed just for you.

BRIAN:

(takes a long drag of cigarette—watches smoke)

Babe, I need you to do me a favor.

JAZELLE:

Sure. What? Anything?

BRIAN:

I need you to be happy.

JAZELLE:

Brian, what are you talking about? I'm happy. We're both happy, remember? We'll be even happier in Tahiti. Where are you?

BRIAN:

I'm sitting on our bridge waiting for sunset.

JAZELLE:

Okay, you're close. I'm coming over to watch the sunset with you. Stay there.

(silence)

Brian? Brian?

BRIAN:

The news vans are here. They'll finally get the show they've been waiting so long for—the final scene from Frank Richardson's son.

JAZELLE:

Why are the news vans there?

BRIAN:

Jazelle.

JAZELLE:

Brian.

BRIAN:

Fall in love, be happy, have kids.

JAZELLE:

Stay where you are. I'm coming to you now. I'm in the car.

BRIAN:

No. If you come, I won't be able to do this.

JAZELLE:

I know. That's why I'm coming.

(she sees his car and starts crying, knowing what he is going to do. She parks and runs to him)

Brian. Please, don't leave me alone. You promised you'd stay with me. Please, Brian. Please.

BRIAN:

Stop running away, Jazze. Be happy. Sunrise to sunset, look for me. I'll always be with you. I love you.

JAZELLE:

I love you more.

END SCENE

The phone message beeped and ended. Jazz took a deep breath then released it slowly. It had been exactly one year since that act played out, but she remembered it as if it were yesterday. She opened her eyes. Tears crept down her face. She stared at the light dipping below the horizon. It was sunset. There were no words. There never were.

"That was you and Brian?" Devon asked, still standing behind her.

"Yes, our last conversation. He dissolved right here in front of me. I didn't know how to help him anymore. Before, when he came to me on location, I'd make him stay with me. When I was done shooting, we'd go someplace crazy and stay for weeks. This time he just wanted to be alone."

"Your brother loved you, and just like he protected you in the club all those years ago, he was doing the same thing."

She nodded. "No one's ever heard that before. Not even my best friend, Savannah."

She turned to him and half smiled. "Hi," she said.

He moved closer and stood beside her. "Hi."

"I guess Savannah told you where to find me."

"She's a good friend. I think I passed her test."

"What test are you talking about?" she asked then paused. "Oh, the whole we-share-everything test?" He nodded. She smiled.

"Jazz…"

"No, Devon, let me say what I have to say first." He nodded. She took a deep breath and began. "My life is crazy sometimes. It's been like that since the day I was born. Being with me isn't easy. I'm sorry about your contract."

"What do you mean?"

"The newspapers and sportscasters said yesterday that I messed up your chances for the five-year contract you were negotiating. I know how much you wanted it. I'm sorry."

"Since when do you listen to them?"

"Since your future in football was on the line."

"My future in football is just fine. I got the contract. They offered me everything I asked for, plus more. I turned it down." She looked at him, shocked and speechless. "Yep, I turned it down. Not all of it, of course. I'm not crazy. The contract is for two years on the field and three years in the front office. I think it's time that I retire the jersey and look toward a different future."

"Are you sure? You wanted to play so badly."

"It occurred to me that football wasn't as important in my life as I thought it was. There's so much more." He stood in front of her and smiled. "There's you. The contract is exactly as I want it to be."

She sighed, heavily relieved by the news. "Then you didn't get cut or lose it because of me."

"No, of course not. As a matter of fact, because of you it's even better than I dreamed. If anything, that story about you and your father in the New York newspapers reenergized the team's efforts to keep me as long as possible."

"I'm happy for you, Devon. Congratulations."

"I'm happy for us."

"Devon, about that…"

"No, now it's my turn to talk." He reached out and took her hand and kissed it. Then he took the small diamond ring from his pinky finger and eased it on to her ring finger. She looked down in awe. He knelt down and looked up at her. There was nothing but love in his eyes. "Marry me, Jazelle Richardson. You are my heart's choice. I love you, and I need you in my life forever."

"Devon," she began. "I don't know what to say."

"Do you need a cue card?" he asked. She shook her head, smiling.

"Devon, I love you, too. I can't run away this time. I tried, but I can't. My heart just won't let me. Yes, I will marry you."

Devon stood and grabbed her up into his arms and swung her around. They kissed. Sunset—that was their new beginning.

Epilogue

EXTERIOR—BEACH—LOS ANGELES

Devon and Jazz patiently waited on the beach for the sun's setting. It had been a full year since they had met and married. She was deliriously happy. Her brother's movie was in post-production and was already getting rave reviews. Devon's football season was a success as he led the Stallions franchise to the playoffs with expectations of a Super Bowl ring in his last season. Movie scripts were pouring in, and her EP in honor of her mother was a huge success. "Are you happy?" Devon asked.

Jazz nodded and smiled. She was happy. For the first time in her life, everything she'd ever dreamed was coming true. "Yes, I'm happy. I'm very happy. What about you? Are you going to miss playing football when you retire?"

"Not at all."

"Really?" she asked.

"Yes, really," he said. "There was a time when I couldn't imagine doing anything else with my life. Football was everything. Now, being married to you and having our first child is more important than anything in the world. I love you, Jazz. I always have and always will."

She smiled. "I love you, too, Devon." She grimaced.

"Are you okay? The baby…"

"…is just fine," she said, finishing his sentence. "He just kicked. I think he's going be an athlete like his father."

"Or like his mother, a star," he said and then reached down to rub her swollen stomach. "All right, little buddy, calm down. We have to take care of mommy, too."

Jazz smiled and leaned back against his strong body. She closed her eyes, and he continued to rub her belly. The baby calmed down. "You have a way with him already. That's not fair. I do the heavy work, and you two get to bond."

"Don't worry. The next one will be a girl, and the little guy and I will thankfully be left out of nail-polishing, lipstick-hunting, mega-shopping girl talk."

"You've been watching too much television. Girls certainly aren't like that anymore."

"Good. I'm looking forward to meeting our next and all the rest, starting of course with this little guy."

"All the rest?" she questioned.

"I'm thinking seven or eight, maybe ten."

"Children?"

"Of course."

She turned around to face him. "And who is going to have all these children?"

"We are," he said. "What do you think about adoption?"

Jazz smiled. "I love the idea." She reached up and kissed him. Afterward, he smiled and shook his head. "What?" she asked.

"I can't believe how blessed I am to have you in my life, and how we almost messed everything up."

"But we didn't. And I have a feeling that Melanie, along with Jessica and Vincent, wouldn't have let that happen. I never really put much stock in the whole matchmaking thing, but…"

"Yeah, there's definitely something to it."

"Do you think Melanie will ever find someone for herself?"

"She seems happy as she is now," Devon said.

"I know she does, but…"

"You're thinking that the matchmaker needs to be matched."

She nodded. "Something like that."

"Let's hope so. One day."

"Soon," Jazz said hopefully. "One day real soon."

A few weeks later, Melanie walked out onto the office veranda with the baby announcement in her hand. She poured coffee into her china cup and took a seat at the head of the table. She looked up at the large, stately home that had been in her family for decades. Still in the afterglow of another success, joy and fulfillment washed over her. She smiled delightedly. Jazz and Devon—she'd done it again. She looked happily at her associates, who had joined her for their morning meeting. "Okay, who's next?" she asked.

END

FADE TO BLACK

* * * * *

THE *MATCH MADE* SERIES

Melanie Harte's exclusive matchmaking service—
The Platinum Society—can help any soul find their
ideal mate. Because when love is perfect,
it is a match made in heaven…

Book #1

by *Essence* Bestselling Author

ADRIANNE BYRD

Heart's ♡ Secret

June 2010

Book #2

by National Bestselling Author

CELESTE O. NORFLEET

Heart's ♡ Choice

July 2010

Book #3

by *Essence* Bestselling Author

DONNA HILL

Heart's ♡ Reward

August 2010

www.kimanipress.com
www.myspace.com/kimanipress

REQUEST YOUR FREE BOOKS!

2 FREE NOVELS
PLUS 2 **FREE GIFTS!**

KIMANI™ ROMANCE

Love's ultimate destination!

KROM10R

L♥VE IN THE LIMELIGHT
Fantasy, Fame and Fortune...Hollywood-Style!

Book #1
By *New York Times* and *USA TODAY*
Bestselling Author Brenda Jackson
STAR OF HIS HEART
August 2010

Book #2
By A.C. Arthur
SING YOUR PLEASURE
September 2010

Book #3
By Ann Christopher
SEDUCED ON THE RED CARPET
October 2010

Book #4
By *Essence* Bestselling Author Adrianne Byrd
LOVERS PREMIERE
November 2010

Set in Hollywood's entertainment industry,
two unstoppable sisters and their two friends
find romance, glamour and dreams-come-true.